MW01534597

HOW TO LOVE A DANGEROUS ROGUE

ROYALS AND RENEGADES
BOOK ONE

SCARLETT SCOTT

HEA
Happily Ever After Books

How to Love a Dangerous Rogue

Royals and Renegades Book One

All rights reserved.

Copyright © 2024 by Scarlett Scott

Published by Happily Ever After Books, LLC

Edited by Grace Bradley and Lisa Hollett, Silently Correcting Your Grammar

Cover Design by Wicked Smart Designs

This book or any portion thereof may not be reproduced or used in any manner whatsoever without the express written permission of the publisher except for the use of brief quotations in a book review.

The unauthorized reproduction or distribution of this copyrighted work is illegal. No part of this book may be scanned, uploaded, or distributed via the Internet or any other means, electronic or print, without the publisher's permission. Criminal copyright infringement, including infringement without monetary gain, is punishable by law.

This book is a work of fiction and any resemblance to persons, living or dead, or places, events, or locales, is purely coincidental. The characters are productions of the author's imagination and used fictitiously.

For more information, contact author Scarlett Scott.

https://scarlettscottauthor.com

For my Sassy Readers. Your daily support and enthusiasm for my work means everything to me.

CHAPTER 1

The King of Varros had arrived.

The approach of the carriage in the streets below had warned her, along with the rustle of frantic movement in the hall outside the chamber, the raised voices, the hastening footsteps. She hadn't expected him.

Not now. Not today. Not yet.

"Perdition," Tansy swore, then added another vicious Boritanian oath for good measure as she plumped the pillows beneath the counterpane on the princess's bed, a fine sheen of sweat on her brow.

She didn't want to see the king without Princess Anastasia acting as a necessary barrier. But it would seem, like much of her life, Tansy didn't have a choice in the matter.

For in that moment, the door opened to admit *him*.

She moved away from the bed instantly, as if the empty piece of furniture had singed her hand, guilt warring with trepidation within her.

King Maximilian was obscenely tall and broad, seeming to take up half the chamber with his entrance. His size, in this instance, was fortuitous, as it meant the guard in the hall couldn't spy the empty bed in which the princess was meant to be reclining as an invalid, nor the pillows that were a poor imitation of her feminine form.

The door clicked closed, and Tansy watched as the king raised a massive paw to latch it in place, trapping her with him.

Alone.

He turned to her slowly, his brown eyes dark and unreadable, mouth grim and unsmiling. "You've a vicious tongue, Lady Tansy."

His English bore the traces of a Varrosian accent but was otherwise flawless.

Sweet Deus above, had he heard her cursing? How? She had been muttering to herself, not shouting. Tansy felt lightheaded at the prospect, knowing full well that he could punish her for daring to utter such an oath in the presence of the king.

Belatedly, she remembered herself, dipping into a curtsy. "Your Majesty."

"Repeat it," he ordered curtly.

Tansy had just straightened to her full height, which wasn't considerable under any circumstances, and most certainly not when in the presence of King Maximilian, who towered over her as mightily as any mountain. But she dipped again, offering him a protracted curtsy, making extra effort.

"Your Majesty," she said.

"Not that." He flicked his hand in a dismissive gesture. "What came before it."

Curse the devil. He *had* heard. She didn't dare repeat the Boritanian oath. Literally translated to English, it meant *May God rot your cock.*

Decidedly not the sort of thing one said to a king, particularly one as menacing and imposing as the monarch before her.

"I beg your pardon, Your Majesty," she offered, bowing her head in a show of humility that she hoped would appease him. "I said nothing else."

He had drawn nearer. Soundlessly, which was impressive for a man so large in stature. With her head bowed, she saw the perfectly gleaming black boots—as immense as every other part of him—a mere foot away. The hair on the back of her neck rose.

"You dare to lie to me?" he demanded, his voice deceptively low.

It was the quietness that frightened her most. The stories of the horrors King Maximilian had visited upon his enemies were legion. He had battled for years to emerge the victor and assume the throne that was rightfully his, sparing no one.

Ruthless.

Pitiless.

Unfeeling.

Those were a scant few of the whispers Tansy had heard about him.

"I would never presume to lie to you, Your Majesty," she fibbed, head still bent, praying he would cease toying with her.

"Look at me, Lady Tansy."

She didn't want to. Particularly not given the king's troubling proximity. So near that she could detect his scent, spice and musk with a hint of leather and citrus. A pleasant scent. Altogether not one she would have expected of a man like him, but she had never previously been near enough to take note. She supposed it stood to reason that brutal warriors might smell as lovely as anyone else.

Tansy took a deep, shaky breath. "Forgive me, Your—"

"I said, *look at me*," he interrupted, enunciating each of the words as sharply as if he wielded a whip.

She lifted her head and wished she hadn't. He was even closer than she had supposed, presiding over her like one of the old gods her ancestors had worshiped. Fierce and fearsome, his face a collection of angular blades—wide jaw, high cheekbones, a stern nose. A fine scar marred the skin above one of his slashing brows, a shocking hint of a past vulnerability. His black hair brushed over broad shoulders, twin patches of silver at his temples. He had amber flecks in the dark-brown depths of his eyes, and his mouth was almost cruel to look upon, sensual and full lips so harsh and unyielding.

And then those lips moved. "Say it again, Lady Tansy."

She swallowed hard, her stomach knotting. Now she had done it. All these years of avoiding the wrath of the usurper Boritanian King Gustavson, and one foolish oath had ruined her.

In a quiet voice, she repeated the curse and then waited, shoulders tense, for a blow. For a cuff to the side of the head for her insolence. Everyone knew how vicious King Maximilian was.

"Are you a sorceress, madam?" he growled, the tone of his voice low and deep.

The question took her by surprise.

Confusion made her brow furrow. "Of course not, Your Majesty."

"Good, for I do not wish for my cock to rot off."

She stared at him, aghast. King Maximilian did not jest. Did he? No, it simply wasn't possible. And there was nary a hint of levity in his immovable countenance. Was there? The man could have been carved from marble, though she very much doubted he would be cool and smooth to the touch. Something told her he would be quite hot.

At the errant and most unwelcome thought, she nearly choked. The result was a strangled sound that was most impolite.

"Are you well?" he asked, his gaze narrowing.

No, she was not well. She was alone with a merciless tyrant who would soon be marrying the princess who had become like a sister to her over the years she had spent as Princess Anastasia's lady-in-waiting. Tansy couldn't bear to hold his gaze. Her head dropped, her gaze falling to the carpet.

"I beg Your Majesty's forgiveness," she mumbled, still stricken by her lapse.

How could she have been so foolish as to exclaim the vile oath aloud?

She blamed the hours she had spent waiting for Princess Anastasia's return, fretting and fearing on her behalf.

"I asked if you are well," he reminded pointedly.

She was aware of him shifting; there was a rustle of fabric, his long arm stretching toward her slowly.

Would he strike her now, then?

"Very well, thank you, Your Majesty," she managed, scarcely moving her lips.

"Hmm," was all he said, his voice fashioned of steel and ice. And then his finger was on her chin, rough and firm and yet surprisingly gentle, urging it upward. Making her meet his gaze again. "I won't hurt you, if that is what you fear. Does King Gustavson strike the women in his court?"

The bloodied lashes she had tended on the princess's back rose in Tansy's mind, and she had to bite back the bile rising in her throat. She should lie, for the tale was not hers to tell. But with his fathomless gaze holding her in thrall, she couldn't seem to find the words. Still, she needed to say something. The king had spoken to her. Had asked her a question.

"I—" she began, only for his finger to settle in the bow of her upper lip, staying further explanation.

"You've answered me well enough," he interrupted.

As quickly as he had reached for her, he withdrew his touch, before spinning on his heel and stalking toward the door. He unlatched and wrenched it open. Then, he strode out, closing it smartly at his back, somehow taking the air from the room with him.

Tansy stared at the paneled door, holding her breath.

The only sounds were more muffled voices and booted footsteps disappearing down the hall, both finally supplanted by the rhythmic ticking of a mantel clock. The jangling of tack interrupted, rising from the street below. And still the door remained closed.

Tansy waited, lip tingling where King Maximilian had laid his finger.

~

KING MAXIMILIAN of Varros was planning a revolution and a wedding. Not necessarily in that order. If the wedding came first, so be it. If the revolution took precedence, that was just damned fine.

What he hadn't been planning was to smash his fist into the nose of a royal Boritanian guard. However, since the sniveling whelp he currently had pinned to the wall wasn't answering him, he was leaving Maxim with little choice.

Maxim drew back his fist. "Has King Gustavson given you leave to use force against the princess or her lady-in-waiting? You've until the count of three, puppy. One, two, th—"

"Yes, Your Majesty," the man gasped, his reddening face turning a shade to rival the royal Boritanian purple livery he wore. "King Gustavson h-has instructed all

6

guards t-to use force if the princess or Lady Tansy es-escapes."

Maxim released some of the pressure on the guard's windpipe. He didn't want to choke the bastard entirely, just to instill much-needed fear. Fear by throttle.

"Do you know why we're in London?" he demanded of the guard.

"Y-yes, Your Majesty," the man sputtered, eyes wide with fear as he scrambled to find footing on the polished marble floor. "T-to announce the betrothal b-between yourself and Her Royal Highness P-princess Anastasia."

"That's correct." He flexed his fingers on the guard's neck incrementally, showing him that there was far more strength he'd yet to unleash, for Maxim had learned long ago just how terrifying restraint could be. "Princess Anastasia and Lady Tansy will be under my protection soon, and I don't like any of my possessions to be touched. Do you understand?"

The sound of the man's soles skidding frantically on the marbled floor was almost comical. Maxim might have laughed if his mind weren't plagued by thoughts of the gray-eyed lady-in-waiting he had left mere minutes earlier.

Lady Tansy Francis.

She had a flower's name. Flowers were easily crumpled in a fist. They faded and wilted after the bloom. Shriveled and died, only to return the following season.

Stupid, useless things, flowers were.

"I u-understand, Your Royal H-highness," the guard squeaked out, clawing at Maxim's hand on his throat.

"Good," he spat, releasing the man so suddenly that he crumpled to the floor in a pathetic heap. "Tell the other guards as well."

With that instruction delivered, Maxim spun on his heel and crossed the hall in easy, long-legged strides. When he reached the staircase, he ascended two stairs at a time, eager to return to the invalid chamber where his betrothed, Princess Anastasia, was meant to be convalescing. There was only one reason behind his impatience, however. *Lady Tansy.* His finger still burned from where it had touched the velvet-softness of her upper lip's maddening bow.

There were no guards at the door now, which was how he preferred it. Hopefully, the worms would wait below while he concluded conducting the rest of his business. He wasn't above choking a few more of them if necessary. Or setting his bodyguard Felix upon them like a hound after unsuspecting hares.

Drawing blood wasn't out of the question, although he didn't want to make the usurper Boritanian king suspicious. No, he wanted to lull the bastard into a false sense of security and then strike.

Maxim didn't bother to knock at the door. He simply entered, finding the lady-in-waiting precisely where he had left her, hands clasped behind her back, gaze wide as it landed on him, her full lips parting.

"Your Majesty," she said, grasping her skirts to dip into a full, elegant curtsy that belied their mutual presence in this grim, closed-off chamber.

She was so damned small that for a fleeting moment, he had a fanciful notion that he might tuck her into his coat and spirit her away without anyone the wiser. Maxim knew he was a great, towering beast, but he had never felt his size more than standing alone in this room with her. He was taller than most men. Taller than all men he'd encountered thus far in London. Thanks, no doubt, to his pillaging ancestors.

"You are to cease curtsying in my presence when we are alone," he told her curtly, irritated at the way his body leapt to attention in her presence. "I dislike ceremony."

She rose, smoothing her skirts, the only indication of her

confusion the slight crease of her brow. "Forgive me, Your Majesty. I did not intend to displease you."

Displeasing him was not the problem. Pleasing him was. Because everything about the woman before him pleased Maxim far too much. And he wasn't meant to be lusting after his future wife's lady-in-waiting. He didn't have time for lust. He had a war to wage.

He grunted. "You are to stop apologizing as well, unless an apology is requested of you."

She was too...subservient. Yes, that was the word.

Frightened of him, he suspected. And while he preferred everyone in his midst to fear him—his court, his men, his enemies most especially—the thought of Lady Tansy being afraid of him made his gut clench.

She swallowed, and he tracked the movement of her creamy throat with great interest. Her neck was dainty and feminine. He could likely wrap his entire hand around it. Not to squeeze, but to hold her in place for a kiss. He was suddenly terribly curious about what her lips would feel like beneath his.

By all the gods.

This wouldn't do.

"Yes, Your Majesty."

"Maxim," he corrected, giving her the name he preferred for himself.

The name that only his closest friends and allies were permitted to use. But then, he was marrying Princess Anastasia. Lady Tansy would become a part of his family. Like a sister to him.

If only his body reacted to hers in a brotherly fashion. That could come with time. He was well accustomed to privation, when necessary.

"I could not presume to be so familiar." Lady Tansy was already denying him.

Maxim was not a man people denied. He had spent more than half of his forty years making certain of it.

"Maxim," he repeated sternly. "In private, it is what you will call me."

A stirring of pink rose to her cheeks. He wondered why. Because he spoke of privacy between them?

Two more steps, and he was upon her, the fresh scent of her perfume invading his senses. He had noted it before, when he had laid his finger over her philtrum in an effort to keep from touching her lips and yet stay her further speech. Floral, just like her name. He leaned incrementally nearer, inhaling discreetly to catch more of it.

"I shouldn't think there will be many occasions for privacy between us," she said, her dark lashes impossibly long as they swept over her eyes to hide her thoughts from him.

He wanted, quite suddenly and irritatingly, to press his lips to the hollow at the base of her throat. To discover if that was where she applied her perfume. To know the warmth of her silken skin beneath his mouth.

"Within these four walls, and within any other walls of my choosing, you will call me Maxim," he commanded.

Because he was king, damn it. And she ought to remember it.

The title had never appealed to him because it had been his by birth and then stolen mercilessly from him. Rather, it was the power of the throne, the might of his armies, the trepidation with which everyone viewed him, that imbued King Maximilian with the right to rule. And he had earned all of those things with his own spilled blood and the blood of thousands of men far better than he.

"I do not—"

"Silence," he interrupted in a harsh bark, because he didn't like her insolence.

She needed to know her place, even if he regarded women far more highly than the court from which she hailed. The highest, in fact. His own mother had been a damned saint. But that was neither here nor there.

"Forgive me, Your—"

"Woman, do you try your hardest to displease me?" he broke in again, tempted to take her chin in hand and force her to hold his gaze when she looked away, and yet hesitant to tempt himself by touching her. "You will be in my court soon. You will be treated with care and respect there. No man shall raise his hand against you, nor cause you any harm. But you will, by God, do as I say. And I say you will call me Maxim and that you will not curtsy or otherwise lower yourself before me when I do not wish it. Am I understood?"

He couldn't say why this was important to him. Why he wanted her capitulation every bit as much as he wanted her to defy him. It was maddening. *She* was maddening. He wasn't meant to notice her. His union with Princess Anastasia St. George, coupled with the revolution he intended to set in motion in her homeland of Boritania, would give him the position of strength he required for his own small island kingdom. Together, Boritania and Varros could be magnificent.

But the only magnificence he was thinking about as he awaited Lady Tansy's response was that which belonged to her alone.

He thought she said something beneath her breath in Boritanian. But that couldn't be—surely she knew he comprehended her language by now, after he had overheard her vulgar curse earlier and made her aware of it. She was not a stupid woman. Rather, he suspected she was far too intelligent. There was a lively light burning in her gaze.

"Am I understood?" he prodded.

"It is wrong of me to be so familiar," she said, her eyes searing his with such bold, unwavering daring that for a moment he could do naught but stare at her, dumbfounded.

Maxim crossed his arms over his chest and glared at her, mostly to keep from touching her as he wanted, for this woman wasn't his, even if his meddlesome cock had other ideas. "It isn't wrong when I command you, Lady Tansy. I am your king."

"Not yet, Your Majesty."

Such spirit. Incredible that it hadn't been extinguished in Boritania beneath the king's vile rule. Perhaps it was only her role as lady-in-waiting that had rendered it possible.

"Your audacity is foolhardy," he said, impressed and annoyed in equal measure.

"You are marrying Princess Anastasia. My first loyalty is, as ever, to her. She will be your queen."

Lady Tansy's dulcet voice was quiet and yet it carried a firm strength. She wasn't wrong either; he appreciated that she was loyal. In his experience, few people were, particularly when motivated by greed. He had known more than his fair share of vipers who had been willing to smile to his face and feign a true kinship or friendship, meanwhile hiding the dagger behind their backs, waiting to plunge it between his ribs.

"And as she will be my queen, your loyalty will be to me as well," he pointed out, absurdly nettled.

This entire dialogue hardly mattered. He had not come here to argue with his future queen's lady-in-waiting. Rather, he had come to speak with his future queen.

His future queen, who remained, quite conspicuously, absent.

Lady Tansy watched him, her countenance immobile, her mysterious eyes more potent than he could bear. Her intense regard was making his prick go hard. Ye gods, when had a woman's mere regard ever made him get a cockstand?

Never.

"Speaking of my future queen," he bit out, changing subjects and tactics abruptly, "where is she?"

That made Lady Tansy blink.

Ah.

Telling, that blink. The lone indication that she was not entirely at ease.

"She has gone on your errand, at your request," she said.

He knew that, of course. Princess Anastasia had taken his carriage. His most-trusted men watched her and kept her safe. The life of the woman who would be his queen was of the utmost importance. And Maxim didn't trust the princess's uncle, King Gustavson, as far as he could throw the bastard. He suspected the king had sent assassins to London to watch the princess and kill her if she proved herself more liability than asset.

Concern brewed within him as he took note of the gray pall beyond the windows. "The hour is growing late, however. Should she not have returned by now?"

"I expect her at any moment," the lady-in-waiting said, her tone dutiful, her voice kept carefully low, lest any of the guards beyond overhear.

And he couldn't blame Lady Tansy. For they all played a dangerous game with Gustavson's guards. Princess Anastasia feigned illness whilst secretly seeking her exiled brother, the rightful king of Boritania and the one man Maxim truly needed to be able to wrest the throne from Gustavson. Because he needed peace in Boritania. He needed the kingdom to prosper and flourish. He needed trade and an alliance between Boritania and Varros that would be worth more than the damned paper upon which it was written.

"I'll wait, then," he said, testing her to see if she was lying on behalf of the princess.

A second blink, and then the small pink tip of Lady Tansy's tongue crept over her lower lip, leaving it glistening. "I am certain Your Majesty has better uses for his time."

The appearance of her tongue had left him briefly bereft of air. A sizzling arrow of lust had landed straight in his groin, and all he was able to think about was how feminine, how lush, how desirable the petite lady-in-waiting was. She had a foul mouth to rival any sailor's, and he wanted to know what other wicked things she might say and do with it.

"I'll be the judge of that," he snapped, irked by his unwanted reaction to her.

Maxim prided himself on his iron rule and his iron control. He was forty years old. This slip of a girl should not tempt him so.

"Of course, Your Majesty," she demurred.

And he couldn't shake the feeling that her humility was false, like a mantle she donned solely for his benefit. That the true Lady Tansy was hidden somewhere beneath her calm, imperturbable mask.

"How old are you?" he asked, needing to know.

"I am of an age with Princess Anastasia," she answered primly.

As if he knew how old the blasted princess was. He stared at the lady-in-waiting, trapped in the mysterious, cool depths of her eyes.

"How old is she?" he asked finally.

"She is your betrothed. I thought Your Majesty would know."

There was a tiny thread of censure wrapped about her tone, as if he had disappointed her with his lack of knowledge about the princess. But he wouldn't feel a crumb of guilt over it. He wasn't wooing the princess. He wasn't some love-sick hound trailing at her heels. He was a king intent upon strengthening his rule and bringing more wealth and prosperity to his people.

"She is young enough to bear me children," he grumbled, running a hand along his jaw to find the prickle of whiskers his man had just shaved that morning already returning. "Her precise age never interested me."

Nor had the princess, aside from what marriage to her would enable him to obtain.

Lady Tansy's gaze traveled to a point somewhere over his shoulder. "Of course, Your Majesty."

She was speaking politely, with such grace and poise, her voice even and sweet. It was a pleasant voice that Lady Tansy had. As pleasant as her face. His own stare dipped to the swell of her breasts beneath her modest gown. And the rest of her too.

But he didn't like the way she said *of course*, as if he had just proven some notion about himself that she had already decided before he had revealed his lack of interest in the woman he was marrying.

"You still haven't told me how old *you* are, Lady Tansy," he reminded her pointedly, jealous of the wall over his shoulder for holding her rapt attention.

He was accustomed to everyone looking at him.

Being in awe of him, whether for his size or his throne or his wealth. He was King of Varros.

"Five-and-twenty," she answered, her eyes still averted.

He wanted those eyes on him, curse it.

He was fifteen years her senior, and he felt every one of his forty years, compared to her youth and beauty.

"Look at me when you speak, my lady," he demanded.

At last, those gray orbs returned to him, but whatever she was feeling and thinking remained hidden. It was then he realized there was a hint of palest blue circling her irises, rather like a sea in the midst of a storm.

"As you wish, Your Majesty."

Her unflappable poise commanded a reaction in him that he couldn't contain. Maxim wanted to ruffle her feathers.

"Better," he allowed grudgingly. "Now come and sit with me while we await the princess's arrival."

Lady Tansy's eyebrows rose. "Sit with you?"

She repeated his request in the manner he imagined she might if he had announced that she must throw herself from the window.

He gave her his most feral grin. "Yes, Lady Tansy. Sit with me."

As he offered her his arm, he knew she had no choice but to take it and allow him to escort her the handful of paces to the sitting area arranged by the fireplace. Her hand settled on his sleeve as lightly as a bird. He placed his hand atop it, keeping her neatly trapped, the warmth of her soft skin a subtle, delicious temptation.

And Maxim had never been adept at denying himself what he wanted, whether a woman or a kingdom.

CHAPTER 2

King Maximilian's hand was incredibly large.
So large that it covered hers entirely on his shot-silk coat sleeve.

And it was hot.

Not as smooth as she would have supposed a king's hand to be. Not that she had spent any time at all considering King Maximilian's hands. No, indeed. The flip in her belly at his touch was a product of her nerves and nothing more.

She was overset, awaiting Princess Anastasia's return. Fearing for her welfare. Yes, that was all. Nervous about the necessity of keeping further company with the king. About the lies she had been telling on the princess's behalf.

King Maximilian guided her to the seating area as politely as if they were at court with the watchful gazes of a hundred courtiers looking on. He was perfectly mannerly. Surprisingly elegant for a man whose barbarous acts on the battlefield and beyond were legendary.

But she wouldn't think of any of those things now, not with him so near, for fear that her countenance would give her away.

"Sit, my lady." His low voice was perilously near to her ear.

With a jolt, she realized he had lowered his head toward hers. Swallowing hard against an odd rush of some unfamiliar emotion, she seated herself with more force than necessary. The impact of her bottom colliding with the cushion made her breasts jostle beneath her gown. To her horror, she saw the king's dark, glittering gaze dip and linger.

An answering fluttering took up residence low in her belly.

Ignoring the unwanted reaction, Tansy made a show of arranging the drapery of her gown around her, flustered beyond measure by his nearness, his voice, his probing stare, his scent. King Maximilian smelled like a Boritanian summer —citrus with a hint of bay. And the more she studied him, the more she was forced to admit just how disturbingly handsome he was.

In a series of sinuous movements that were far more graceful than she would have anticipated from a man of his size, the king seated himself opposite Tansy. The effect was almost comical—the armchair could scarcely contain him. He stretched his long legs before him, crossing them at the ankle, looking comfortable and quite at home, as if he expected to remain there for an indeterminate span of time.

How she hoped and prayed Princess Anastasia would climb through the window soon, and for more reasons than merely her concern for her friend's safety. The king was still far too near. She shifted on her seat, her discomfort growing, her cheeks warming beneath his steady regard.

"Will the guards not wonder at how much time you have spent within the princess's chamber?" she asked, plucking at her skirt to occupy her restless fingers and mind both.

He drummed his own long fingers on the stuffed armrests of his chair. "It's none of their concern."

"But the princess is unwell," she quietly reminded him of their carefully crafted lie. "Surely it is unusual for you to linger in the sickroom for so long. It will be remarked upon."

And her unspoken fear was that any remarks that went back to King Gustavson in Boritania would fall upon all their heads with the weight of a hundred boulders. Every bit as deadly too. Tansy had seen, firsthand, the death and destruction the king was capable of. He was systematically killing the St. George line. She feared the princess was next, despite Gustavson having arranged the match with King Maximilian and agreeing to send her to London for the pomp and circumstance of a formal betrothal announcement.

But King Maximilian did not seem to be afflicted by the worries that had been plaguing Tansy ever since the marriage decree had been given by Gustavson several months ago in Boritania.

He shrugged indolently. "I am the King of Varros. Let them remark."

"Word could reach King Gustavson," she tried again, unable to shake the misgiving haunting her, for it was her duty to protect the princess as well as serve her. "The damage of scandal and gossip would not taint you. It would, however, affect Princess Anastasia."

"I very much doubt that word will reach him of anything that occurs here in London." A small, lethal smile curved his lips, as if he found the notion amusing. "My reputation precedes me."

His reputation was terrifying. It was said that he had gouged out his enemy's eyes with his own bare fingers. Difficult to comprehend when her gaze flitted again to those tapered fingers now, their blunt-tipped nails clean and neatly cut. It was also said that he had smeared the blood of enemy soldiers on his face to terrify his opponents on the battlefield. He had won Varros from a cousin with dubious claims to the throne, but the war had raged on for many years before he had finally done so. Tansy had ceased reading accounts of the king and his misdeeds after a point, too sick to her stomach to continue.

She swallowed hard against a rising surge of disquiet, wondering how it was possible for a man to be so beautifully formed, so handsome and debonair, and yet harbor the soul of a merciless monster beneath his façade.

"Of course, Your Majesty," she managed.

"*Of course,*" he repeated, a new sharpness entering his voice, though he spoke quietly to keep his voice from carrying. "You say that a great deal, my lady. I suspect it is to keep yourself from voicing your true opinion on matters."

His observation sank its teeth into her like the fangs of a serpent, unexpected and deadly. Worse, he was not wrong. As a lady-in-waiting, she was accustomed to being overlooked in the royal court. She was on the periphery. A gilded adornment to the princess, there for her in every way necessary. No one noticed her.

Not until this man.

She offered him a tight smile. "I haven't an opinion on matters. It is not my place to do so."

He leaned forward, bracing his elbows on his well-muscled thighs, his expression intent. "What lies you spin, Lady Tansy. Do you think me a fool?"

Tansy's shoulders tensed. "Of—" She paused, inhaling swiftly as she realized she had been about to say *of course* yet again. "I do not, Your Majesty," she corrected.

"But you must, or else you would not...what is the word...*patronize* me."

They were conducting their conversation in English, for it was as familiar to Tansy as Boritanian, a language that was commonly used at court. She spoke no Varrosian. King Maximilian, however, possessed a fluency in all three languages. And there was something about the way he uttered that lone word, *patronize*, rolling the *r*, that slid over her like warm honey. Like the wicked promise of more when she knew she could not trust it.

"I would never patronize Your Majesty," she reassured him, inwardly issuing yet another fervent prayer that Princess Anastasia would return imminently.

In the next second, preferably.

But a glance at the window proved that her request had gone unanswered.

"You would, and you have."

His insistence had her jerking her gaze back to him, finding him studying her as if she were a mystery he intended to solve. His dark eyes glittered as they clashed with hers. She wished she could read the emotion in their brown-black depths, and yet she could not any more than she could understand him. The king was an enigma.

A dangerous, fearsome, tremendous, vexingly *handsome* enigma.

"I must beg Your Majesty's forgiveness for any slight I have paid," she managed past the myriad of emotions threatening to clog her throat and steal her voice.

"How will you beg it?" he asked, raising a brow as if in challenge.

For a moment, she had no answer. But then she clung to her sangfroid, which had stood her in good stead through King Gustavson's court of vipers.

"How would you have me beg it?" she returned, refusing to wilt beneath his stern countenance and frank regard.

"I have many ideas, my lady," he drawled, reaching into his coat. "However, as none of them would be wise, I have an alternative solution." He extracted a golden, gem-encrusted flask from his coat and held it aloft. "A drink."

She eyed the flask, wondering at its contents. No doubt, it contained spirits. Speaking of unwise...partaking in anything with a king who was betrothed to the princess seemed foolhardy indeed. And Tansy could not shake the impression that there had been an overt sensuality in his words.

I have many ideas.

No, she must not think of them. Nor entertain the inexplicable spark of warmth in her belly at his presence and nearness and the way his bold gaze traveled over her form, as lingeringly as a touch.

"If it pleases Your Majesty," she agreed, reaching for the flask against her better judgment.

As she took it from him, their fingers grazed, and a new frisson leapt past her wrist, up her arm, and then down her spine.

"Much would please me, Lady Tansy. Beginning with you calling me Maxim."

Maxim.

The name, like the invitation, like the man, felt dangerous.

Holding the flask more tightly than was necessary, she opened it and brought it to her lips, tipping it back. Cool liquid sluiced over her tongue; the flask was fuller than she had anticipated, leaving her with a mouthful. A foul-tasting mouthful.

She jerked the flask from her lips and forced herself to swallow the dreadful concoction. Her eyes watered as she struggled not to choke and sputter.

A low rumble interrupted her misery.

It was coming from the king, watching her with hooded eyes. Laughter, she realized. He didn't seem a man who was capable of levity, and yet he was laughing. At her. Tansy's cheeks went hot, embarrassment creeping over her.

"What is it?" she managed, her voice raspy.

"Scotch whisky. Have you never tried it before?"

"Never," she croaked, wishing she could spit the taste of the vile stuff from her mouth. "Nor can I see the allure."

His lips turned up into a smile.

And for a searing moment, Tansy forgot the flavor coating her tongue. Because when King Maximilian of Varros smiled, her breath caught, seizing in her lungs. Every part of her body became exquisitely aware of him as a man. His handsomeness was austere and forbidding, but when his mouth curved and the grooves at the corners of his eyes deepened, his masculine beauty was nothing short of arresting.

"Perhaps it's a spirit that one must try several times to garner an appreciation."

His tone was low, almost intimate. As was his gaze, lingering on her lips as she licked them to rid them of the terrible flavor of his Scotch whisky.

She almost said *of course*, her usually unassailable nerves rattled by this man and his mercurial personality. But she bit back the words at the last moment.

"Perhaps," she allowed instead, offering the flask to him.

He accepted it, and unless she was mistaken, deliberately caused their fingers to brush once more. Holding her stare, he brought the flask to his lips, making a show of placing them where hers had so recently been, and taking a long pull of the awful spirits within. She watched as his Adam's apple dipped twice whilst he swallowed. A ring on his finger caught her attention—it was fashioned of gold with a red stone at its center.

He lowered the flask and offered it to her again. "Test our theory, Lady Tansy."

Our theory.

There was something equally intimate about the word *our*, the implication that they were somehow secretly united, even if only for the purpose of something as trivial as sharing a drink. The air surrounding them certainly felt intimate. They were alone, his long limbs spread out so that his booted feet nearly touched her gown's hem. They were in a bedchamber.

The *princess's* bedchamber, she reminded herself sternly as she accepted the flask with great reluctance. "I'm not certain I should. I very much fear my mouth shall never recover if I ingest another sip of your foul brew."

He drummed his fingers on his thigh, the ruby winking from his ring like a taunt. "If you aren't daring enough for a second taste, I understand."

He questioned her mettle?

Tansy raised the flask to her lips, holding her breath as she poured another measure down her throat, hoping she wouldn't regret her capitulation.

And somehow suspecting she would.

～

The act of sharing a flask had never filled Maxim with unadulterated lust.

Or, at least, it hadn't until now.

But there had been something damnably erotic about placing his lips on the cool metal where Lady Tansy's had been. And watching her as she attempted to prove her daring to him by choking down another swallow of his whisky was its own form of sensual torture. Because her defiance, her bravado...ye gods, they were mesmerizing. The quiet little lady-in-waiting possessed the fortitude of steel.

And he liked it.

Liked the sharp intelligence hiding in her eyes. Liked the way her shoulders went back and her spine stiffened before she met his challenge. Liked that she was willing to swallow his *foul brew*, as she had called it, just so that he wouldn't think her weak.

Liked *her*.

And curse it all, that was a problem. Because he wasn't meant to like the lady-in-waiting of his future queen. He was meant to like the woman he would wed.

The one who was still presently missing.

Lady Tansy lowered the flask to her lap, wrinkling her nose as she swallowed loudly enough that the indelicate sound broke the peacefulness of the chamber.

"It's still perfectly vile," she announced with a moue of distaste.

He tried to recall the first time he'd ever tippled. It had been so long ago.

"I thought the same when I had my initial taste," he told her and then wondered why the hell he was confiding in a woman he scarcely knew.

A woman he ought not to know any better. And yet, he couldn't seem to help himself.

"How long have you been drinking it?" she asked, surprising him with her soft query.

With her interest in him as well.

No one asked him questions that were of a personal nature. At least, no one, save his rascal brother. But Nando was likely debauching a bored wife of the *ton* at this very moment. Perhaps even two at once.

Maxim reminded himself of Lady Tansy's question, forcing his mind to return to long-ago days that seemed a lifetime away, days that were forever out of reach. "I was a stripling of fourteen at the time, and I'm a man of forty now. I reckon it has been a long time."

"Fourteen seems terribly young for a man to drink such stringent spirits," she said, still holding the flask in her dainty hand.

He could not tell if she was reluctant to return it to him or if she had forgotten she yet held it.

Likely the latter.

"My sire gave me the whisky. His mother was Scottish. A Graham." The warmth fled him as he recalled the reason for the drink instead of the heritage that had supplied it on the far-flung, sun-drenched island of Varros. "We were at war with my uncle. I had just watched my first man die. His blood was yet on my hands when my father gave me the whisky and told me to drink, that doing so would help to numb the shock."

Lady Tansy's countenance had grown taut with compassion, her brow furrowed. "And did it?"

He shook his head. "No. It didn't. That wasn't the first lie my father told me, nor was it the last."

Gods, why was he telling her this? He wasn't even slightly soused. He had no decent excuse.

"I don't remember my father," she said, her voice small. "He died when I was quite young."

And then she surprised him by bringing the flask to her lips and taking another healthy sip.

"I'm sorry, my lady," he offered, knowing it was woefully inadequate. He had lost his father in the early half of the Varros Great War, and he had never entirely recovered from it. "I still miss my own sire," he added, "though he has been gone these last twenty years."

Lady Tansy nodded solemnly and extended his flask. "Loss doesn't grow easier with time, does it? Everyone tells you that it will, that passing years soften the sting of the blow."

"But they do not," he agreed, accepting her offering. "Nothing can."

He took a healthy swig from the flask, feeling for a moment as if they were the only two people in the world, sharing secrets and whisky. Each witnessing a part of the other that no one else had been permitted to see.

"You loved your father, did you not?"

Her soft voice cut through the quiet, the question like a blade slicing to his black, ash-filled heart.

Maxim thought of the fearless, stoic warrior he had known. The man who had cut down enemy soldiers without pause and yet who had sung him the same Gaelic lullabies his own mother had sung to him years earlier when Maxim had been naught but a lad. He had been soft and yet hard, his father. He'd been what the world had made him. And Maxim was no different.

"He was a good man," he rasped instead of answering her question directly, for doing so felt far too raw and personal. "He should have been king."

And yet, his father had never lived to ascend the throne that had rightfully belonged to him. Instead, his father's half brother, born from an annulled marriage and disavowed by the Varrosian church, had gained the support of powerful members of parliament through bribery and had seized the throne when Father had been a naïve young man himself.

He had paid dearly for his trust in his own kinsman.

And so had many loyal members of the House of Tayrnes, their lives lost during the endless, bloody years of the Varros Great War.

"That is the reason, then," Lady Tansy said quietly, as if making sense of something.

Perhaps speaking her thoughts aloud unintentionally, with a bit of aid from the whisky she had consumed. He had only the finest delivered to Varros from his grandmother's family. Potent and smooth.

"The reason?" he prodded, though he suspected he well understood what she was suggesting.

"For your betrothal," she elaborated. "For the rest."

By *the rest*, Lady Tansy meant his plot to find the exiled Prince Theodoric St. George, the only man he trusted to restore law and order to Boritania in the wake of the revolution Maxim intended to sow. As the closest and most-trusted female in Princess Anastasia's circle, Lady Tansy was privy to Maxim's plot. Her assistance and silence were necessary, given the dangerous nature of their plan. Gustavson had seen his own sister-in-law, Princess Anastasia's mother, tortured in the dungeons and sent to the gallows for execution. He had also almost certainly murdered his nephew. He had tortured the exiled prince they sought to find.

Maxim inclined his head, taking another pull from his flask and swallowing before answering. "There are many reasons, Lady Tansy."

He offered her the flask, suspecting she would refuse. But when she reached for it, her fingers yet again glancing against his, he was shocked.

And impressed.

She plucked it from his grasp and raised it to her lips with a bravado he recognized all too well from his years on the battlefield. Lady Tansy Francis was attempting to prove herself to him.

Sweet Christ above, he was experiencing something far worse than an inconvenient hard cock just now. He was experiencing...

Admiration.

That was the word for it. Foreign and familiar at once, for so few of his acquaintance had managed to earn it.

She lowered the flask, only the slightest hint of her

distaste for the whisky visible on her lovely countenance now. "Tell me, then." She paused and, as if remembering their disparity of stations belatedly, she added, "If it pleases Your Majesty to do so."

He could think of many, many things that would please him more, but that was base lust inside him, his prick thinking on behalf of his brain. He tamped down such wayward thoughts, unwanted longings.

"Now isn't the time for such revelations, my lady," he forced himself to say.

For he didn't dare lay bare the full extent of his plotting. Not to this lady-in-waiting who tempted him beyond measure. Nor to anyone. His time at war had taught him well.

Trust no one but yourself.

"I should not have been so forward as to ask." She handed the flask back to him, her voice subdued.

He accepted it, raising the vessel to his lips for a longer draught, but nothing would numb the twinge deep inside him at the change in her demeanor. A change he was responsible for. Nor could he tamp down the stupid, futile urge to confide everything in her.

Perhaps it had been too long since he'd known the comfort of a feminine presence in his life as well as his bed. His mistress Lucinda had never been capable of soothing him the way Mina had.

"I give you leave to be forward with me," he said, wiping his lips with the back of his hand.

The gesture was crude, far more worthy of the battlefield than a private tête-à-tête with a woman as regal and refined as Lady Tansy.

Color blossomed, pale pink in her cheeks, and he belatedly realized the double entendre in the invitation he had just issued. If he were a better man, a polite man, he might have hastened to correct his words. Or to apologize. Since he was neither of those, he did nothing.

"Why have you come, Your Majesty?" she asked quietly.

The reminder was unwanted.

"To pay a call upon my betrothed." Holding her stare, he took another pull from the flask.

A polite smile curved her lips, and he couldn't shake the notion that it was forced. "Perhaps you should return tomorrow."

Was she *dismissing* him? Did she dare to reject his presence here? Emotion stirred deep inside him. Not lust. Not mere admiration. But something else, something far more dangerous.

Slowly, he lowered the flask, taking great care to replace its lid. "Mayhap I should. When would be a better time to pay her a visit, Lady Tansy?"

They were dancing about the truth, unable to speak it. Princess Anastasia was presently seeking her long-lost, exiled brother. When she would sneak back into the chamber was a mystery to which he hadn't an answer. But he wondered if the clever lady-in-waiting did.

Her pause and the flick of her pink tongue over her lips just before she answered him told the tale well enough. Lady Tansy was nervous. And she didn't know when to expect the princess's return.

Damn it, he needed Princess Anastasia. Without her, his chances of finding her brother Prince Theodoric were grim. To say nothing of persuading the man to aid his own cause, should he locate him. The princess—and her welfare—was priceless to him.

"Tomorrow evening," the lady-in-waiting suggested. "After your obligations."

He tucked his flask back inside his coat, knowing it would be far better to finish drinking its contents later—alone. "I'll return then, my lady. Be certain to tell your princess just how much I value her health when she *wakes*."

The last was said for the benefit of Gustavson's guards, should they be anywhere in the vicinity. But the warning within it was purely for Lady Tansy. A great deal was resting upon the shoulders of Princess Anastasia. And she had damned well better prove her usefulness to him.

Or else.

"I will be certain to extend your felicitations," Lady Tansy said, utterly imperturbable as she rose and smoothed her skirts, all the intimacy they had shared in those stolen moments effectively obliterated.

Grinding his jaw in irritation, he rose, towering over her. "Until tomorrow, madam."

She dipped into as fine a curtsy as he had ever seen at court. "Your Majesty."

She had once more reverted to pure, icy reserve. If he hadn't heard those perfect lips of hers uttering such vulgarities earlier at his entrance, he wouldn't have believed her capable of it.

But he had, and now he knew that there was far more to Lady Tansy Francis than he had previously supposed.

May the gods rot his cock for it.

CHAPTER 3

$\mathcal{M}$axim was pacing the entry hall when his brother swept in from the mews with a dripping greatcoat and a half-sotted grin.

"The hour is late," he told Nando curtly in their native tongue, for although English was as familiar to him as Varrosian, when he was in a state, he preferred their language.

"Too late to be marching, brother," Nando said, removing his hat and sending a shower of water droplets to the polished floor.

"Is it raining again?" he asked needlessly, ignoring his brother's pointed remark.

Nando knew him too well. Only Mina had known him better, but he had been a vastly different man then. In the fifteen years that had passed since her death, Maxim had changed so much that he doubted she would recognize him. The thought was not without the omnipresent bitterness that haunted him, along with the stinging lash of blame. For what had happened to his sweet, lovely Mina was Maxim's fault alone.

"It is always raining," Nando remarked with a devil-may-care shrug. "One only need fret over it when one ventures out of doors. And why venture beyond four comfortable walls when there is so much beautiful entertainment to be found within?"

"Within the walls of some countess's bedchamber, no doubt," he muttered, his foot tapping on the floor to the rhythm that soothed him.

If he ceased his measured pacing, then he had to move *something* or else his cravat choked him and his skin felt too tight and his entire body felt as if it were crawling with insects. But that was only when his fits took hold of him. He had been doing his utmost to battle them, waging an inner war.

One he was currently losing.

"She was a duchess," Nando said glibly. "Her friend may have been a countess, however. Lady Such-and-Sundry, if I'm not mistaken."

Maxim slid a finger between his cravat and his throat, creating an incremental space that seemed somehow vital for continued breathing. "You were carrying on exactly as I supposed you would be this evening, then."

"Where are all the servants?" Nando frowned as he looked about, sounding perplexed. "My hat and greatcoat are dread-fully sodden."

"They're abed," Maxim growled, trying not to feel irritated with his brother and failing. "It is half past three in the morning."

"Is it?" His brother tossed his top hat away as if it were an insult, the felt brim and crown traveling end over end to land with a damp thud some feet away. "Ye gods. London ladies keep disreputable hours."

Oh, to be as carefree as Nando, with his head of blond curls and his sea-blue eyes that forever had the ladies swooning. Nando seducing whomever he wished. Nando flitting about at night without a care as to kingdoms or thrones or alliances or exiled princes or revolutions.

Or beautiful, gray-gazed ladies-in-waiting who were forbidden.

Maxim tapped his foot and crossed his arms over his chest, pinning his brother with an unimpressed stare. "Indeed."

"Hmm," Nando hummed, shucking his greatcoat and sending a fresh flurry of water to the floor. "Whatever happened to the carpets?"

"They were ruined," he said simply, thinking it best not to trouble his younger brother with the entire truth.

The blood had proven too difficult to remove from the woolen rugs covering the polished wood. In the end, they'd been rolled up, neatly concealing the body within.

"Ruined how?" Nando countered, surprising Maxim with his persistence and curiosity both.

"It hardly signifies." Maxim waved his hand dismissively.

Tap. Tap. Tap.

But his brother's eyes narrowed, dropping to Maxim's restless foot. "Something has happened."

Yes, something damned well had. *Something* had been an enemy infiltrating the haven of the town house he had leased for this infernal betrothal announcement. An announcement he was only making to further his goal of securing peace and prosperity for his kingdom and his people.

"It has been dealt with," he said simply. "You should go to bed."

Nando raised a lone, dark brow. "And leave you alone in this state? I think not, brother."

In this state.

Maxim clenched his jaw and rolled his shoulders at the words, the implication. The unspoken acknowledgment that something was inherently wrong with him. He supposed he should be grateful that Nando hadn't uttered the word that truly incited him to abject rage—*madness*.

"I'll remind you that I am your king," he said sternly.

But despite his proclamation, he still couldn't stop tapping his damned foot. Because when the fits came, his body was not his own. It was as if it belonged to another.

"You are my brother first," Nando said, throwing his soaked greatcoat in the same direction as his abandoned hat.

It landed with a heavy thud on the newly revealed parquet.

Maxim stared at the coat and hat, noting a small smear of red on the wall that had been missed by his assiduous servants in their earlier efforts at cleaning. Shooting a man was so blasted messy. Tomorrow, he would see the last trace of what had happened upon his return from visiting Lady Tansy removed. For tonight, he couldn't stomach wiping the blood from the plaster himself for fear of the effect it might have upon him.

He hated blood, a fact which had never bothered the gossips who had claimed he'd smeared the blood of his enemies on his face in battle.

Hated its hot slipperiness. Hated its metallic scent, the taste of it in his mouth. The splatter of it on his face and hands in the midst of a battle. His own soldiers' life source...

His stomach clenched violently.

Tap. Tap. Tap.

He clenched and unclenched his hands at his sides, the itchiness becoming overwhelming. He had to start pacing. Moving. He couldn't continue standing still thusly.

"Brother?"

Nando's familiar, calming voice stole him from the grips of whatever ailed him, forcing his gaze back to his brother. His reckless, careless, wonderful brother. The battlefield had left them both wounded and scarred in more ways than one, but they shouldered their burdens differently.

Maxim swallowed hard against a rising surge of bile. "I need to walk, Nando."

It wasn't an explanation, nor was it an acknowledgment. Rather, it was a bitter confession. A vulnerability from a man who couldn't afford to possess one.

The desperation edging his voice must have been sufficient, for Nando nodded, striding forward until they were shoulder to shoulder. "I'll walk with you."

The gesture made something unfurl inside him. His throat grew tight.

"You needn't," Maxim managed, though there was no one else he would trust to see him in such a state.

"We are all the family each other has in this world," Nando reminded him needlessly. "I will walk with you through the fires of Hades if necessary."

And Maxim knew that, for all his rakish ways and endless seductions and careless ease, Nando meant those words to his marrow.

So he managed a nod, his throat tight. "If you must."

"I must."

They fell into a familiar stride, side by side, shoulder to shoulder, their feet moving in time. He couldn't say why one of the most brutal memories he possessed—the march across the Tayrnes forest and through the mountain pass, when they had lost their mounts and had been forced to travel by foot—should also be the source of an act that soothed him. And yet, it was. Life was mysterious, but the affliction he suffered was more so. The royal physician had neither a name for it, nor a cure.

They traveled three lengths of the entry hall before the rising panic inside Maxim subsided enough for him to attempt speech.

"A duchess and a countess, you say?"

"One sitting on my face whilst—"

"Fucking hell," he interrupted. "I have no wish for details, brother. I was merely trying for polite conversation."

"Polite, you?" Nando laughed lightly. "I wouldn't have thought it possible."

Fair enough. Neither would he have. Maxim hadn't attempted pleasantries or the pageantry of court since assuming the throne. Gentility and gallantry—even polite conversation—had always felt hollow and foolish without Mina. She had been the sole thread binding him to civility.

And now...

Now, he would soon have a new wife, even if his mind was currently stumbling upon someone else. That, too, would pass.

He was sure of it.

"I can be polite," he countered as they turned in tandem and resumed marching down the entry hall, their booted footsteps falling in perfect timing.

It was a balm to his ragged soul, those steady, rhythmic taps. The action was familiar and calming.

"Brother, your manners are woefully lacking."

"I wasn't the one with a duchess on my face earlier," he pointed out, the darkness fogging his mind receding.

"It was the countess on my face, if you must know," Nando drawled. "The duchess was sucking my—"

"Silence," he interrupted. "Kindly keep the details of your misadventures to yourself."

"As you keep yours to yourself?" Nando's tone, like his question, was razor-sharp.

His brother wasn't fooled by his lack of explanation about the missing carpets. Nando might be a rakehell of the worst order, but he was also damned intelligent. Still, Maxim didn't want to talk about what had happened. The seizing in his chest was finally beginning to abate.

"Ask Felix if you must know," he said instead, referring to his deadliest guard.

The one who, as it happened, had been responsible for dispatching the spy who had dared to infiltrate the house with the intent of sending word back to King Gustavson in Boritania. When the bastard had been confronted, he had extracted a vicious-looking blade from his coat, wielding it against Maxim. Fortunately, Felix had acted with his customary haste and precision.

"I will in the morning," Nando said, still keeping the steady rhythm as they paced the length of the entry hall in the opposite direction. "I'm too tired to seek him out this evening, and I have a suspicion hearing his tale will only make it more difficult for me to sleep."

That was something they had in common—the dreams that haunted them and the darkness that made it impossible to find peace.

"Your suspicion is correct," he said curtly, trying to keep his mind from the gruesome details.

Trying to think instead of the pleasing floral scent of Lady Tansy. The softness of her skin when he had touched her. The awareness that had flared between them. The tingling in his lips when he had laid his where hers had been. The secrets and whisky they had shared, as if they were old friends instead of wary strangers.

"You should try to get some rest, brother," Nando told him quietly, sounding worried.

He was accustomed to his brother's concern for his welfare. And grateful he never elaborated. The shame that threatened to drown him along with his demons was never far.

"I cannot yet," he admitted, sighing heavily. "Perhaps I'll play a game of chess."

"With yourself?" Nando scoffed. "If you won't sleep, then neither shall I. But fair warning. I'll crow when I trounce you."

Relief washed over him, chasing more of the disquiet. "We both know that I always win, brother."

"Lies." Nando neatly led them down the hall to the library where Maxim's favorite chess board, brought from Varros, had been laid in preparation for just such an occasion.

Hours later as the sun rose in the sky and Maxim finally laid his head on his pillow, it wasn't thoughts of the dead man haunting him, nor was it memories of war. Rather, it was a pair of sparkling gray eyes.

～

"YOU SHOULD EAT MORE," Tansy told Princess Anastasia as she pushed aside the tray of sickroom fare that had been brought to her chamber that morning by one of the English servants.

Blessedly, it hadn't been one of King Gustavson's guards. The less Tansy saw of those scoundrels, the better off she and the princess were, for there were fewer risks of their deception being unraveled. No curious eyes attempting to peer over Tansy's shoulder as she accepted the tray either.

"I cannot eat more," Princess Anastasia said. "You know why."

Of course Tansy knew the reason her friend didn't dare to consume any more than a few bites of toast and some sips of tepid tea. If they wanted her uncle's guards to believe their farce—and they very badly needed them to, for their lives were in danger otherwise—then the princess could not be eating her breakfast as if she were healthy. They couldn't afford for any suspicions to be raised, nor for word to reach the king if there were. Tansy didn't doubt that Gustavson would have them both killed without the slightest hesitation.

A shiver passed down her spine.

"It isn't good for your constitution," she countered anyway. "Surely you must be hungry."

"I am hungry for justice," the princess said softly.

"And something decidedly less noble," Tansy said wryly, though she knew she shouldn't speak of the plan her friend had confided in her.

Not only was it not her place to do so, she would be wise to forget the princess's whispered plot. However, she was worried about her friend. Princess Anastasia was in a position of grave danger, both from her uncle's guards, from her uncle the king, and from her betrothed, King Maximilian.

Thinking of the man who had seated himself by the fire with her the day before made an odd flutter come to life in Tansy's stomach. He had scarcely seemed as ruthless and terrifying as his reputation suggested when he had been sharing his whisky with her. But then, what did she truly know about him?

More than she should, she thought with instant regret and the stinging lash of guilt. For she had been far too familiar with the king.

Princess Anastasia sighed heavily, her blue gaze seeking Tansy's, her countenance unfettered and honest. "You've made no secret of your disapproval. But if you would meet Mr. Tierney yourself, I know you would understand. There is something about him that is…"

"Rakish," Tansy supplied when the princess faltered in her description of the man she had met the evening before with King Maximilian's blessing.

Her friend's lips twisted. "No."

"Disreputable?" she suggested next, hating the notion of

the princess making any manner of ill-advised bargain with an English rogue.

"Magnetic," the princess said with great feeling and another sigh. "The English word was eluding me. And handsome, of course. He is a powerful man."

"As is the king you will wed," Tansy reminded her primly, taking up the tray her friend had scarcely touched.

"Need you mention *him* now?" the princess asked, wrinkling her nose.

Tansy almost revealed the king's visit the day before. She should, she knew. She had always been nothing but honest and loyal to Princess Anastasia. And yet, there was something about King Maximilian's call the day before that felt distinctly intimate. As if it were a secret best kept between the two of them instead of shared with anyone else.

"No good will come of your plan to offer yourself to this man," Tansy whispered, ever cognizant of the guards lurking in the hall. "If the king discovers—"

"How should he discover?" the princess interrupted, shaking her head. "He won't, Tansy."

"He is an intelligent man," she argued, for she had witnessed his keen intellect the day before.

The king saw everything and everyone. He was not the sort of man who would fail to realize he was being betrayed. His keen stare had seemingly bored deep into Tansy's very soul. Nor was he the sort of man one should cross.

"Do you think he would fail to take note if his wife were not a virgin?" she whispered again furiously, feeling her cheeks go hot at the familiarity of her question.

"And how would he know the difference?" Princess Anastasia demanded, frowning mightily, making a dismissive gesture with her hand, the motion somehow flawlessly elegant.

"He would know," Tansy insisted, thinking of the

forbidden book she'd discovered at a shop in Boritania just before they had left for London.

It was written in English, and it was incredibly descriptive and informative in all matters carnal. She was still working her way through the volume, taking care to carry it with her always, lest one of Gustavson's guards should discover it. The consequences of such a detection didn't bear further contemplation, for she knew they could only have one response.

She shuddered.

"Have you taken a chill?" Princess Anastasia asked, her voice tinged with worry. "It is so very damp and cool here in England. A servant should attend the fire."

"I will tend the fire myself if you are cold, Your Royal Highness," she offered dutifully, thinking that the princess must be chilled.

"It isn't your duty to do so," Princess Anastasia said with a frown. "A servant should."

But they both knew that admitting a servant could prove ruinous. If a chambermaid looked too closely at the princess, she would no doubt take note that she didn't appear pale and weary, that she didn't seem ill at all. And if they allowed another servant within, the guards would likely view it as proof that the princess's illness was not as deadly as Tansy had reported. Either way, it was certain that questions would be raised. Word would be sent to King Gustavson. Princess Anastasia's search for her exiled brother would come to a halt.

Tansy shook her head. "We cannot risk it. I'll stoke the flames myself."

She moved to go to the fire, but the princess caught her elbow in a staying grip. "It is beneath you. You are not my servant, Tansy, but my loyal and trusted lady-in-waiting. Beyond that, you are my friend and the sister of my heart."

"I don't mind, Princess." Gently extricating herself from her friend's grasp, Tansy carried the tray to the door.

Laying her ear to it, she listened carefully for sounds in the hall. When nothing reached her, she opened the door, finding the space beyond blessedly bereft of Gustavson's guards. She placed the tray on the floor and snapped the door hastily closed before moving to the fireplace, where the flame had indeed dwindled low.

She knelt at the hearth, making short work of adding kindling and agitating the hot ashes so that new flames were sparking to life, filling the chamber with some much-needed warmth. When she was satisfied with her task's completion, her face hot from her proximity to the fresh fire, she turned back to the princess, who had risen from the bed in her dressing gown.

"Were they out there?" the princess whispered.

The guards, of course.

"No, Your Royal Highness," Tansy reassured her. "I do believe your uncle's minions must be otherwise occupied at the moment."

Another sigh left the princess, this one distinctly relieved. "Wonderful. I wish they would occupy themselves elsewhere every second of each hour. Or better yet, that they would throw themselves from the roof or drown themselves in the Thames."

Tansy's lips twitched with suppressed mirth. "I fear we won't be so fortunate."

"Of course we won't." The princess folded her in an impulsive embrace. "Oh, Tansy. I don't know what I would do without you here with me. Pray don't be displeased with me for wanting to carry on with my plan. It is the only thing I will have done solely for myself in as long as I can recall."

Tansy returned her friend's embrace, understanding her

all too well. "I fear for you, Your Royal Highness. It is my duty to protect you and serve you in all ways."

"I wish you would call me Stasia," the princess said, her voice sounding small and sad.

And once again, Tansy understood. "But you are my princess, and one day soon, you will be my queen."

It was an important distinction, one she couldn't forget.

Even if she had during those intoxicating moments with King Maximilian the day before. As Tansy gave the princess another reassuring squeeze, she vowed to herself that she would never be alone with the king again.

CHAPTER 4

A sudden, jarring knock at the door stole Tansy from the distraction of the book she had been halfheartedly attempting to read. *The Tale of Love*, with its lewd and shockingly descriptive chapters, had been entertaining her previously—a much-needed source of amusement despite the risk she took in reading it. But with her thoughts and heart heavy, she was no longer finding the wickedness within its pages nearly as intriguing as she previously had.

"Who comes?" she called in Boritanian, her heart leaping into her throat as she snapped the volume closed.

The bed behind her was empty, pillows neatly arranged into a princess-shaped lump once more. How she hated these hours of subterfuge, when the risk of discovery was brutally heightened by the princess's glaring absence. They were one knock, one opened door, one curious guard away from all their efforts coming undone. And should that happen, from the inevitable punishment that would follow.

Certain death.

"King Maximilian to see Her Royal Highness, Princess

Anastasia," came the gruff response from the guard, cutting into her worried thoughts.

The pronouncement didn't alleviate any of her concerns.

He had returned, and earlier than she had expected. Tansy had been hoping that Princess Anastasia would be here when he paid his call. Praying that she would.

"No," she muttered to herself, rising from her chair and depositing the book upon a nearby table. "No, no, no."

Why had Princess Anastasia yet to return? How long would she be gone? And would the king suspect something was amiss and that the princess intended to give herself to the man she had paid to find her missing brother?

Tansy felt dizzied, her entire body alight with a strange sense of half panic, half excitement. He was here, and she would have to face him.

"Just a moment, if you please," she called loudly to the guard, casting a frantic glance around the chamber to make certain everything was in its place.

The window was closed, the curtains neatly closed. The bed looked occupied. She strode to it anyway and plumped the pillows, arranging the counterpane to her satisfaction. Delaying the inevitable.

She walked across the room, telling herself that she could survive one more encounter with King Maximilian. But then she opened the door a small sliver and saw broad shoulders, a massive chest, and a knowing, dark stare, and all the reassurances she had offered herself promptly died a swift death.

"Your Majesty," she murmured, awareness washing over her like molten honey.

"Lady Tansy."

The way he said her name in his deep voice made it sound like a sin.

She swallowed hard. "The princess is sleeping."

He raised a brow, his lips tightening incrementally. "I'll wait until she wakes."

She stepped back with great reluctance, allowing him just enough room for entrance, his large body shielding the empty bed from the guard's view beyond in the hall. When he closed the door at his back, she retreated swiftly, putting some necessary distance between them.

For despite all her fervent vows to herself, she was once again alone.

With the king.

His stare traveled up and down the length of her body, and she knew a fleeting, foolish urge to check her gown for wrinkles and her hem for tears or stains. "Good evening."

She dipped into a curtsy. "Good evening, Your Majesty."

He was already walking when she straightened, his long-limbed strides taking him across the chamber to the princess's bed. With a swift, efficient motion, he peeled back the bedclothes, revealing the lumpy assortment of pillows beneath.

"As I suspected," he drawled.

His countenance was as hard as if it had been hewn in stone; there was no softness to King Maximilian. Not even a spare hint of flesh on his lean, muscular form. And his implacable stare was upon her, as if she were responsible for Princess Anastasia's failure to return promptly enough for his call.

Her suspicions over the princess's tardiness made Tansy's ears go hot.

The king's gaze narrowed to glittering obsidian slits as he let the bedclothes drop back into place. "You know something you aren't confiding in me."

He issued the words as an accusation rather than a question.

She swallowed hard. "Of course not, Your Majesty."

King Maximilian approached her in a predatory prowl. "What did I tell you yesterday about all your *of courses*, Lady Tansy? Could it be that you've already forgotten?"

His voice was soft to keep it from carrying to the hall, and yet it bore an underlying strength that was as hard as granite. She clasped her hands together before her and resisted the urge to retreat from his imposing form as he stopped near enough to touch. She had a wild, fleeting thought about what it would feel like to place her hand on his massive chest, to test the strength of his arms. But then she hastily dashed the unwanted curiosity away.

"Naturally, I have not," she said. "Your Majesty said that you suspected I used the phrase to keep myself from offering my true opinion on a matter. However, as I said yesterday, I haven't any opinions. It is not my place to do so."

"Are you telling me that I am *wrong*, my lady?" he asked sharply.

He had certainly laid a neat trap for her. Any answer she could give would pay him insult.

"I would never deign to do so," she told him solemnly.

"Hmm," he said, that disapproving hum he had given her the day before.

Not a growl, at least, nor a grunt. Dare she consider it an improvement?

"Are you a liar then, as well as a lady-in-waiting?" he asked shrewdly, and she had her answer.

Decidedly not an improvement.

"I do not count myself a liar, Your Majesty," she answered quietly.

He seemed somehow harsher today. The slash of his jaw was tense, and he looked very much like a man who carried the weight of the world upon his shoulders. No doubt, he did carry the weight of his kingdom and his people. For a wild, fleeting moment, she knew a pang of guilt at the secret she was keeping from him, but then she banished the unworthy emotion. Her loyalty was to Princess Anastasia above all else.

"You've a secret," he said firmly, insistently.

His gaze was hard and glittering. Probing and penetrating.

There was something about this man that made her intensely aware of him. It was as if her body were somehow commanded by his presence, making a traitor of her with every moment they spent alone.

"I have no secrets, Your Majesty," she said, giving him the somber answer that she knew she must.

"You haven't any secrets just as you haven't any opinions," he said, his voice low and deep and somehow smooth and cutting all at once. A slow smile curved his lips, and the transformative effect it had upon his already handsome countenance left her breathless. "And yet, you claim not to be a liar."

He took another step closer, bringing with him the tempting hint of leather and citrus and musk. And he was towering over her now in truth, near enough to touch, the three gold buttons on his white linen shirt within easy reach. They bore his insignia, she realized for the first time.

King Maximilian was a devilishly handsome man.

She could admit it to herself. From his black hair with the blazing silver at his temples to his massive form and sensual mouth to those dark, knowing eyes.

"Yes, Your Majesty," she answered simply, her eyes slipping to the Aubusson at her feet, for she couldn't bear to continue holding his gaze.

It was like staring into the sun.

"You will call me Maxim from this moment forward."

It was the command of a king. Of a man who knew his dictate would not be questioned. A man who was powerful and understood it, who wasn't afraid to flex his proverbial muscle.

"I cannot," she denied him just the same.

"You can, and you shall." He leaned down, the heat emanating from him palpable, so near that she felt his breath coasting over her neck and his lips grazed her ear. "What is it that you're not telling me?"

The soft brush of his mouth over her skin shook Tansy. Her nipples went instantly hard beneath her stays, a jolt of awareness gliding through her to land low in her belly. For a moment, she was frozen, trapped in the astonishing effect his nearness and touch had upon her. The thought of him lowering his head a scant inch and pressing his lips to her throat flashed through her before she banished it.

"Why should you think I have a secret?" she managed to force past the inconvenient longing still holding her in its relentless clutches.

To her utter frustration, the king did not straighten to his full height, nor did he step away from her.

"You don't ask the questions, Lady Tansy," he growled darkly. "I do." And then he did move, but not in the manner she would have preferred, giving her some much-needed distance from his massive presence and equally large, masculine form. He lifted his head just enough that they were almost nose to nose, his breath falling over her mouth as if it were a kiss, his dark stare burning into hers. "Now tell me what it is that makes such shadows hide in those gray eyes of yours."

She was thinking of Princess Anastasia's determination to give herself to the man she had hired to help find her brother. It was a bold plan, a foolish and reckless one. For Tansy feared that on King Maximilian's wedding night, he would discover the truth and there would be hell to pay. She feared for the princess.

Feared that even now, the princess's lack of punctual return signaled that she had cast herself headlong into ruin. But Tansy didn't dare make any such revelations to the handsome, sinful king.

He was her enemy, and she must not forget it, even if he was far too handsome and her unwanted attraction to him wouldn't abate.

"You noticed the color of my eyes," she said instead, feigning a boldness she didn't feel. "I am honored, Your Majesty."

Not only had she failed to answer him, but she had also refused to refer to him as he had demanded.

A small smile curved his lips, and he tilted his head, as if to study her better. "So, that is to be the way of it between us, then."

She disliked the way he said *between us*, implying that the two of them were anything more than strangers. Somehow adding an underlying intimacy that made her heart pound faster and made yearning pool in her belly. It was a yearning that must never be answered.

Tansy held his regard, unflinching, willing herself to remain as impervious as stone. "That is very much the way of it."

Had he doubted it would be any different? She was the lady-in-waiting to his future queen. They had been inseparable since they had both been young, naïve girls. Before the world had changed and jaded them. And Tansy did not just consider Princess Anastasia the sister she had never had; she owed the princess her life. Without the St. George family, Tansy would have been adrift in the vast sea of the Boritanian court, without a home or anyone to care for her.

She owed the princess nothing less than her pure, constant loyalty. And that was what made her uncontrollable reaction to King Maximilian all the more infuriating. She hated herself for the way she felt in his presence. For the restless urge to touch him, to be touched by him.

"You do know that you are speaking to your king, do you not?" he asked then, tearing her from her ruminations.

"You will not be my king until you marry Her Royal Highness, Princess Anastasia."

They stared at each other, each of them unwilling to relent. His hand rose, and she could not contain her flinch at the sudden movement. Her instinctive reaction made him frown severely.

"Have I given you reason to believe that I would strike you?" he demanded.

She bowed her head, feigning subservience in the hope that it would calm his ire. "No, Your Majesty."

Fingers were on her chin as they'd been the day before. The pads of his fingertips were callused. And the way he touched her...

He forced her head up, not harshly, and yet unrelenting. Forcing her to look at him.

"I don't harm women, Lady Tansy."

He stroked his thumb over her jaw, a place she had never previously been aware would be so responsive to a touch. And yet, she couldn't deny the reaction the simple caress evoked. Her knees trembled.

"You're safe with me," he added.

Only, she recognized his assertion for a lie at once. Because being in his presence was the greatest peril she had experienced. Not to her person, but to her loyalty to the princess. She was desperately drawn to King Maximilian, and it seemed there was nothing she could do to change that.

"I don't *feel* safe with you," she whispered, the admission torn from her.

She hadn't intended to make it.

"Why not?" His forefinger moved slowly, stroking the underside of her chin, the steady glide a seduction in itself.

"You are a dangerous man, Your Majesty."

"Perhaps." He continued his light caress, holding her captive with scarcely any effort. "But I am also just. Which is why you should tell me what you're keeping from me before you make me cross. I assure you, Lady Tansy, that you don't wish to see me when I'm cross."

His baritone was as soft and tantalizing as his touch.

"What happens when you are cross?" she asked, inwardly chastising herself for the breathless quality of her voice and the rapt fascination with which she watched him, as if she were his to touch, to play with.

To tease.

As if she were his lover.

She wondered stupidly, wildly, how he treated the women he took to bed. Did he touch them as tenderly, with such care that seemed at odds with his massive size and his brutal reputation? Had he earned the calluses on his hands from fighting on the battlefields he had conquered?

"When I am cross, I do everything in my power to vex my enemies." He smiled then, a beautiful smile, truly, that revealed the full extent of his white, ridiculously even teeth.

Did all the men of Varros look so splendid, or was it merely this one?

Belatedly, his claim occurred to her. "I am certain you could not vex me, Your Majesty."

"And I'm equally certain I could. Do you wish to try me?"

She had no other choice.

"I suppose I must."

His smile deepened, making grooves at the corners of his dark eyes and sinful lips. "Consider yourself warned, spitfire."

~

HER SKIN WAS SO DAMNED soft. And she was so stubborn. So tempting. He had never wanted to kiss her more.

Everything within Maxim was clamoring to take her mouth. To claim her. To sweep her into his arms and carry her away like the spoils of war, to strip her bare and use his lips and tongue and teeth and cock to please her until no more stubborn resistance remained.

Lingering here and clashing verbal swords with the beautiful lady-in-waiting was stupid, and he knew it. Only yesterday, an assassin intent upon killing him had been slain in his entry hall. He was likely standing within the lion's den, with Gustavson's guards within a shout's distance at all times. And there was also the matter of the ever-elusive princess he was to wed.

She had been due to return an hour ago by his calculations.

But he hadn't become King of Varros by failing to seize what he wanted. And he very much wanted Lady Tansy.

She had thrown the gauntlet between them. He was merely taking it up.

To that end, he released her with great reluctance and turned to a book abandoned upon a nearby table, retrieving it. She had been reading the volume, he knew. The contents mattered not to him; what did matter was that it belonged to her. He folded himself into one of the uncomfortable armchairs by the fire and flipped the book open to its frontispiece.

She flew after him like a little bird intent upon chasing a predator from her nest of eggs. "What are you doing?"

He gestured calmly with his left hand. "Reading."

"But that is my book," she sputtered, her fingers tangling

in her gown as if to keep from snatching the tome from his grasp.

"Is it?" He raised a brow, giving her an unconcerned look. "Not any longer. Now it is mine."

With that pronouncement, he turned his attention to reading. The book was in English. Its title, *The Tale of Love*, was decidedly intriguing. Was it a bawdy book, then?

His stubborn prick twitched to attention at the possibility.

"You must not read it," she said, sounding rather frantic, catching her lower lip in her teeth.

His cock hardened, pulsing with eagerness. She was beautiful, hovering over him with an expression of utter concern on her lovely countenance. He flicked his gaze away from her, turning his attention to the source of her apprehension. What did the book contain?

Using his thumb, he opened the volume and flipped through a few dozen pages, words catching his eye as he worked his way through dense blocks of text. A handful of words jumped out at him.

Nipples.

Globes.

Stiff.

Staff.

Pleasure.

"Ye gods," he murmured aloud, allowing the book to fall shut as he jerked his gaze back up to meet hers. "Is this, perchance, the secret you've been keeping, Lady Tansy?"

"It does not belong to Her Royal Highness, Princess Anastasia," the lady-in-waiting was quick to say.

"You've already told me it is yours," he reminded her, far more intrigued about the Boritanian beauty than he had been previously.

"What did you read?" she demanded.

He opened the book and sifted through a few pages until his eye caught on more interestingly indecent prose. "His hand swept over every part of me, beginning with my throat and shoulder, then passing down over my breast, his thumb rolling one ruby nipple until an arrow of pleasure most exquisite—"

"Enough," she interrupted, her cheeks going a fetching shade of pink, her bosom heaving beneath the sudden frenzy of her embarrassment.

He would have been amused were his cock not presently as hard as iron.

"You asked me to tell you what I had read," he said with mock innocence. "I was merely attempting to edify you, my dear."

"Trying to embarrass me is more apt."

"Are you embarrassed by the word *nipple*, my lady?" he asked, showing her no mercy. "Or is it the description of the act itself? The thumb attending to the lady's pleasure is, I confess, what intrigues me most. Tell me, is it followed with a tongue, or does the gentleman pleasuring his companion relegate himself to the use of his fingers alone?"

She was still blushing furiously as she closed the distance between them, clearly intent upon stealing the book from him so that he could not further antagonize her by reading its lustful adventures aloud. But as she leapt at him—there were no other means of describing her act, so very out of character for the proper lady-in-waiting—she failed to take note of his legs, crossed and stretched before him.

She tripped and went tumbling forward, a high-pitched squeal tearing from her throat. Her eyes were wide, arms flailing for purchase. But Maxim was prepared. His hands spanned her waist and hauled her into his lap with ease, saving her from the disaster of crashing to the floor.

Not, however, from the disaster of his insistent prick

prodding her backside. She felt his ardor. No question of it, for her back instantly stiffened, and she moved to flee.

But now that Maxim had her here, he wasn't inclined to allow her to leave with such haste. His grasp on her tightened just enough to keep her where she was.

"I do believe you lost your balance, Lady Tansy."

"Release me," she cried, squirming on his lap.

The act did nothing to assuage the ache in his groin. Rather, the friction only further incited the riot of lust roaring within him.

He strengthened his hold. "Stop moving if you please. It was your own recklessness that landed you here, and now you must pay the forfeit for your lack of grace."

"Lack of grace? You tripped me, you…you…Varrosian oaf!"

For some reason, her attempt at paying him insult amused Maxim.

He chuckled. "Do you know what you sounded like when you fell, spitfire? You sounded like a little piglet."

"A p-piglet?" she sputtered, her outrage nothing short of endearing.

She was delicious. Intoxicating. He wanted to bask in her fury. Wanted to hold her here, kicking and fighting and wounding him with razor-sharp verbal barbs. And then he wanted to kiss her until she was sighing and using all her scorching flame to seduce him instead of to flay him alive.

"Mmm," he said, admiring the way the candlelight danced in her dark hair, bringing to life shades of cinnamon and gold hidden within the rich depths. "A very small, very charming, very angry one."

"How dare you compare me to a beast?"

"Lower your voice if you don't want Gustavson's guards to run into the chamber and find you sitting in my lap," he warned lightly.

In truth, he had no doubt they would remain where they were, fear not just of himself but also the princess's mysterious illness and the possibility that it was catching keeping them in the hall. But he hardly wanted one of the blackguards to race into the room, intent upon discovering the reason for her outraged demands. The guards Gustavson had hired were not nearly as vicious as the assassin, but Maxim wasn't inclined to spill blood just now.

Lady Tansy stilled at the mentioning of the guards, her spine stiffening. "I am not seated here of my own free will," she said, her voice significantly quieter, though still laced with the sharp snap of irritation.

He disliked the implication of force, for he had maintained his hold on her only to shake her polish and poise. And yet, he could admit to himself that he liked having her in his lap. Liked the soft, womanly weight of her, the heat seeping through her layers of petticoat and gown to burn him. Liked the swell of her rump nestled against his cock.

"I saved you from tumbling to the floor," he said mildly, flexing his fingers on her waist.

"And then called me a piglet." At last, she turned her head toward him, her lips pursed, angry fire dancing in those mysterious eyes.

"I might have called you something worse," Maxim pointed out.

"And you also might allow me to stand."

"Or I could keep you here," he countered.

He liked that idea. Far too much.

Her lips parted, and he thought for a moment he had shocked her speechless. But then she regained her wits, for her hands landed atop his and she made another ungodly wriggle that ground his cock more firmly against her bottom.

"And what would Princess Anastasia say if she were to find me thus?" the lady-in-waiting demanded, breathless.

He would give his left eye to know why.

"I'd prefer not to think of her just now," he answered with complete honesty.

For while he had been determined to discover why his future queen had yet to return from her visit with the man she had hired to find her long-lost, exiled brother, his thoughts were decidedly elsewhere now. Admittedly, his interest in the princess had always been solely in the benefits of an alliance. The icy, reserved Princess Anastasia had never appealed to him. But there was something about Lady Tansy that made him long to have her in his bed. To have her beneath him. Astride him. On all fours.

The possibilities were as endless as they were enticing. Would she be as much of a spitfire in bed as she was outside it? He had never wanted a woman to put up a fight in bed until now. Perhaps he was more depraved than even he had realized.

Maxim would blame his inconvenient attraction to her upon the bawdy book she'd been reading, but that would be a lie. He'd been drawn to her from the moment their paths had first crossed at court in Boritania.

"We *must* think of her," Lady Tansy argued. "This position is vastly indecorous."

"It could be more indecorous." He paused, flashing her an evil grin. "As indecorous as reading books containing descriptions of nipples being fondled, for instance."

Defiance blazed in her eyes. "Why should the books I read be any concern of yours?"

"Because you will be in my household, a part of my court. Because you are the closest ally of my future queen. Your influence over her is undeniable."

He omitted the truth: that he found it fascinating and

rousing as hell that she was sneaking about with vulgar books. He wondered what else it contained and what she did after she read them. But then he forced himself to cease all such veins of rumination for fear it would only make his cockstand more rigid.

"Release me," she said, tugging at his hands to no avail.

He was far stronger than she was, and he wasn't letting her go until he had what he wanted from her. "I'll have your promise first."

"What promise?"

"That you will tell me what you've been keeping from me."

"I'm not keeping anything from you. Now release me."

They glared at each other, at a stalemate.

A knock sounded at the door, and Lady Tansy instantly stiffened, her back going rigid. Reluctantly, Maxim guided her to her feet. The absence of her soft, feminine curves pressed against him nettled more than it should. But nothing irked him more than the indication that she feared Gustavson's guards.

"What is it?" he called curtly in Boritanian.

"It is me, brother," came Nando's familiar voice from the other side of the door, speaking in Varrosian.

Maxim's gut instantly curdled. If Nando was here instead of wallowing in bed with some willing London lady, that meant trouble was afoot.

"I'll be right there," he said grimly, before turning to Lady Tansy with an ominous promise of his own. "I'll return to see the princess another day."

CHAPTER 5

"*A* duel?" Maxim roared.

Nando winced as the carriage rumbled away from Gustavson's town house. "You needn't shout so loudly, brother."

He loved his brother.

Nando was the only family he had left.

But Maxim also wanted to thrash the ever-living hell out of him.

He ground his molars so hard that his teeth ached, trying to calm himself before he responded. Trying to tamp down his inner rage. Telling himself that Nando cared. He wasn't trying to put everything Maxim had worked for—the prosperity of Varros—in danger. But anger was boiling up inside him, taking root like an evil tree.

And it wouldn't be answered until he slammed his fists into the squabs at his sides, the satisfying crash of his knuckles into the oiled leather making his brother jump.

"Maxim?" Nando prompted, looking equal parts shame-faced and wary. "You aren't speaking."

"That is because I fear what I'll say," he bit out tightly.

He had been warned by his closest adviser in his privy council that Nando was reckless. That his recklessness could prove dangerous to their cause and that he should be left behind in Varros. But what his privy council didn't know—what no one knew, save Nando—was that Maxim needed his muttonheaded, wench-loving brother to help him stay sane.

"Oh," Nando said with feeling, lacing his hands together in his lap before him as if in prayer.

Perhaps he was.

Maxim narrowed his eyes. "Are you praying?"

Nando swallowed hard, his Adam's apple bobbing. "Mayhap."

"Then you may as well say a prayer that I don't kill you for being so stupid," Maxim said harshly.

The instant the words left him, Maxim regretted them. Nando crumpled before him like a kicked puppy.

"I'm sorry, Maxim."

"You ought to be sorry," he said sharply, trying to control his ire. "I asked you to exercise care in your dalliances, did I not?"

"She said her husband would never know." Nando's expression was a study in guilt.

Understanding dawned.

"Ye gods, Nando. Tell me the husband didn't walk in on you in bed with his wife."

A second wince. "I try never to lie to you, brother."

"Fuck," he growled before he could leash his tongue.

Nando had been bedding the cuckold's wife, the cuckold had interrupted them, and now the cuckold had challenged Nando to a duel. Maxim was busy trying to find an exiled prince, avoid being assassinated, keep his future queen safe, and orchestrate a revolution in a nearby kingdom, and Nando was getting caught bare-arsed by angry husbands. Maxim's fists landed in the leather squabs again.

"And now the husband has demanded you meet him with pistols at dawn," he elaborated when he could once more control his temper sufficiently.

"I'm afraid so," Nando admitted weakly. "You needn't worry, Maxim. I'll find a second and meet him. I'm a crack shot."

"No, you won't, damn you. I've enough to worry about without you killing some English lord because you couldn't get your prick wet with a proper strumpet."

"You do know that strumpets aren't proper, by the very definition of their nature of work, do you not?" Nando dared to ask him, clearly attempting to make light of the circumstances facing them.

But Maxim wasn't in a laughing mood. He was in a make-heads-roll sort of goddamned mood. A mere half hour ago, Lady Tansy had been in his lap, her lush feminine curves a delicious temptation pressed against him in all the right ways. Her scent still haunted him even as they made their way through the horse-dung-covered streets. And he had been rudely torn away from that idyll by his brother's endless, careless propensity for wenching.

"Do you think this is the time to make jests?" he returned. "Need I remind you that I am your king and that you are tasked with helping me here in London rather than hindering me?"

Nando frowned. "I am *trying* to help you, curse you. But you scarcely entrust me with any information. You're always either hiding in the study with Felix or off somewhere attending gods know whom. A fellow eventually suffers from sufficient ennui, leading him to seek entertainment and enlightenment."

"Up a married woman's skirts, apparently," he muttered.

Nando had always been a scapegrace. But this—dallying with a married woman beneath her husband's nose while

Maxim was undertaking a very important and very dangerous series of missions in England—was the most foolish bit of nonsense in which he'd found himself yet. And the timing could not have been worse.

"Perhaps if you found your way up a woman's skirts now and again, you wouldn't be so blasted angry all the time," Nando suggested.

And just like that, all the fury Maxim had been endeavoring to control roared to life once again.

"Apologize," he bit out.

His brother sighed, looking instantly contrite. "I'm sorry. I shouldn't have spoken of it. Forgive me."

"No, you should not have," he agreed tightly, for the subject, like the war, was one about which they had agreed to never speak.

After Mina's death, Maxim had lived like a monk for many years, until Lucinda had come into his life. But he had found solace in Lucinda's arms and her welcoming bed. Not true and abiding emotion, nothing deeper than a mutual need for each other's company and the release it provided. Lucinda could never compare to the woman he had loved and lost, what now seemed a lifetime ago.

Unbidden, thoughts of Lady Tansy intruded, along with a tantalizing question that felt like a crude betrayal of what he'd shared with Mina. What if Lady Tansy could compare? The wayward notion didn't matter, he told himself sternly. He was marrying Princess Anastasia, not her lady-in-waiting.

But he wouldn't lie. The prospect of taking Lady Tansy as his mistress held sudden, tremendous appeal. He couldn't recall being so stirred by a woman. Not since Mina.

"I'm sorry about the duel," Nando was saying, bringing Maxim back to the present with a jolt. "It was never my intention to cause you problems here in London. I was simply trying to occupy myself, to keep out of your way. Perhaps if you would entrust me with a more important position, I wouldn't need to seek out diversions."

Maxim forced his clenched fists to open. Pummeling inanimate objects was beneath him, and it didn't solve anything. But he was beginning to think he had misjudged his hellion brother.

"Are you suggesting that if I placed a greater weight of responsibility on your shoulders, you wouldn't go about shagging every woman in sight?" he asked crudely.

Nando brushed at the sleeve of his coat, red staining his high cheekbones as he cleared his throat. "It is hardly every woman in sight. I do have requirements."

"Quite a reassurance." He drummed his fingers on the bench at his side, trying to keep his anger restrained as he reminded himself that Nando had good intentions. He just tended to go about them all wrong. "The more pressing matter, for now, is what you intend to do about the duel."

"As I said, I'm going to meet the Earl of Levering tomorrow morning at dawn," Nando said, as if it were a matter of course. "You can't order me about."

"The devil I can't. I may be your brother, but I am also your king. You will do as I say." He paused, taking a deep breath and reminding himself this was not the battlefield, even if, in some ways, the plotting he'd been orchestrating here in London made it feel that way.

Already, he could feel the hair beginning to stand on end on his arms, his heart starting to pound harder, his mouth going dry. That wouldn't do. He couldn't have one of his fits now. And not so soon after the last one. He had known that the dangers swirling around him would produce a strain, but he hadn't realized they would affect him so strongly and so quickly.

"What is it you command me to do?" Nando asked dourly,

dredging Maxim's thoughts from the grip of impending madness.

"We will find the earl and persuade him to nullify his challenge," Maxim said, one of his booted feet tapping in a marching rhythm.

There, that served to take the edge off his discomfiture.

He rapped on the carriage roof, issuing new orders to his coachman.

"And how will we do that?" His brother wanted to know, mulish as ever.

"Simple." Maxim flashed his brother a grim smile. "Bribery."

⁓

"King Maximilian has promised he will return to see you," Tansy warned Princess Anastasia as she worked a bit more of the soothing balm she had made into the small bruise on the princess's throat.

A bruise she had spied the evening before when the princess had returned late from her assignation with Archer Tierney. Initially, Tansy's heart had leapt at the thought that her friend had been set upon by one of London's notorious footpads. But the princess had quickly dispelled the notion.

"Why would he wish to see me?" Princess Anastasia asked, frowning. "I'm an invalid."

The vibrant, lovely woman before Tansy was as far from an invalid as one could reasonably get.

"Perhaps to lend credence," she whispered, careful to omit any incriminating words.

"To pretend he is a doting suitor, you mean?" the princess asked quietly. "Hmm. Perhaps, though I hardly think it in keeping with his reputation. He's known for his cold ruthlessness. It is what carried him through on the battlefield all those years of the Varros Great War."

The king's legendary battle prowess had, indeed, been reported widely. His victory over armies that had outnumbered his and his sheer defiance in the face of certain death had rendered him a figure both fearless and fearsome. How strange it was to think of him in those terms now, after she had spent time in proximity to him, after they had shared whisky and secrets. After she had sat upon his lap yesterday and felt his heat and muscled strength beneath her.

And another part of him as well.

The unwanted intrusion of the memory of his massive length pressing against her bottom was enough to make Tansy drop her pot of cream, which landed on its side on the carpet below. Licking lips that had gone dry, she hastily bent to retrieve her ointment before it spilled in its entirety.

"Oh dear," she murmured to herself, guilt tangling her stomach in a knot. "Forgive me for my clumsiness."

And for thinking about your future husband in an impure manner, she thought to herself, hating that she could not seem to stop. King Maximilian was forever beyond her reach. He was going to be the husband of her dearest friend, the woman she considered a sister. What was the matter with her?

"Shall I fetch a cloth to mop it up?" Princess Anastasia asked, blissfully unaware of the inner struggle waging within Tansy.

"No, of course not, Your Royal Highness," she denied, shame threatening to swallow her. "I made the mess, and I will clean it."

She reached for the nearest item at hand that could be of use—a handkerchief Tansy had been embroidering during her vigil in the supposed sickroom. Aside from the book she had been reading, she needed some way of occupying her time.

She reminded herself again that it was her duty to attend the princess.

Her duty to be loyal.

Her duty to put her needs, wants, her very life, aside.

It was decidedly not her duty to desire the king to whom the princess would soon be married. Nor to think about what his lips might feel like pressed against hers, whether he was capable of softness, of tender seduction.

The very thought sent such a pang of yearning through her that she upturned the pot a second time, spilling more onto the rug.

"Oh dear, you must let me help," Princess Anastasia said, moving to retrieve a small towel at the washbasin before kneeling and helping Tansy.

"Such a task is beneath you," she felt compelled to remind the princess. "I am perfectly capable of cleaning the spilled balm."

"Perhaps, but you were kind enough to make it for me, and already it has done wonders to fade the mark."

The reminder of the reason for the bruise had Tansy scrubbing the carpet harder, quite soiling her handkerchief. "I hope you will consider my warnings."

"I will consider them as always, dear friend," Princess Anastasia said with a mysterious smile.

One that told Tansy she had no intention of abandoning her plan to lose her maidenhead to the Englishman tasked with helping her find her exiled brother.

"It is dangerous," she whispered. "I wish you would not continue to flit about in the night as you've done. Surely you've provided all the information he needs."

"You worry too much, Tansy," Princess Anastasia said

without bite, giving her hand a reassuring pat. "This is my last chance for freedom before…"

Her words trailed off and she grimaced, as if her future as King Maximilian's queen were too wretched to consider, let alone voice. And Tansy hated herself in that moment for thinking about what being married to such a man might entail—sharing his bed. Hated herself for the forbidden longing it sparked to life deep inside her.

Hastily, Tansy finished cleaning the rug and straightened, pot of balm in hand. "Promise me you will be careful, Your Royal Highness. Boritania is depending upon you."

Princess Anastasia rose as well, her countenance turning serious and hard. "I know they are, and I promise you, Tansy, there isn't anything I want more than to see my kingdom and its people prosper again. Support me in this one whim, giving myself to a man of my choosing. It's all I ask for myself."

Tansy nodded, humbled by the princess's depth of sacrifice. She was putting herself in grave peril for the good of Boritania, and Tansy admired Princess Anastasia for that and so many other reasons. It wasn't that she thought the princess was unworthy of making her own choices, but rather that she very much feared the repercussions of those choices.

One, in particular.

But she didn't want to think about why she was so concerned about King Maximilian and his response, should he discover what the princess had been about with Archer Tierney. Nor did she want to think of him as a man with emotions and desires at all, for doing so rendered him far more tempting than he already was. No, indeed, she would be well-served to keep her mind and heart rooted firmly in duty and loyalty to her princess and kingdom where they belonged.

Tansy raised her fingers to her lips in the traditional salute, then lifted them into the air. "For Boritania."

"Thank you for being such a good, steadfast friend to me for all these years. I couldn't have asked for a better lady-in-waiting at my side." The princess returned the salute, solemn. "For Boritania."

And Tansy did her best to tamp down the worry and guilt festering in her belly.

CHAPTER 6

*S*omething mysterious was afoot.

And Maxim didn't like mysteries. Or liars.

Or princesses who were meant to be taking his carriage as transport and yet inexplicably turned it away.

"You're certain?" he asked again of his coachman, who had returned early with an empty carriage and the news that the lady he'd been meant to squire to Archer Tierney's town house that evening had declined the use of the carriage and walked away.

"I'm certain, Your Majesty," the coachman said. "The lady said she wouldn't be needing the use of the carriage this evening, but that she would arrange for a different night."

Yes, something was definitely wrong. Either the princess was engaged in deception of some sort as he suspected, or her nighttime activity had been discovered. And if the latter was the case, the princess's life was in danger. Not just hers, but her lady-in-waiting's as well.

His gut clenched. He had to go and see for himself. Messages could be intercepted or misconstrued.

Maxim thanked the coachman and gave him directions to

take him back to the town house where Princess Anastasia was staying. Essentially where the coachman had just arrived from. But if the man questioned the reason or found it odd, he gave no indication. And that was why Maxim paid him so well.

He settled on the squabs, crossing his too-long limbs that were never at home in a carriage, and tried to practice patience as the carriage rocked into motion. He was weary to the bone, having spent the night before chasing an earl across London to avoid a disastrous duel. Bribery had, as he had suspected, won in the end. Nando hadn't met anyone at dawn this morning with pistols, and he'd also been forced to assure Lord Levering that he would avoid Lady Levering for the duration of his stay in London.

Nando had sighed on the carriage ride home, objecting to being banished from the countess's bed, even if he had understood the reason for it. Maxim had narrowly avoided giving his brother the thrashing he deserved. In the end, no members of the aristocracy had been maimed or hurt—the only damage had been to masculine pride. And that was precisely how Maxim wanted it, because he had far more important matters to attend to.

Namely, where the long-lost, exiled Prince of Boritania was. And why the devil the princess had turned his carriage away.

He couldn't lie—the closer the carriage drew to his destination, the greater his anticipation, and to his shame, it hadn't a thing to do with either the exiled prince or the princess he would be marrying. Rather, it had everything to do with Lady Tansy Francis, the gray-eyed spitfire he couldn't stop thinking about.

She had damned well better be safe, he thought as the carriage finally drew to a halt outside the town house.

The prospect of harm befalling her lying heavy on his

chest, he leapt from the conveyance before it had completely come to a halt, calling out his order for the coachman to return and collect Felix, his trusted bodyguard. A man he decidedly shouldn't have come here without, he thought wryly as he approached the front walk and rapped at the door. His need to solve the mystery of the princess's refusal of the carriage had spurred him on, supplanting all else. Even the thought of his own protection.

But he couldn't lie to himself. It had also been the need to make certain nothing had happened to Lady Tansy. His protective instinct where she was concerned was as strong as it was baffling.

The door opened to reveal the English butler Gustavson had hired, a perfectly placid gentleman who hadn't the slightest notion he was working for a cutthroat, deadly usurper king.

"His Royal Highness, King Maximilian of Varros for Her Royal Highness Princess Anastasia," Maxim announced unnecessarily, for the fellow knew damned well who he was.

This was the third evening in a row Maxim had arrived at this very door, paying a call. Moreover, he was a king. He didn't imagine it was every day that the butler greeted royalty, even if Maxim hailed from a tiny island kingdom that was below the notice of most.

"Of course, Your Majesty," the butler intoned, bowing. "Follow me, if you please."

Maxim stepped inside, listening for any hint of unrest within and hearing nothing untoward. All was silent as a tomb, which was generally the prevailing mood within the town house upon his every visit. He waited in the entry hall while his visit was announced to the guards and then proceeded up the by-now-familiar staircase and down the hall to Princess Anastasia's room, passing the guard he had warned two days before. The fellow lowered his head as

Maxim strode by him. He hoped to hell the fear of him would last until he could pry Princess Anastasia and Lady Tansy from these walls.

At last, he reached the door and knocked smartly, not bothering to request a guard do so. The farther away those bastards stayed, the better.

"Who comes?" Lady Tansy called in almost flawless English.

For the benefit of the servants, no doubt.

"King Maximilian," he announced in return. "To see Her Royal Highness."

Although he listened closely for the slightest hint of a curse, the only sound that reached him was a faint floor creak and then the rattle of the door latch as she pulled it open a tiny crack, revealing one eye.

"Her Royal Highness is sleeping," she announced coolly.

"I'll wait," he returned smoothly, flattening a hand on the paneled door and gently but firmly pushing it inward.

Lady Tansy had no choice but to allow him entrance, and they both knew it. Still, as Maxim stepped over the threshold and snapped the door closed at his back, he couldn't deny a certain sense of pleasure unfurling in his chest.

Pleasure at seeing *her*, he realized.

Lady Tansy's dark hair was swept into a chignon, a few curls coming free to frame her face. She dipped into an elegant curtsy instantly. "Your Majesty."

He wanted to correct her, to tell her to call him Maxim as he had commanded, but first, he needed to get to the heart of the matter. He stalked to the bed with its artfully arranged pillows once more plumped to replicate the outline of the princess. With one hand, Maxim flipped up the counterpane, revealing the subterfuge.

"Sleeping," he repeated, turning to Lady Tansy with a raised brow.

Lady Tansy frowned at him. "You are surprised?"

He took her hand in his, pulling her to the farthest point in the chamber from the door and any chance a passing guard would overhear. The awareness that shot through him at the contact was undeniable, but he forced himself to ignore it for now. He needed to learn where the princess was and why she had declined the use of his carriage this evening.

"What are you doing?" Lady Tansy demanded, her voice a harsh whisper, her expression ferocious as she attempted to disentangle her fingers from his, as if his touch burned her.

Maxim released his hold, taking pity on her.

"Finding a place we can converse without fear of listening ears," he told her quietly, calmly.

"Why should we need to converse? I do believe we have said everything to each other that needed to be said."

He gave her a small smile. "How wrong you are, spitfire. Where is she?"

"On your errand." Lady Tansy's brows drew together. "Where else?"

"Somewhere that didn't require the use of my carriage," he explained. "She sent my coachman away. I came here immediately, fearing the worst."

And finding the same tableau that had greeted him upon his previous visits. A pile of pillows being watched over by a tempting lady-in-waiting with determination and stubbornness forged in steel. He would give anything to take her mouth with his. To know the supple give of her luscious lips. To discover if she would respond.

Maxim suspected he already knew the answer to that particular question.

"As you can see, nothing is amiss," Lady Tansy said, her tone lacking conviction.

Unless he missed his guess, she was worried. But she also knew more than she was saying.

"I see the opposite, my lady," he countered. "Something seems to be distinctly amiss. The princess is not here, and she is not in my carriage, under my protection. Where the devil is she?"

Her chin went up in a rather defensive gesture. "The guards spotted your carriage by the mews. I learned that questions were being asked. The princess thought it prudent to avoid traveling in it, given the suspicion."

"Fair enough," he allowed, stroking his jaw as he considered Lady Tansy with grave care. "How did the princess arrive at her destination, then?"

She gave him a tight smile. "I believe she arranged for another conveyance."

Lady Tansy was lying. His instincts never failed him, and everything—from her false cheer to the stiff set of her shoulders—suggested she was not telling him the truth.

Interesting.

Maxim smiled back at her, feeling wolfish. "I appreciate Her Royal Highness's sense of caution."

"I am glad," Lady Tansy said faintly. "Princess Anastasia is nothing if not circumspect. She understands how important this is. She would never do anything to hinder your mission."

He ran his hand along his jaw some more, considering her. "I would never doubt it."

Also a lie.

He was suspicious of the princess. He trusted her only as much as he needed to—she was the sole person who could convince her exiled brother to return to Boritania at great peril to his own life and limb. Maxim needed to marry her for the power such an alliance would bring. But something decidedly odd was afoot, and he was determined to get to the root of it.

One way or another.

"I am grateful for your confidence in Her Royal Highness," Lady Tansy chirped with more false brightness.

Prevarication ill suited her. Perversely, it rankled Maxim that she was deceiving him even if he wasn't being honest with her. It was as if she were taking the side of Princess Anastasia when he very much wanted Lady Tansy to be aligned with him.

In all ways.

But he couldn't think of that now. He had another reason for paying this call, and it was far more important than his inconvenient lust. Ye gods, he was no better than Nando.

"There is news from the Boritanian Court," he told Lady Tansy quietly, carefully. "My spies have sent word that Gustavson grows suspicious at the delay in announcing our betrothal. There is word he may travel to London himself."

Which meant that they would need to make a formal announcement soon, whether the princess was able to find the exiled prince and rightful king or not. The notion didn't sit well with him, but there was no other solution.

Lady Tansy's eyes widened at the news. "I'll pass on your warning to Her Royal Highness."

He nodded. "Our time lessens by the moment."

Her gaze dipped, and unless he was mistaken, landed on his mouth, lingering there like a touch. Everything inside him turned to instant flame.

"Will that be all, Your Majesty?" she asked, her eyes flying back up to his, a slight tinge of pink coloring her cheeks.

Did she think to dismiss him? The daring of the woman knew no bounds.

"No," he said, even though he knew he shouldn't. "That's not quite all, Lady Tansy."

∾

TANSY BRACED herself for what the king would say next.

"How else may I be of service to you?" she asked, trying to maintain her composure.

Doing so was a struggle, given the intensity the king exuded. Being in his presence so soon after she had been on his lap the day before was a challenge all its own. She had spent every moment of their interaction thus far achingly reminded of the large, thick length of him pressing into her. He made her feel restless and reckless, two traits she had never previously believed herself capable of possessing.

From the moment she had been taken beneath the sheltering wing of the St. George family, Tansy had maintained her gratitude and humility. Never desiring anything for herself. Certainly never desiring anyone.

"Come and sit with me," the king said, his tone one of august command.

He didn't ask. King Maximilian issued orders, and everyone around him was expected to comply without question. The instinct to deny him was strong. Every minute she spent alone with him took her sixty seconds more perilously close to disaster.

"I would prefer my own chair this evening," she told him tartly instead.

Without waiting for his response, she swiftly moved to the armchairs flanking each other before the fire crackling in the grate. She seated herself primly on the edge, not about to allow herself to become too comfortable, for she didn't recognize herself when King Maximilian was in proximity.

Mere moments ago, she had been staring at his stern yet finely sculpted mouth, wondering what it would feel like if those lips claimed hers.

It was an inherently wrong curiosity—and traitorous, too.

The king stalked across the chamber in a handful of long-legged strides and sank into the chair at her side, his dark eyes searching as he reached into his coat. "How are the guards treating you, Lady Tansy?"

The question took her by surprise. She had expected he would engage in further interrogation. He seemed so very suspicious of the princess, and she couldn't blame him. No doubt Princess Anastasia had possessed an excellent reason for turning away the king's carriage this evening. But Tansy couldn't fathom what it could be. If she had to hazard a guess, she would reckon it had something to do with Archer Tierney.

"The guards are treating Her Royal Highness well," she answered, relieved that she'd had the presence of mind to hide *The Tale of Love* earlier that day.

"I didn't ask how they were treating the princess," he drawled, "although I'm pleased to know it. I asked how they are treating *you*, my lady."

She swallowed against an unwanted rush within; his interest in her should hardly matter. It was likely nothing more than perfunctory. "They are treating me well."

"They damned well better be." He had extracted his flask from his coat, she realized, and now he was bringing it to his lips. "Whisky, Lady Tansy?"

She remembered the burn of it on her tongue, down her throat. The way it had seemed to make her feel loose-boned and lighter than a feather, the way it had felt to place her lips where his had so recently been.

Dangerous. So very, very dangerous.

Tell him no, urged an inner voice of caution. *It's hardly befitting of a lady in your position.*

"Yes, please," she said, reaching for the flask, spurred by some hint of inner wickedness she hadn't previously known she possessed.

His fault, she was sure.

A sudden smile kicked up the corners of King Maximilian's lips. Not quite a true smile, she thought, but a hint that he was pleased by her capitulation.

"You surprise me," he said, the low timbre of his voice undeniably pleasant.

He relinquished the whisky to her, and she brought it to her lips for a sip, feeling bold and defiant and free. The princess wouldn't return for hours. Tansy had been trapped in the chamber for most of her days since arriving in London, supposedly tending to the invalid Princess Anastasia. Here was an opportunity for distraction, however unwise.

She took a hesitant sip of the whisky and then returned the flask to him, licking her lips. "Thank you."

He brought the flask to his own lips, seemingly taking care to place them precisely where hers had been. The king took a long pull before swallowing, holding her gaze all the while. A flush crept up her throat, the heaviness of desire making her feel languid yet needy. It was a complex combination, and to her detriment, she couldn't seem to banish the memory of his member, hard and firm and so very large, prodding her yesterday.

What did it mean? The king was a massive man. It stood to reason that he was also similarly sized in other portions of his anatomy that remained hidden. But she couldn't shake a more intriguing possibility—that the king was attracted to her. That the length beneath her had been the result of his own pent-up desire, not so different from hers.

These were thoughts that were unworthy of her. Thoughts she had no right to entertain. For the king was going to marry her oldest and dearest friend. The woman who was like a sister to her. The princess she had sworn her loyalty and life to.

"Tell me, my lady, what is it that you do with your time when you are hidden away in this chamber?"

His request dashed her ruminations, bringing her back to the present with a jolt.

"I read," she blurted before she could think better of it.

The king grunted. "I'm aware."

"I also sew," Tansy added, inwardly cursing herself for being so foolish as to mention reading, for it had clearly reminded him of the book she had gone to great pains to hide.

"You certainly possess the patience for such an art." He took a small sip from his flask.

She didn't know if he was offering her praise or insult, but she decided to believe it was the former. "Thank you."

"What else do you do?" he asked next, as if reading and sewing were insufficient pastimes.

"I attend to my duties," she answered honestly, surprised he would issue such a question.

She was a lady-in-waiting. It was her primary obligation to assist the princess in all matters.

His regard was solemn, his gaze probing and far too intimate, making her feel as if he saw her in a way no one before him had. "You're adept at hiding your true self, I suspect. Who are you truly, Lady Tansy, beyond a lady-in-waiting?"

Once again, his question surprised her. Largely because she didn't have an answer, and that was most shocking of all. She didn't know who she was aside from Lady Tansy Francis, lady-in-waiting to Princess Anastasia St. George. Her life had been dedicated to the role. She hadn't sufficient time to concern herself with anything else.

"I am as you see me," she said faintly. "No more, and no less."

"That's hardly an answer, my lady," the king observed shrewdly.

She shifted uncomfortably in her seat, wishing she could escape his intensity, and then folded her hands primly in her lap to give herself a source of distraction. "It is the only answer you shall have."

King Maximilian made a low sound. "What pleases you?"

"Solitude," she answered pointedly. "Quiet."

He bit out a bark of laughter, the sound undeniably pleasant to her ears.

Your laugh, she thought then. *Your laugh pleases me greatly.*

For there was no denying the effect it had upon her. She felt his levity as acutely as if he had brushed his hand along her bare spine. Better still, she had earned it. He struck her as a man who had little use for humor.

"Touché, spitfire," he said, giving her a smile that made her stomach perform an odd little flip as he raised his flask as if in salute before sliding it back inside the pocket in his coat.

"What pleases you?" she asked, suddenly desperately curious, even though she knew that she shouldn't be.

That she had no right.

His smile faded, his dark gaze burning into hers. "A gray-eyed lady-in-waiting with a sharp tongue I'd like to put to better uses than flaying me alive."

Her breath caught. "What uses?"

She shouldn't have asked. Shouldn't want to know.

"Kissing," he said simply. "And other uses I shouldn't describe to a maiden, even if she delights in reading filthy books."

Molten heat pooled between her thighs. Understanding struck her like a bolt of lightning arcing from a stormy sky to claim her. It was wrong. It was wicked. She was ashamed of herself.

But she wanted King Maximilian of Varros. Wanted his stern, forbidding mouth on hers. Wanted to know if his kisses would be as bold and unforgiving as he was or if they would be tender and seductive.

And she couldn't lie—it nettled her that he was treating

her as if she were too innocent to know his other intentions beyond mere kissing.

"What if I'm not a maiden?" she asked brazenly, spurred on by the whisky and the sudden, uncontrollable desire blossoming inside her.

He stood abruptly, rising to his full, tremendous height. For a moment, she feared she had gone too far and he was intending to leave. Until he held out his hand to her in offering.

She stared at his hand, so big, so powerful. The hand of a king. The healed scars on his rugged palm suggested it was also the hand of a warrior. Tansy shouldn't take it. To do so was inviting ruin. But the whisky and the way he made her feel were potent and heady, and her body took on a will all its own, her hand settling neatly in his. Long, callused fingers wrapped around hers, and with one swift tug, he hauled her from her seat.

She landed against the hard, muscled wall of his chest. And it felt good, his heat burning into her. It felt right, his spicy scent curling around her. It felt like everything she had ever wanted without knowing, and it felt like everything she could never have.

He cupped her cheek, such gentleness in his touch. "Then you should kiss me, spitfire. Learn what other uses I have for that barbed tongue."

Tansy shouldn't kiss him.

She knew it.

Kissing him would be a traitorous act. A betrayal of Princess Anastasia from which she could never return.

But he was staring down at her, so fiercely magnificent, the silver at his temples lending him a dignified air that filled her with longing.

"Only if you dare," he added.

And for the first time since going to stay at the August

Palace as a girl, Tansy did what she shouldn't. She reached up, setting a tentative hand on the king's cheek, feeling the prickle of the whiskers shading his angular jaw. Warmth swept up her arm, a jolt of connection so deep that she trembled beneath the force of it. Different from the mere linking of hands, and so very far removed from the casual game of cat and mouse he had played with her the day before.

He was so beautifully stark and austere, and yet as awareness of him seeped into her, she was no longer thinking of him as a king. Rather, her body was attuned to his, woman to man. Everything else was stripped away at the feeling of his face beneath her palm—such raw intimacy that was forbidden between king and commoner. It didn't matter that she was a lady born and gently raised within the confines of the August Palace. He was still a king—her king, soon—and incredibly powerful. No one had the right, the privilege, to touch King Maximilian as Tansy was touching him now.

And yet she couldn't stop. Didn't want to. Her thumb traveled the high ridge of his cheekbone, finding a scar she hadn't noticed, small yet deep, almost hidden in the faint grooves at the corner of his right eye.

"You've a scar here," she said.

"A glancing blow from a saber."

"So close to your eye." The observation fled her, worry for the danger King Maximilian had faced in his past making her stomach tighten.

The king held her stare, unrelenting. "My enemy intended to run his saber through my eye."

A shudder passed over her, knees going weak at the notion.

The king released his hold on her cheek and idly traced the outline of her lips with the lightest, most tantalizing graze of his forefinger, dark eyes glittering as they followed the path of the lone digit. "You needn't worry, my lady. I stopped him before he could, else I wouldn't be here today."

Tansy had heard the many stories of his battlefield prowess. And yet, it had been easy to see him in his London finery, surrounded by the trappings of the English aristocracy, as king rather than warrior. Yet here was undeniable proof that he was both. That he had not just defended himself in battle but emerged the victor.

"I am glad," she told him, meaning those words to her core.

He made another low, deep sound—this one of approval or perhaps thwarted need. She couldn't say which, nor did she have the chance to further examine it or care. Because in the next moment, the king lowered his head, and his lips sealed over hers.

CHAPTER 7

*L*ady Tansy's lips were all he had dreamt they would be beneath his and more. Full and warm and lush.

And, ye gods, *sweet*. So fucking sweet. She tasted like whisky and woman and mysteries and determination and the forbidden. Everything he couldn't get enough of. Everything he had ever desired without fully knowing it.

Maxim wanted to consume her. He wanted to kiss her until he hadn't breath left in his lungs. Wanted to strip her bare and take her soft, feminine body beneath his. To sink inside her, to claim her, to make her his. A fierce sense of possession swept through him, mingling with the desire that had been building to feverish heights from the moment he had first entered this room days ago.

To the devil with anyone else who had touched her before. No one would ever lay a finger on her again. Not in his court. Nor in his kingdom. All Varros would know that she belonged to him. Hell, who was he fooling? His tiny nation wasn't enough. No one would ever kiss her or touch her or bed her for as long as he lived. Not in this damned world.

He parted her lips and gave her his tongue. She made a husky, sensual sound, welcoming him. The hand on his cheek slid to thread through his hair, and her other hand found purchase on his cravat. He despised the fashionable linen neckcloths so unanimously adored in England, but he wore them in an effort to keep from looking as if he were a brutal barbarian from a foreign land, even if that was precisely what he was. Maxim had always been more at home on the battlefield than in the throne room.

Yet when Lady Tansy's fingers curled in the snowy-white cravat and tugged him closer, he vowed he would wear the constricting piece of fabric every day if it meant she would pull him nearer and return his kiss as if her life depended upon it. He would have his man tie it into a hundred knots just for the chance to have her clinging to him thus again. For the ripe press of her breasts into his chest, the heat and the softness of her.

Because Lady Tansy's mouth, her lips, her silken sigh, her surrender, her seductive curves molding to him, her scent invading his senses better than any marauding infantry ever could…

It was heaven. Pure, unadulterated heaven.

He had never known a kiss like this one, for the way it changed him. Lady Tansy's kiss made him forget. Reminded him he was a man of blood and bone, of desire and need and so much pent-up longing, instead of the regal king and battlefield warrior fashioned of ice. He had kissed other women before her. And yet, it was the frustrated capitulation and undeniable desire of the woman in his arms that unraveled him more than any of those experiences combined.

It made no sense, the effect this small lady-in-waiting had upon him.

But she was meant to be his. He felt it to his soul.

And suddenly, he had to have her closer. Her lips were insufficient.

His hands settled on her waist in a possessive hold, and he lifted her, their mouths still feasting on each other. She made a noise of surprise, clutching him tighter, wrapping her legs around him as if he were a tree. He wished for the absence of the barriers of her petticoats and gown and his trousers. Wished he could slide into her then and there, without regard for consequence.

His need for her was raging out of control.

His cock was harder than marble.

He wanted so much more than he could have. So much more than these four cursed walls would allow, the guards just beyond, the princess about to return. Thinking of the woman he would make his queen served to quell some of his hunger.

But then Lady Tansy nipped his lip, and he forgot everything but her.

Her sharp teeth on him were exquisite. A wildness lurked beneath her refined elegance, and here was proof. How he loved the dichotomy, the restrained, perfectly poised lady-in-waiting who *bit* him.

His prick surged against her, seeking, thwarted by all the damnable layers keeping them apart. He pulled back just enough to catch the fullness of her lower lip in his teeth and return the tug with a little bite of his own. She moaned, her fingers gliding through his hair, nails raking over his scalp.

Maxim was overwhelmed by the raw, unrestrained urge to fuck.

Not just to fuck.

To fuck *her*.

To fill her with his cock and then with his seed.

His feet traveled with a mind of their own, unerringly seeking the bed across the chamber. He didn't even need to tear his lips from hers or raise his head to see where he was going. His body *knew*.

He reached the bed, its coverlets tossed aside from his earlier revelation, and deposited her in the heaps of pillows. She lay there, mouth kiss-stung, dark hair in stark contrast to the bed linens, the most tempting sight he'd ever beheld. Her breaths were ragged, her breasts rising and falling with each inhalation, her eyes slumberous from passion, pupils dilated. He settled himself into the invitation of her parted legs, pushing hems up silken calves and thighs until they were bunched at her waist and his cockstand was notched against her hot, beckoning sex.

And then he took her mouth again, kissing her ravenously, showing her without words just how badly he wanted her. Telling her with his tongue that she was his to claim, that from this moment onward, she would only ever belong to him.

With a needy sound, she clung to him, feeding on his kisses as if he were her life source. And he kissed her in the same fashion, because that was what it felt like. He didn't want air in his lungs or the sun shining down on him or a beat in his heart. All he wanted was her beneath him, her tongue dueling with his and her body supple and pliant and threatening to burn him to ash with the fire she brought to life inside him.

How he needed her, more desperately by the second.

She was intoxicating. Like a poison in his blood.

Maxim was going to take her, but first, he wanted her to know that she would have no worries in his care, that he would provide for her generously when they arrived in Varros. Everything he had would be hers.

He tore his mouth from hers with great reluctance, resting his weight on one forearm to keep from crushing her, and used his free hand to caress her cheek. "I'll protect you.

Whatever you want, whatever you need in Varros, it shall be yours."

Her brow furrowed, confusion flashing in the depths of her eyes. "What do you mean?"

Maxim struggled to speak over the raging lust coursing through his veins. "I'll take care of you. You will be provided with your own house and servants. I'll shower you in jewels. Every man, woman, and child in the kingdom will know who you are and kneel to you."

Yes, he liked the notion of her waiting for him, naked, fistfuls of fine gems sprinkled over her ivory skin. Or better still, a necklace of his choosing glistening around her throat and nothing more. She was too beautiful to be a lady-in-waiting. She deserved all the finery his wealth could provide. She deserved an army of attendants to do her bidding, every member of his court bowing and scraping to her. She deserved to be revered and adored, worshiped like the goddess she was. His goddess.

For a fleeting moment, he imagined her as his queen, but he quickly banished the tempting notion. He owed the people of Varros peace after so many years of protracted and bitter war, and the surest means of achieving it was an alliance with Boritania. That meant he had no choice but to wed the princess, even if he wanted another more.

But something had suddenly changed in Lady Tansy. The dreaminess had fled her countenance, and she was stiffening beneath him, her arms falling away so that she no longer embraced him. The loss produced an ache deep inside Maxim.

"Your mistress?" she hissed. "Is that what you would make me?"

"My woman," he corrected, for there was an important difference.

A mistress was a temporary lover. But the lifelong position of power and respect he offered her was one he had never given another. She would have every bit as much importance in his kingdom as his queen. Perhaps even more.

"No," she said, planting her palms on his chest.

Maxim was sure he had misheard.

"No?" he repeated.

"No," she growled at him, suddenly an angry cat with razor claws instead of a drowsy kitten who had been content and pliant. "I'll not be your kept woman. Get off me."

"Not a kept woman," he attempted to explain, rolling to his side to accommodate her request, although doing so nearly killed him. She belonged to him, was meant for him, his by right as much as the throne of Varros was. "*My* woman. The king's woman. I will give you everything."

"Everything but your respect," she spat, rising from the bed and shaking out her skirts as if she expected to find them filled with vipers.

"I respect you greatly." Frowning, Maxim rose to his feet as well, towering over her, taking great pleasure in the sight she presented, so thoroughly mussed and kissed, despite her ire. "That is why I would give you a house and carte blanche, servants to do your bidding, and the loyalty of everyone in my kingdom."

Perhaps she didn't fully understand. Boritanian ways often differed from Varrosian traditions. Now she would accept his proposition and allow him to kiss her again, he was certain of it.

But Lady Tansy's eyes were still flashing with stubborn fire.

"You do not respect me at all, or you would not wish for me to step down from a position of honor to lie in your bed in a position of dishonor."

He stared at her, bemused by her outrage. "The position is one of great honor. You will want for nothing."

Her chin rose, and he couldn't deny the picture she presented—a gorgeous beauty, regal as any queen—affected him deeply, despite her angry rejection.

"I must decline Your Majesty's offer," she said coolly. "My loyalty is to the princess, and I have failed her this evening."

Maxim was suddenly, absurdly jealous of Princess Anastasia. He wanted the fealty Lady Tansy gave to her to belong to him alone. He wanted her to accede to his wishes. To give them both what they so plainly desired. He hadn't mistaken the restless way she had moved against him and clung to him, nor the half-dozen breathless sighs and soft moans she had given him, the answering glide of her tongue against his, the seductive nip of her teeth.

The wet heat of her sex, tantalizing him through the barrier of his trousers.

"You will change your mind," he vowed.

To Lady Tansy. To himself.

She was his, and she would know it. The damned *world* would know it.

But he was a man who had spilled the blood of others on the battlefield, and he knew when it was time to retreat.

"I won't," she denied.

Of course she did.

He would fight her anyway. Fight her and win.

"Oh, but you will. And I will greatly enjoy earning the word 'yes' from your pretty lips. Just as I'll enjoy being deep inside you, making you mine, watching you come undone for me." Maxim bowed, the blood thundering in his veins. "Until next we meet, spitfire."

He turned away from her and all the temptation she presented. Turned his back upon the unmade bed where he had nearly fucked her in the mound of pillows. And with each step that took him farther from Lady Tansy, Maxim's determination to have her rose until it became insurmountable.

He had never accepted defeat in all his forty years of life, and he didn't intend to begin now.

~

TANSY WAITED on a chaise longue for what felt like a lifetime, drowning in a vast sea of guilt and longing. The two made for a devilish combination. Long after King Maximilian had left her, he had been all Tansy had been able to think about.

The memory of his lips on hers, bringing her to life.

The delicious weight of his big, masculine body covering Tansy's, pinning her to the bed.

The rigidity of him, pressing in demanding fashion between her legs where she had ached for him—where she still ached for him.

The torment of it all threatened to swallow her whole.

But then there was the sharp, stinging anguish of the betrayal she had committed against the princess. It mattered not that Princess Anastasia harbored no tender feelings for the king. He was still the man who would be her husband. And Tansy had kissed him. Not just kissed him—she had lain with him, and in the princess's bed, no less. Had felt him intimately aligned with her. Worst of all, had he not broken the spell of lust he'd cast over her by asking her to be his mistress, she would have allowed him anything.

Would have given herself to him.

She shut her eyes miserably against the flickering candlelight, which itself seemed a recrimination.

Until the subtle scraping at the window alerted her to the return of Princess Anastasia.

Relief washed over her—relief that the princess was safe.

Concern, too, over where she had been. But there remained the sickening guilt as well.

"You were gone for hours," she observed quietly.

The princess sighed. "I thought you would be abed by now."

"As well I should have been," she said, thinking of other things she should have done and hating herself all the more. "As should you."

Princess Anastasia cleared her throat. "You know why I was gone."

Tansy rose from the chaise longue, moving across the chamber in the princess's direction. "Your original purpose should not have required all evening and half the hours of the morning," she reminded her quietly, fearing that the worst had happened and that Princess Anastasia had given herself to Archer Tierney.

She didn't like to consider the reason for her concern, that she was every bit as much nettled by the realization that Princess Anastasia would betray the king as by the danger her friend so openly courted with her rash behavior.

If her uncle were to discover what she was doing…

Tansy shuddered, not wanting to consider the repercussions.

The princess opened the fastening of her cloak, giving Tansy the opportunity to sweep it away, grateful for the distraction from her whirling thoughts. Calm, mindless tasks and duty supplanted the guilt and worries for a moment.

"He served me dinner," Princess Anastasia said then. "I hadn't realized how very hungry I was after largely refusing the trays sent to me."

The worries instantly returned, for Tansy recognized a lie when she heard one.

"For seven hours?" she asked softly. "Pray, Your Royal Highness, do not mistake me for a fool."

"I would never think you a fool," the princess said, her gaze searching as she reached for Tansy's arm. "Something is amiss. What is it?"

Was her guilt written upon her face, then?

Oh, how she hated herself for her pathetic weakness where the king was concerned. Why had she not been stronger? Why had she not resisted his advances? She should have been impervious to his charm, secure in her loyalty. Instead, she had been carried away by raw, unfettered yearning. She had allowed herself to feel far too much, to take what could never be hers.

"Of course something is amiss," she said, agitated, as she withdrew from her friend's grasp. "You are placing yourself in grave danger, acting as recklessly as you are."

And I have been acting with equal recklessness.

The princess frowned. "Have my uncle's guards come to check upon me whilst I was gone?"

"No," Tansy reassured her, knowing she had to reveal the awful truth to her friend and face the consequences. "*He* came," she added, unable to force herself to say King Maximilian's name aloud.

"My brother?" the princess asked.

There was no hope for it. She was going to have to say it after all, just as she was going to have to confess.

"King Maximilian," she elaborated grimly.

"He called? Why would he do such a thing?"

"You returned his carriage," she explained, working while she talked, untying tapes and helping the princess to step out of her gown. "He wished to know why. I was forced to meet with him on your behalf."

"Deus," Princess Anastasia whispered. "He didn't harm you, did he, Tansy?"

No, indeed, what he had done was worse than harming her. He had turned her into a traitorous wretch.

"What would you do if he had?" she asked, the anger in her voice aimed at herself.

The princess's eyes narrowed. "Did he hurt you?"

Tansy struggled with her answer, working instead at Princess Anastasia's petticoat, sending it to the floor in a whisper of sound.

"Tansy," Princess Anastasia pressed, sounding impatient.

Tansy's fingers tangled in a knot that had been tied thrice on the princess's stays. An unfamiliar knot—she had only tied it twice this morning.

"This knot isn't mine," she observed instead of replying, knowing what the new knot meant.

The princess had removed her stays while she had been away. Or perhaps it wasn't the princess who had done it, but someone else.

Her friend turned about unexpectedly, countenance troubled. "Tell me what happened," she demanded. "Please."

Such concern for her, and Tansy knew she did not deserve it. She wasn't worthy. How to tell the princess the whole of what had happened? How to admit the depth of her own depravity, her stunning lack of loyalty, her inexplicable weakness where the king was concerned?

"I told the king that his carriage had been spied by the guards near the mews and questions had been raised," Tansy began haltingly, recalling the portion of King Maximilian's call that had occurred before those sinful kisses had turned her mind to ash and dashed her loyalty to bits. "His Royal Highness was grateful for your caution. He was careful to play the part of concerned suitor. The guards were easily fooled. He wished for me to pass on the warning that his spies in Gustavson's court have sent word that your uncle grows suspicious by the delay in announcing your betrothal. There is word he may travel to London himself."

Stasia exhaled slowly, some of the urgency fading from her expression. "That is all?"

Tansy's stomach clenched. She was going to have to confess her sins and pray the princess could find it in her heart to forgive her and one day, perhaps, trust her again.

"No," Tansy forced out. "That is not all."

"Did he strike you?" Princess Anastasia demanded. "Did he threaten you or hurt you in any way? You must tell me, Tansy. I will not allow you to suffer because of me."

It would have been better if he had, for then she would never have found herself in such an untenable predicament.

"No, King Maximilian did not." She swallowed hard against a stinging rush of shame before continuing. "He did something far worse."

"What can it have been?" the princess asked, sounding panicked now. "You must tell me, Tansy. Please."

One deep breath. She was going to have to do it.

"He kissed me," she admitted.

And so much more than that, but she couldn't find the words, couldn't summon the strength to tell the woman who was like a sister to her that her future husband had asked Tansy to be his mistress. That for a wild moment, she had considered his offer until her conscience had banished all the lust fogging her mind and sent it on its way.

"He kissed you," her friend repeated, sounding shocked. "He forced himself upon you?"

"No." Tansy shook her head, remorse making her throat go tight as she thought of the role she had played in the wicked tableau earlier, of how she had welcomed the king's every advance. "There was no force. Your Royal Highness, I am so sorry for what happened. I pray that you will forgive me and that I may regain your trust."

Princess Anastasia stared at her wordlessly, her mouth dropping open.

"I never meant for it to happen, Your Royal Highness," Tansy rushed to add into the silence, bowing her head, too afraid to look at her friend for fear of what she would see in her eyes. "I must beg you for mercy, which I do not deserve. I promise you that it will never occur again."

"He did nothing to hurt you?" Princess Anastasia asked.

No, indeed. Everything the king had done had been exquisitely pleasant. Much to her shame.

"Nothing," Tansy said, staring down at her fingers, laced together as if in prayer, so tightly that her knuckles stood out in stark white relief.

"You are forgiven," the princess said quietly, without a hint of anger.

Tansy jerked her head up, tears stinging her eyes, gratitude pouring forth like a river bursting over its banks. "Thank you, Your Royal Highness."

"Stasia, if you please," the princess told her kindly. "You have always been like a sister to me, Tansy. That shall never change."

More compassion she was not worthy of receiving.

"You are the only sister I've ever known," she said thickly, emotion rising as she thought of the parents she had lost at such a tender young age, of the siblings she had longed to have as a girl and had been denied by the deaths of her mother and father.

Of how she had been raised alongside Princess Anastasia instead. She owed the princess her very life. But so much more than that as well. Tansy vowed to herself that she would never again so much as look upon King Maximilian, let alone touch him. If he paid another call at the town house, she would bar the door and deny him entrance. Heavens, she would climb out the window herself to escape him.

Anything to keep from falling back under the spell of desire. To keep from surrendering to the promise of sin and foregoing all she held dear. Tansy had always wondered why a woman would lower herself to becoming a man's mistress instead of demanding her place as a wife. But now she understood. How shockingly easy it was to be tempted by a man like the king.

The princess took her hand then, giving it a reassuring squeeze. "We shall weather this storm as we always have. Together."

Tansy nodded, still frowning as she thought of how unbearable the future seemed, her place in the king's court rendering it all but impossible to avoid him when they reached Varros. And then she thought of all the perils facing Princess Anastasia as the king's plan continued to unfold beneath her uncle's nose.

"But you need to take greater care," she warned the princess, fretting anew over all the mysterious hours her friend had spent in Archer Tierney's care. About that blasted knot and the implications of it. "The danger grows stronger, and I am not certain how much longer we can continue to fool the guards or King Maximilian."

"Just a bit more time," Princess Anastasia said. "Soon, everything will fall into place, just as it is meant to be."

Tansy continued her ministrations, wondering how the princess could be so stoically accepting of the knowledge that the man she was about to wed had been kissing another. The very thought of King Maximilian's mouth on any woman's but hers filled Tansy with jealousy that was as unwanted as it was unfounded.

There was one thing she was certain of—this madness had to cease.

CHAPTER 8

One dead body was inconvenient.

Two dead bodies were a problem.

Particularly when one of the men in question bore an uncanny resemblance to his uncle.

Maxim tapped the sole of one of the unfortunate fellow's boot. "Who do you suspect was behind this latest attempt?"

Felix paused in the act of wiping the remnants of blood from his blade with a black handkerchief. "Lingering loyalists. These two aren't Boritanian, though they took care to wear the Boritanian colors."

"Charles has been beneath the dirt these last three years," he reminded his bodyguard. "Why would his supporters come for me now, and why here in London?"

Felix resumed the cleaning of the vicious-looking blade, which he had recently removed from the body of the nearest man. "They want you dead, Your Majesty. You're beyond the protection of your court here, and they know it. They likely believe the betrothal celebrations will distract you, make you vulnerable to attack. And if they further sow the seeds of discontent by wearing Boritanian colors, they cannot lose even if they give their lives to their cause."

Bile rose in Maxim's throat as the scent of blood, so familiar and so detested, filled his nose. After so many years of war, he was beyond weary of it. Exhausted by endless battle, losing too many good men. Tired of blood and death and the ceaseless quest for vengeance that had once been his own driving force until he had finally emerged the victor. But could there be a victor, truly, when there would forever be shadows waiting in the darkest night for him to be alone, hoping to sink their daggers between his ribs or slit his throat?

His heart was pounding hard, his mouth going dry. All signs that one of his fits loomed. No. He couldn't afford to lose control now. Not when so much was at risk—the peace he had worked so damned hard to achieve, his alliance with Princess Anastasia, his chance to overthrow King Gustavson.

Lady Tansy.

He didn't know where the last thought emerged from. But suddenly, all Maxim could think about was the dark-haired Siren who had denied him the night before. What if he risked bringing further danger upon not only himself, but Lady Tansy and the princess as well? He had to concentrate. To keep the demons at bay.

He inhaled through his mouth, trying not to breathe in the scent of the blood.

"This one resembles Charles," he acknowledged grimly, giving the dead would-be assassin's boot another sound tap. "Likely a by-blow."

"Your uncle had more bastards than there are hours in the day," Felix agreed, finishing cleaning his blade and restoring it to its hiding place inside his boot. "He could be one."

There was so much blood on the floor. Pooled around the bodies, seeping into fabric and carpets alike. He was going to have to replace the Aubusson in this chamber as well. It was an odd concern, he knew. He ought to have had a thought for the dead men on the floor. Perhaps he would have done, had the pair of them not been hiding in the study, intending to stab him mercilessly to death.

"This makes three," he pointed out needlessly, for Felix could count the number of men who had sought their way into the house intending to slay him just as well as Maxim could.

"Three dead men," Felix agreed.

Death. Blood. Bodies. Gore. The sound of cannons roared in his ears. Or maybe that was the pounding of his heart. Screams filled his mind. That was the ugly, ruthless, terrible consequence of warfare—the battlefield never left a man. Years could pass. A lifetime, even. But the memories remained, forever haunting, emblazoned upon his mind.

Maxim began tapping his foot. His cravat was so tight, choking him. He wanted to breathe, but his lungs felt as if they had been seized by an invisible fist, and he didn't want to smell the metallic tang lingering in the air.

"Do you suppose there are more?" he asked his most-trusted man.

"If there are more, they'll meet the same fate," Felix said calmly, his tone one of eerie reassurance.

And Maxim believed him. They had fought in hand-to-hand combat at each other's sides during the Varros Great War. There was no braver man, nor any deadlier, than Felix.

Tap, tap, tap. The frantic movement of his foot was not sufficient. He wouldn't be able to breathe if he remained in this room another moment, surrounded by death.

He nodded. "I need to—"

"Brother?"

The untimely interruption of Nando's voice had Maxim turning to find his brother at the threshold of the study, his gaze pinned upon the dead men, his face taking on a sudden pallor.

"Fucking hell," Nando muttered.

Maxim stalked across the chamber, relieved for the distraction and the opportunity to turn his back upon the ghastly sight. "Close the damned door."

His brother belatedly did as he commanded, snapping the portal closed. "What's happened?"

"Assassins," he said succinctly, stopping before his brother. "Felix discovered them before they found me."

"Deus," Nando said, still looking pale, his gaze lingering on the dead men over Maxim's shoulder.

"You've returned early this evening," he observed instead of offering further explanation.

"What will you…" Nando's words trailed off and he swallowed hard, as if struggling to continue. "What will you do with them?"

"It's best you don't know, Your Royal Highness," Felix said calmly.

"I…" Nando paused, swallowing again, as if doing his utmost to keep from casting up his accounts. "I suppose so." He turned his unsteady gaze upon Maxim. "You weren't injured?"

"Thankfully not," he reassured him. "I was not at home until after they were already dispatched."

Because he had been out doing, of all things, shopping. It was embarrassing to admit, even inwardly. King Maximilian did not reduce himself to the ranks of lowly pages by wandering through shops for bits and baubles to impress a lady. Whenever he had made a gift to Lucinda, he had always foisted the task of the selection and purchase upon one of the young servant lads in his employ.

And yet, that was precisely how he had spent the entirety of his afternoon and a goodly portion of his evening. He had been investigating bookshops and the massive Bellingham and Co. and every other corner of London where he might find suitable gifts to woo Lady Tansy.

He had yet to work out just how he would secret ten books, a fur, an ivory fan, a pair of gloves, a sapphire parure, and a dashing hat inside the sickroom. But that was a problem for later, when he wasn't trapped in a room of death with the only two men in the world he trusted.

"You could have been killed," Nando said, looking as if he might crumple at any moment.

"Ye gods, Nando," he grumbled. "Are you going to swoon like a woman?"

"Might we talk elsewhere?" he asked faintly. "Whilst Felix takes care of…the rest?"

Sometimes it was easy to forget that Nando had not witnessed the atrocities of war as Maxim had. His brother had been young, so very young, when the Great War had begun. By the time he had been old enough to fight at Maxim's side, the ugliest years of the war had already been behind them, and victory had been on the horizon. Cognizant of the need for the House of Tayrnes to carry on, Maxim had been intentionally careful about Nando's position on the battlefield; he had always been far from enemy soldiers, secured in a field tent.

Maxim cast a glance back at Felix. "You will see the mess cleaned up?"

Felix bowed. "Always, Your Majesty."

He nodded. "Thank you." Maxim turned to Nando. "Go before I'm forced to fetch hartshorn."

He was being unkind and he knew it, for he was every bit as affected by the death and blood as his brother was. But for Maxim, it was different. There was a certain hell that lived inside him, one he would never be able to banish, and sometimes, it reared up to claim him.

They left the study in silence, reaching the outer hall where Maxim could breathe again. His cravat remained a constriction, his lungs still seized, but he no longer felt as if he needed to scratch his way out of his own skin.

"What did you need to speak with me about?" he asked Felix as they settled into a familiar marching pattern, their feet moving in rhythmic beats that began to help soothe the ragged pieces inside him.

Gratitude hit him like a blow. Nando was a scapegrace, but he knew Maxim so well. Better, perhaps, than he knew himself.

"I've forgotten," his brother said, his voice weak.

"Not another cuckolded husband?" he asked sharply, thinking of the blasted duel that had only narrowly been avoided.

They marched neatly to the rear of the town house, past the staircase, and then pivoted, returning from the direction they had just come. Servants moved about in a flurry of activity, guards slipping in and out of the study at Felix's direction. The town house was a beehive of activity and people.

"No," Nando reassured him. "I've learned my lesson."

That remained to be seen.

"One would hope," he drawled, trying not to think about the lifeless forms in the study.

About the blood.

About the obvious proof that he had yet to snuff out the entirety of the loyalists fomenting rebellion in the name of Charles.

"Ah yes," Nando said, his voice sounding less peculiar now as they marched back toward the staircase.

Step, step, step, step.

There was comfort in the familiar, in the regimented, the routine.

He could breathe again.

He cast his brother a sidelong glance when he didn't continue. "You've remembered?"

"I have," Nando said lowly. "It's about Lady Tansy Francis."

His shoulders tensed. "What of her?"

It was all he could do to keep from roaring that she was his. That his brother should keep his rakish, philandering ways far from her. But then he remembered that he was scarcely any more worthy of her. He needed to marry another, after all.

"I was thinking that perhaps I ought to court a lady who is unattached. And who better than Princess Anastasia's lady-in-waiting? She is lovely, and it will be a furthering of the alliance. Naturally, I wanted to ask your permission first."

Nando sounded quite pleased with himself.

But Maxim was clenching his jaw with so much force that he feared his molars might crumble. "Not her," he barked.

Nando's footsteps faltered, and he shot Maxim a searching look. "Why not?"

"Because you scarcely even know her," he forced out instead of blurting the embarrassing truth, that he wanted Lady Tansy for himself.

"I've spoken with her on several occasions now," Nando corrected him, frowning. "She is quite intelligent and kind. I have no reason to believe she wouldn't make an excellent wife."

Maxim was absurdly jealous of the time his brother had spent in Lady Tansy's company without his knowledge. What had been said? Had he made her laugh? Ye gods, if he had touched her...

"You cannot dally with the princess's lady-in-waiting," he snapped, hating the idea.

"I don't wish to dally," his brother countered. "As I said, I think that perhaps the time has come for me to settle down with a wife. It would certainly cause you fewer problems, and I'm of an age that I ought to do so. I thought you'd be happy, brother."

He was happy with the notion of Nando no longer causing him headaches with married women and irate husbands and every other nonsensical scrape in which he'd found himself over the years. However, there were hundreds of unattached females at court who would be eminently more suitable choices.

Specifically, who would not be *her*.

"I am pleased you are expressing a desire to take on more responsibility," he allowed grudgingly. "However, the lady-in-waiting of my future wife can't marry a prince of the realm."

"Why not?" Nando asked, a bit petulantly.

"Because I said so," he snapped. "Find someone else. Anyone but her."

Nando stopped marching and spun to face Maxim, his expression one of mulish stubbornness. "You may be the king, but you can't command me. I've a free will. I can court whomever I want."

"Yes, you may," he agreed tightly. "Just not her."

"I'm afraid you'll be destined for disappointment, then, Your Majesty," Nando said bitterly. "Because I've decided that Lady Tansy is the only woman I want."

With that pronouncement, Nando stormed away, rather like a petulant lad who had just been denied a favorite toy. Maxim watched him go.

It would seem they found themselves in the same predicament, he thought grimly.

Because Lady Tansy Francis was also the only woman he wanted.

And therein very much lay a problem that was somehow

even larger and more frightening than the men who'd wanted him dead.

~

KING MAXIMILIAN HADN'T RETURNED.

But another visitor had.

One who had climbed the tree beyond Princess Anastasia's window just as she did each night when she escaped her confines to roam the city in search of her brother the exiled prince. This visitor was a man who claimed he had come at the directive of Archer Tierney.

One who had a message for her.

Tansy held the hastily scrawled missive in the meager candlelight, her heart leaping into her throat as she read for the third time the news that it contained.

Princess Anastasia had been wounded.

She was being attended by a physician, but her injury had rendered her unable to return this evening. Tansy inferred that meant the princess couldn't climb the tree. Which meant her injury was significant enough to impair her movement.

"Mr. Tierney says I'm to await your response," the man whispered, hovering at the periphery of her vision.

Her hands shook as she extracted a fresh sheet of paper and dipped her pen into the inkwell, scratching out her reply.

My loyalty, as always, is to Her Royal Highness. I'll do my utmost to keep others from discovering her absence, but I recommend three days at most before suspicions rise, though sooner if at all practicable.
Respectfully,
T.

PS: I must insist that if an infection sets in, you notify me at once.

SHE FOLDED the epistle thrice before entrusting it to the man who waited in the shadows. Silently, she handed him the response.

With a tug at his forelock, the man slipped back out the window into the night, leaving her alone.

Alone with her panic.

Princess Anastasia had been somehow injured this evening. And although Tierney's vaguely worded note had intended to reassure her, Tansy felt anything but calm. She felt utterly helpless and powerless. In a state of abject despair, in fact. She was deeply worried for the welfare of her friend. If she'd been seen by a doctor and couldn't return, that meant something significant had occurred. Tansy didn't know Archer Tierney from any other man in London. Was he trustworthy? What if his note was a lie and he was holding Princess Anastasia captive?

More questions swirled, a long line of them as Tansy paced the length of the chamber.

How was she to keep the guards satisfied indefinitely? One false move, and their deception would be discovered, and Tansy would be in certain danger as well as King Maximilian.

If the reason for their subterfuge were ever to become known...

If something were to happen to Princess Anastasia...

No, she couldn't think about that now. She had to remain calm and formulate a plan.

Tansy halted suddenly, staring at the empty bed where she had artfully placed pillows and rolled-up garments to resemble the princess's sleeping form. A sudden realization hit her. She needed help, and there was only one man in London she trusted.

King Maximilian.

But the hour was very late, far beyond the time he had ever paid a call. The servants and guards were likely abed. If she wanted his aid, she was going to have to go to him.

She hastened to the bed, making certain the counterpane was pulled over the pillows, and then she took the missive from Tierney, tossing it into the fireplace, watching it burn to ash. If she were to leave the chamber, there was a risk she would be seen. However, unlike the princess, who was believed to be ill, Tansy's movements within the household wouldn't be remarked upon. She could likely slip away with ease and find herself in the mews. The only risk would be in someone venturing inside the room while she was gone.

But it was one she was going to have to take. For the princess's sake as much as for her own and King Maximilian's. Everything they had been working in secret to build was in grave peril.

Tansy retreated to her room and gathered her cloak, preparing to venture out into the dangerous night.

CHAPTER 9

"*Y*our Majesty."

"What is it now, Felix?" Maxim demanded in a snarl from his position slumped on a chaise longue in the small town house library before a contrarily merry fire. "I told you I'm not to be disturbed for the rest of the evening."

"Of course, Your Majesty," his bodyguard said from the threshold, his voice placating. "However, there is a visitor come to pay a call, demanding an audience."

"Tell the visitor to go to the devil," he growled, lifting a glass of whisky to his lips and taking a long draught.

After the loyalist rebels had been dealt with—their bodies weighted and delivered to the River Thames—he had slunk away to the relative solitude of the library to be alone with his spirits and his demons. Nando had left in search of diversion between some Englishwoman's milky thighs. The household had settled into an eerie calm.

But Maxim hadn't settled at all. He wasn't fit company for anyone, even if he were expecting a visitor at half past midnight.

Which he decidedly wasn't.

"I've suggested to the lady that she isn't welcome," Felix said, lingering, although he'd been dismissed. "She begged me to tell you it is a matter of grave importance concerning Her Royal Highness, Princess Anastasia St. George."

Maxim shot to his feet. "The lady?"

He was already moving, striding across the library, intent upon his course. It had to be Lady Tansy who had come calling upon him at this late hour.

Felix attempted to block his path. "Your Majesty, it may be a trap. I don't think it wise for you to meet with her."

Felix was not wrong. Maxim halted in his single-minded pursuit of the woman whose kisses had been haunting him since his lips had last left hers.

"What does she look like?" he demanded.

"She is small of stature," Felix said, "with dark hair."

"Gray eyes?" Maxim pressed. "A face so lovely it hurts to look upon it?"

The last question fled him before he could think better of it, his tongue no doubt loosened by the whisky he'd been using to drown himself.

Felix coughed, looking distinctly uncomfortable. "I'm sure I didn't look that closely, Your Majesty."

"Let me pass," he ordered curtly, for there was his answer. Felix simply didn't want to admit that he had admired the lady in question.

If it wasn't Lady Tansy, Maxim would eat his fucking banyan for breakfast.

"Your Majesty."

"Let. Me. Pass."

His bellow was likely unwise, given the fact that Felix had saved him from murderous assassins no fewer than three times this week. However, he was nettled. He wouldn't be stopped from seeing her.

He needed to find out why she had taken such a risk, placing herself in great peril to call upon him in the darkest dregs of the night.

Felix obliged him, stepping aside. "Of course, Your Majesty."

"Where is she?" he asked, even though he was moving in the direction most likely, the front of the house.

"In the entry," Felix called after him.

He moved with lightning speed, finding her waiting at the door enshrouded in a dark cloak, her beautiful face pinched with worry. She started forward when she saw him and then belatedly appeared to remember herself, dropping into a curtsy.

"Your Majesty."

He wasn't interested in ceremony with her. Not tonight, not ever.

"Rise, Lady Tansy." Maxim took her arm in a gentle hold and started down the hall past Felix.

"Your Majesty," Felix protested.

"Lady Tansy is welcome at any hour," he told his bodyguard.

The only danger she posed to him was a decidedly different sort than the men who wanted him dead. More perilous as well, but Felix couldn't protect him from it. No one could.

"Of course, Your Majesty," Felix said. "Forgive me my caution."

His bodyguard was entirely forgotten when Felix pulled Lady Tansy into the library with him. Her scent wrapped around him, utterly intoxicating. He wanted to take her in his arms and carry her to his bed so that he could make love to her all night long.

But he also wanted to know why she was here at this hour.

"What has happened?" he asked, not releasing her, even though he knew he ought to. "And why are you out at this hour of the night, my lady, paying a call upon me alone? Have you no notion of how perilous it is to wander London at this time of night?"

The softness of her was too good to resist.

"Princess Anastasia has been wounded," she blurted without preamble.

Ah, hell.

His gut clenched. "How? When? Where is she?"

"I—I couldn't say," Lady Tansy said. "I received word telling me she was unable to return and that I must keep the guards away."

"Who did you receive word from?" he demanded, trying to make sense of the bits she had told him thus far. "Has anything happened to you? Have the guards hurt you?"

"I am well," she said, biting her lip. "As well as I can be. It is the princess who is in danger. I am told she was attended by a doctor."

"A doctor?" He caught Lady Tansy's chin in a gentle grip between his thumb and forefinger. "Who sent for the doctor? Where is she now?"

Lady Tansy nibbled at her lip. "I...I don't know for certain."

She was keeping secrets for the princess again, and Maxim damned well didn't like it.

"Tansy," he said urgently, dispensing with her title and formality. "Do you think me stupid? I can see that you know very well where she is. You must tell me."

The future of Varros depended upon the princess's safety. He needed her, not just as his queen, but to secure her exiled brother's support. He needed Prince Theodoric to join him in challenging King Gustavson. The kingdoms of Varros and Boritania would be stronger together. Such an alliance would further increase his power and go a long way toward forcing lingering Charles loyalists to realize the futility of their cause.

"I cannot tell you." Tears glistened in her eyes, forming rivulets that ran down her cheeks. "My loyalty is to Princess Anastasia."

"Your loyalty should be to me," he told her, frustrated by her refusal to give him the information he sought and bothered by the anguish in her voice. "As your king."

"Wh-what will happen if she doesn't live?" Tansy asked. "I warned her of the dangers. I begged her to take care."

More tears rolled down her cheeks. The hood of her cloak had fallen down her back, and the glow of the lamplight in the small, intimate confines of the library caught in her dark hair, revealing the red and gold hues that were hidden within. She was so lovely, so obviously torn, and he couldn't bear it any longer.

"All will be well," Maxim soothed. "You were right in coming to me."

He realized the importance of that action with impossible clarity. In a moment of panic, when she feared her world would come tumbling down around her, she had found her way to *him*. Freely and despite her outrage at him the day before. She trusted him.

Because he couldn't go another moment without her mouth beneath his, he kissed her.

Chastely at first, tasting the salt of her tears. And then, when she opened for him, with greater urgency. He had only intended to comfort her, to offer distraction from her upset, perhaps even to persuade her that she should tell him everything she knew.

And yet, the moment her hands settled on his shoulders and she responded to him, he was lost. He hauled her against him, the decadent crush of her breasts into his chest enough to bring him to his knees. She made a soft whimper of need that went straight to his cock. He licked the seam of her lips, and she sighed, giving him the opportunity to intrude. His tongue sank into the velvety heat of her mouth, and her fingers dug into the muscles of his shoulder as she rose on her toes to align her lips more firmly with his.

He wasn't meant to be kissing her.

What he truly needed was to find out what she knew about the princess, the extent of her injury, where she was this night.

But none of that seemed to matter, because Tansy was in his arms, and her scent was filling him with a raging fire that would only be doused in one way. He didn't bother to think. He was mindless now, driven by instinct and raw, animal need.

Maxim lifted her with ease and carried her across the room, taking her to the chaise longue he had so recently vacated, and sat on it, bringing her into his lap without breaking the kiss. He tangled his fingers in the silken web of hair at her nape.

Her lips left his to trail a path of scorching kisses along his jaw. Reverent, hot gifts of her mouth on his undeserving skin. He tilted his head back to allow her exploration, vulnerable for her in a way he would never allow himself to be for another.

"Your Majesty," she whispered against his skin.

"Maxim," he corrected gruffly, because he wanted his name on those lips. Had to have it.

Especially when he was deep inside her. There would be no titles between them then. Surely she understood, on an elemental level, how inevitable it was that they would be together.

"Maxim," she murmured, kissing her way to his ear, her

lips grazing over the whorl in a place he'd never known he was so damned sensitive until this moment.

His name on her lips, her mouth fluttering over his skin. Ah God. It was the most exquisite seduction he'd ever known. His length strained against his trousers, drawn by the promise of her sweet weight in his lap, the tantalizing proximity.

She had come to him, and she was here now, exactly where he wanted her. The worries and duties weighing upon him were thrust aside by the driving need to have this woman. He would worry about the rest later.

"I'm here, sweeting," he murmured, his hands coasting over her everywhere they could.

Waist, hips, along the stubborn delineation of her spine. He memorized the shape of her with his palms and fingers, tracing her curves and softness.

"I'm afraid." She shuddered against him, burying her face in his neck and inhaling deeply, as if to drag his scent into her lungs.

He hated the helplessness in her voice, the tremor of fear making her body quake against him. But he was also perversely thankful that she had come here, that she believed he would protect her.

Because he damned well would, with every modicum of power he possessed.

Maxim kissed her forehead. "You needn't be afraid with me. I'll protect you."

Her eyes were closed, fresh tears seeping from under her spiky lashes. "I want to tell you, but I can't."

She was speaking of the princess and her whereabouts, he knew.

"It is for your own good as well as hers that you do," he told her solemnly.

For that was the truth. He couldn't protect Princess

Anastasia if he didn't know where she was hiding or what secrets she had been keeping, and he knew just how loyal Tansy was. Her faithfulness was one of her finest traits. He simply wished it were directed at him instead of the princess.

Tansy's eyes opened, her lips parting on a quiet sigh.

"Tansy," he pressed. "Tell me."

"She is with Archer Tierney."

The man who had been hired to help find Princess Anastasia's exiled brother, Prince Theodoric. Maxim wasn't surprised for his suspicions to be confirmed. He should have asked Felix to assign a detail to watch her movements after she had declined the use of his carriage. He could only blame his lapse upon the twin distractions of the assassins intent upon carving him up and the blazing desire he felt for the woman in his arms.

"Tierney," he repeated, thinking he would need to pay the man a call. "That is who sent you word about the princess being wounded?"

Tansy nodded. "Yes. I didn't know what to do, whether I could trust his word. That is why I came to you."

"You've done just as you should," he said, cupping her cheek with one hand and catching a falling tear with the pad of his thumb. "Aside from putting yourself in danger by traveling on your own. How did you come to me?"

"I hired a hack."

"Fucking hell," he swore viciously, thinking of all the harm that might have come to her, taking a hired hackney alone at midnight. "You took a dangerous risk with yourself."

"I had no other means of reaching you," she said. "I didn't dare trust a message to anyone, and even if I had, all the servants were already abed."

He caressed her cheek, sweeping a stray tendril of hair behind her ear. "I'll make certain one of my men stays in the house at all times moving forward, so that if you should have to reach me, you needn't place yourself in peril."

She shook her head, selfless to the last. "You don't have to do that."

"Yes, I do. You're mine, and I will protect you however I see fit."

The wrong words to say to his spitfire.

Her expression turned stubborn. "I'm not yours."

He would prove to her just how mistaken she was on that account. With words, with deeds. However he could.

"Tell me you don't feel what is between us," he said instead, caressing lightly along her jaw, trailing his fingers down her smooth throat until he found the closure of her cape and swiftly undid it.

The garment slid from her shoulders, pooling on his lap around her in a whisper of sound.

Her eyes widened. "Your Majesty."

It was a protest and a return to formality, and he wouldn't allow it.

He kissed her, swift and hard, before retreating. "Maxim."

"Maxim," she agreed again, her dulcet tone dripping with reluctance. "There cannot be anything between us."

"Very well," he said agreeably, following the modest line of her decolletage until he reached the place where her heart thumped frantically beneath his touch. "Then tell me you don't feel it. Tell me I'm alone in this raging desire. Tell me I'm the only one who burns with need."

Her lips parted, a soundless sigh falling from them, the warm rush of air hitting his lips in a phantom kiss. "You ask too much. More than I'm willing to give."

He would change her mind.

"The words should be easy enough to speak if it's how you feel," he pointed out, already knowing her answer.

She felt it too. He sensed it in the way she responded to

him. Her body melted beneath his touch, regardless of how much her mind did not wish it to be so.

"I…" she began, only to falter.

"Say it," he commanded, so close to kissing her again.

"Please." Her eyes pleaded with him as surely as she did.

But he was unrelenting. Merciless for her in this alone, because he wanted her more than he had known it was possible to want another. A mere handful of days with her, and she was like the breath in his lungs. He needed her.

"Why is it so difficult, spitfire?" he taunted softly, pushing her as he knew she needed to be pushed. "If you don't want me, then tell me."

She stared at him for what felt like an eternity but must have only been a scant few seconds before she capitulated.

"I feel it too," she conceded at last, so quietly that he had difficulty hearing her.

He finally kissed her then, unable to exist a moment more without his mouth on hers. The sound she made, low in her throat, a feminine hum of surrender, spurred him on. All the ravenous desire for her that he had been restraining rushed forth.

She was his. She knew it. Her kisses, her words, her actions told him she did.

And he was going to have her.

His hands moved of their own accord, finding their way beneath her gown and petticoats, past her chemise and up her stocking-clad legs, beyond soft garters with neat bows. To bare skin.

He gave her his tongue as he reverently skimmed his hands over her inner thighs. She was clutching him to her as if she feared he would leave, clinging to his shoulder with a tight grip, her other hand sliding into his hair to cup the base of his skull, her fingers threading through his hair. And she was kissing him back, feasting on his lips and tongue. The proper, infallible lady-in-waiting had come undone.

What a treasure she was.

Maxim deepened the kiss, gliding his left hand over her skin to settle at her hip while he slid his right to her sex. He cupped her there, gently, possessively, offering her a slight bit of pressure when her hips jerked instinctively into his touch.

He wanted to remind her that she was his, that he was claiming her now. That this night, her coming to him, her concession, changed everything. But words were lost in a tangle of kisses. Everyone beyond the four protective walls enshrouding them ceased to exist. There was only the warmth of the fire, the heady floral scent of her in his lungs, the taste of her on his lips and the wet heat of her cunny searing his palm.

He moved his hand slowly, torturing himself as much as her, withdrawing to trace her cleft with his middle finger before finding her plump little bud and teasing her with light, feathery strokes.

She gasped, hips undulating.

So responsive, his spitfire.

He had known she would be.

She felt so good that his cock began to leak. From nothing more than touching her cunny. Maxim was lost. It didn't matter. She was his salvation. He was sure of it. His gray-eyed Tansy with a will of pure iron.

He traced her seam, needing more. Needing to be inside her. If not with his cock, then with his finger. And she moved, accommodating him, rising on her knees to grant him a better angle. His fingertip found her entry, slick and beckoning, and he rubbed over it in slow, lazy circles until she was panting into his mouth.

Until she ended the kiss, breathless, her eyes glazed with passion. "Maxim."

"I want to feel you," he told her fervently. "I want inside you."

Her eyes widened. He pressed slightly and yet did not advance. He would await her permission, even if it killed him.

"I...oh...we shouldn't."

Not what he wanted to hear. He applied his thumb to her clitoris, rubbing.

"Ah," she said, hips moving again. "Maxim."

"That's my name, sweeting. Say it when you come." He brushed his lips over hers. "Now tell me you want to feel me inside you too."

"I shouldn't." She was so beautiful, her skin flushed with desire, her lips parted, her pupils large and black in her stunning eyes. So torn between duty and loyalty and what she desired. He knew the feeling all too well. It had haunted him for most of his life.

"But you want to," he said, needing more.

Needing everything she would give him.

"Maxim." Her tone was one of protest, but she didn't make a move to withdraw from him.

Too much blasted loyalty for an undeserving princess who had abandoned her to her fate. But he wouldn't think of that now, nor of the woman he was honor-bound to make his queen. Because there was only one woman he wanted, one woman who brought him to his knees, and she was here with him, a miracle fashioned of seductive feminine curves and hot, wet flesh and husky sighs.

He worked her pearl with dedicated precision, his thumb fluttering over her in relentless pulses until her hips were chasing his touch and she had forgotten all her objections. Or at least, he hoped to God that she had.

"Tansy, sweeting. Let me inside." He paused, his aversion to begging warring with the furor of his desire. "Please."

"Yes," she whispered.

"Yes?"

She nodded, catching her lip between her teeth. And he kissed the indecision from her mouth as he probed through her folds, his finger sliding inside her tight sheath.

Her muscles gripped him, threatening to push him from her body. And fuck, if it wasn't the most erotic moment of his life, feeling her so wet and hot, her body so ready for his. He sank his finger deeper, her cunny clenching hard on him. So slick and needy.

And greedy.

His cock pulsed, yearning for what his finger had.

He wanted to thrust mindlessly into her, to fill her with his cock until she screamed out her pleasure and drowned him in a river of her sweet dew.

They were staring into each other's eyes, their ragged breaths mingling, their gazes clashing. And he was inside her cunny. Just his finger. He eased it out and then slid it back inside, wanting to give her as much pleasure as he could. Unable to keep from fucking her. That was how good she felt, how right, how perfect.

"Oh," she gasped as he deepened his thrusts, keeping his thumb swirling over her bud in tight circles. Her head fell forward until her forehead pressed to his. "You...this...oh God."

Yes, it was heavenly. Words couldn't begin to do justice to the sensation. His finger moved with a determination his prick envied. Sliding in and out, thumb working her. She was gasping, writhing, close. So close. Wild, too. She'd lost her prim air, and in its place was a sensual goddess.

He loved it.

Maxim buried his face in her throat, breathing in the

heavenly scent of her, determined to give her pleasure. Needing it.

And she gave him what he wanted in a long moan, her upper body bowing into his, a tremble rushing through her as her cunny clamped on his finger.

"So damned lovely," he whispered to her, and he was so far gone that he couldn't be sure which language he used.

It didn't matter. He doubted Tansy even heard him. Her body was still trembling beneath the force of her release. And although the hot clench of her on his finger was delicious, his cock was straining wildly, desperate for release.

He withdrew from her but didn't remove his touch, slicking her dew over her bud and earning another seductive gasp.

"You make me…"

Her words trailed off.

Words he wanted.

Words he had to have.

He was jealous of her mind for housing them, of her tongue for keeping them from him.

"Tell me, spitfire, how do I make you feel?" he prodded, rubbing his stubble on her skin, wanting—needing—to leave his mark on her.

"As if I am someone else entirely," she murmured with great feeling. "Someone who wants what she should never want."

"And what is that?" he asked, raising his head to search her gaze for answers to the mystery that was Lady Tansy Francis. "What is it that you want?"

"You," she whispered, lowering her gaze.

"You can have me," he told her, wishing suddenly that he could offer her that promise in every sense, each definition.

But that was a futile, foolish wish, because he was the king and he had to live for his kingdom and the good of his people. Not for himself and his own selfish desires. He had to make an alliance that would further secure peace, and that meant marrying another.

"I can't," she denied, as if hearing his thoughts.

But she could. Perhaps not in the way either of them would have preferred, but she could have him. He could make her happy. He would give her everything. He felt it in that moment, his hand trapped in her soaked heat, her body welcoming him even as her mind would not.

"Look at me, Tansy," he commanded gently.

She was stubborn, hesitating a moment despite the order he'd given. But then her gaze came up.

"Let me show you," he said.

"Your Maj—"

"No," he interrupted, growling. "You'll not call me that when I'm touching your cunny." And if he had anything to say about it, not any other time either. "Call me Maxim. I give you leave."

He gave her leave to do everything and anything. But he wasn't a fool, so he kept that to himself. What was it about her that so undid him, made him more vulnerable than he had felt in years?

"Maxim," she whispered.

And the answer to his question no longer mattered.

CHAPTER 10

*H*is name felt wonderful on her tongue.

His hands felt wonderful on her body.

And his mouth, when it closed over hers in a greedy, voracious kiss, felt beyond wonderful. It felt...shockingly, alarmingly perfect. With Maxim, she felt safe. Protected. Everything felt possible, even desiring him, when his lips were claiming hers.

You can have me, he had told her, and those sinful, tempting words echoed in her mind now, repeated in every thrum of her heart.

She wanted him; there was no denying it. Not to herself. Not even to him. He knew, as if he understood her body better than she did.

The relentless ache was still between her legs, building again, rising to that perilous crescendo he had guided her through not long ago. But now his hand withdrew, his finger leaving her aching bud.

Perhaps he'd changed his mind as she ought to change hers. As her honor should make her do. But now that the walls of her resistance had begun to crumble, they were fast turning to ash. She was mindless in her need of him, this man, this king who could never truly be hers, regardless of the soft promises he whispered.

She felt her skirts sliding up her legs, bunching at her waist, the lick of warm air radiating from the fire on the part of her body he'd revealed. He was dragging her gown and petticoats and chemise higher, moving them to the side so they presented less of an encumbrance.

His lips moved from hers, trailing hot kisses along her jaw. "I need you."

His raw confession sent a surge of desire through Tansy. How impossible to believe that this powerful, massive man would need her. To know that the desire burning through her veins matched his own.

Was he asking her permission? She couldn't be certain.

"Yes," she agreed, shuddering as he fastened his lips on a sensitive part of her throat and then dragged his teeth along her skin.

One of his hands was between them now, the other on her bodice, cupping her breast. She arched into that touch, her nipple hard and tight, the motion making her intimate flesh graze against his fingers. And then she felt the fall of his trousers giving way, his length springing forth against her.

This was what he had meant when he had said she could have him. He was giving her his body. And heaven help her, she wanted it. Wanted him. Wanted everything she should not want.

"Yes?" he repeated, his breath humid, making her shiver as his lips brushed over the shell of her ear.

There it was. The question. She could tell him *no*. She knew him well enough to understand that he would never force her, nor hurt her. He was an imposing man, a joyless one, perhaps even merciless too. But he was not the sort of man who took pleasure in another's pain.

How could she deny him? How could she deny either of them? She had come to him tonight, and whilst this hadn't been what she had been seeking, she was helpless to do anything but seize what she longed for. To answer her desire.

Just one time, she promised herself.

No one but the two of them would ever know, and it would never happen again. Here was her chance. Her lone chance.

"Yes," she agreed on a sigh, her hips moving in an instinctive rhythm, seeking, searching.

The blunt head of him grazed her folds, then rubbed over her aching bud. He made a low sound, not a grunt, but a swift moan of appreciation and, still gripping himself between them, ran his length up and down her sex, tantalizing her with the promise of more.

Until, suddenly, there was more. Much more.

He brought his cock to her entrance. There was pressure, a great deal of it. He was a massive man. Too large. The pressure turned into a burning sting as he surged up, stretching her body in a way that was foreign and yet not entirely painful. Her breath caught.

She knew enough of the rudimentary aspects of congress between a man and woman to understand what was happening, to know what *would* happen. And yet, her mind had proven woefully inadequate. She hadn't been prepared for the shocking intimacy of him entering her body, the hot sting of his length sliding deeper, claiming her thoroughly in a way she'd never been claimed before.

The hand that was on her waist urged her downward, and she wanted to follow his lead, but she was also afraid he might break her in two.

His head fell back against the chair, his dark gaze questioning as he stopped, his cock thick and stiff inside her. "You're so tight. Relax and let me in."

"I did," she said, astounded that he could not feel himself inside her when he was all she felt.

The thickness of his length, impaling her. The heat of him. The strength. It was overwhelming. She felt as if she were full, so full, surrounded by him, invaded by him, possessed by him.

"I'm only partially there, sweet," he said, further surprising her. "Lower yourself if you can and take me to the hilt. I want to be buried so deep inside your sweet cunny that it feels like I'll never leave."

His voice was low and pure, molten seduction. Velvet and sin and every wicked thought she'd ever had in the dark of night and the solace of her own private chamber. His words filled her with a flurry of mad wanting.

Deep inside me. Never leave.

"Yes," she said, and then before she could further consider the ramifications of her actions this night, she did as he asked, lowering herself in one full motion. The pain that seized her was unexpected. It was sharp, splitting.

She gasped with shock, falling into his broad chest, tears pricking her eyes.

After so much pleasure, the full effect of him inside her was unexpectedly unpleasant. Was it his size? Had she been too rough? Had she done something wrong?

"Sweetheart." His lips were at her temple, soothing, reassuring, one of his hands sweeping comfortingly up and down her spine in rhythmic motions. "Talk to me."

She swallowed hard, burying her face deeper into his throat, his cravat tickling her nose and distracting her from the twinge of pain throbbing between her thighs. "I'm... I've not..."

"Hush," he murmured consolingly, apparently taking pity

on her stammered attempts at explanation. "I know, my beautiful spitfire. You should have told me the truth. I would have been more careful when I took your maidenhead."

He knew.

She hadn't fooled him, then. But of course she hadn't. Why would she have imagined for an instant that this magnetic, enigmatic, intelligent ruler would have believed her when she had just given him ample evidence of her lack of experience?

But then the rest of what he'd said occurred to her.

I would have been more careful when I took your maidenhead.

Those words meant that it wouldn't have mattered if she had been a virgin or not; the king wanted her, and the king would have taken her. He would have made her his, regardless.

Although it was wicked of her, that realization sent a fresh wave of desire to chase some of the lingering pain. Her inner muscles clenched on him, and it felt different. Strange and yet good.

He was still lodged deep inside her, thick and hard and hot. She sat up straight again, the movement setting her alight.

"Oh," she said, bemused by the complex, entirely foreign combination of sensations. Pain, pleasure, fullness. He was stretching her, taking her. But the discomfort continued to ebb, and in its wake were new pangs.

Pleasant ones.

And there he was, his handsome face before her, his dark eyes locked on hers, so much tenderness in his expression.

He cupped her cheek, running the rough pad of his thumb along her skin in one swift sweep. "How is it?"

"Strange," she admitted.

His lips quirked into a half smile. "Not precisely a testament to my ability as a lover. I'll have to rectify that."

"I didn't mean insult," she hasted to reassure him. "It is only that I've never—"

"I know, spitfire," he interrupted gently. "I know. Let me make it better for you. Will you do that?"

She wasn't certain he could, but the softness in his voice made her want to believe him capable of anything. He might have asked her to jump from the nearest window to her doom below, and she likely would have done so in that moment.

"Yes," she said.

Still cradling her face in one big hand, he drew her lips to his, kissing her slowly, languorously. As if they had all the time in the world to explore each other's mouths. And how she wished they did. For this intimacy—lips pressed together, mouths opening, tongues tangling—was every bit as necessary and personal a joining as the rest. Tansy relaxed, surrendering herself to the way he made her feel, to the masterful pressure of his mouth claiming hers. He tasted rich and sweet, like whisky and man and something else that was uniquely him.

Maxim.

Not King Maximilian. Not the icy, aloof stranger she had believed him to be. But a man who shared his flask with her and told her secrets. A man who concerned himself with her welfare, with her pleasure. A man who kissed her so sweetly.

She trusted him.

She wanted him.

Wanted, more importantly, to give herself to him. It was wrong to do so, and yet it was right. So very right.

Tansy threw herself into the kiss, and the pain receded. And then his hand slid beneath her skirts again, finding the place where all her pleasure seemed so very heightened, that responsive bud. The first brush of his fingers over her had her rocking into his touch, seeking more.

She concentrated on his lips, the glide of his tongue against hers, the knowing pressure of his fingers on her where she needed him most. It didn't take long for her to want more. For her hips to move, for her body to know what to do.

"Yes," he murmured against her lips. "Ride me, sweetheart. Find your pleasure. Take what you want."

Take what you want.

No one had ever given her permission to do so before. She'd spent the bulk of her life following in another's shadow, grateful for the roof over her head, the bed in which she slept, the clothing she wore, for her honored place in society when she might have been any other orphan, relegated to the noblesse oblige of distant relatives who didn't give a damn about her.

But here, now, in the arms of a king, she was being told for the first time not just that she could take what she wanted, but that she should.

And so, she did.

She threw caution and honor and loyalty aside, surrendering herself to the need for him. Surrendering herself to the wild, forbidden moments of passion between them.

All she could ever have.

Later, she would think about the consequences.

Later, she would worry over what her princess would think should she discover what had happened.

Later, she would agonize over her actions.

Tonight, all she wanted was to follow her instincts. Feeling bolder and braver than she ever had, she kissed him harder, her body moving, rising, following the path his guiding hand assigned her: up and down, his length nearly slipping from her and then sliding deep. Beneath her, she sensed that he waited patiently, allowing her to find her way.

But the muscles beneath her grasping fingers were tighter than the coils of a watch spring. He was holding himself in check for her sake.

The realization only made her want him more.

She tore her lips from his, breathless, wanton, fearless. "Make me yours, Maxim."

It was an edict given to a man who was ordered by none. He was king. Others bowed and scraped to his whims. He was a ruthless man who had fought on the battlefields for years, decimating his enemy. But he was also the man who touched her as if she were as fragile as newly fallen snow. Who kissed her as if he would die if he didn't have her lips beneath his.

And he answered her order.

With a possessive growl, he tightened his grip on her. For a moment, she feared she had gone too far, that her words would thrust him over the edge. But he quickly proved her wrong. His every touch and movement were careful and yet deliberate, bringing the fires of her desire to a raging height until all the pain of his initial breaching of her maidenhead was long gone and forgotten.

Until all that remained was what happened between them. Bodies moving together, lips searching and seeking, hearts pounding. They found a rhythm together, tentatively at first and then faster, as if they were in a race and each of them was desperate to emerge the victor. He continued working her bud until she was tensed and ready to split apart anew. She learned how good his cock felt, sliding inside her, then almost slipping free, how she could control the pace, the pressure. And in so doing, the pleasure.

He had given her free rein, she realized, and she was taking advantage. Riding him. Rocking against him. Kissing him, touching him. So much hardness to her softness. He was so large, so strong. And yet, he was beneath her, allowing her so much power over him, giving her the freedom to do what he had said.

Tansy was mindless now, driven by the primitive need for fulfillment, her body taking control. Faster, faster. Higher, higher. Her body was acutely aware of everything. His hand between their bodies moved with harsher motions, almost jerky now as he approached the edge of his own loss of control.

And then, it was happening again.

She splintered apart into a thousand tiny, shimmering shards. Or at least, that was how it felt. The pleasure started between her legs, and then it radiated outward in an explosion of pure, unadulterated bliss. This time as it overtook her, she tightened hard on his length, the sensation unfamiliar and yet oh-so good.

Oh-so right.

She cried out into his kiss, and he swallowed her every sound with his greedy mouth, as if he couldn't get enough of her. Beneath her, his body stiffened, and then there was a hot rush within her. He made a low sound of raw need.

All the passion that had been spurring her on began to retreat, and she collapsed against his chest, surrounded by his heat and strength, by the spicy masculine scent of him. Maxim, a man who could never be hers again beyond this lone night.

He ended the kiss, stroking her hair, murmuring words softly to her in his own language, words she didn't understand. But then he pressed his lips to her temple with a reverence that almost broke the dam inside her.

He switched to English, which they both understood fluently. "I'm glad you've changed your mind, spitfire."

Instantly, the contentedness within her dissipated, replaced by the heavy weight of dread.

She jerked her head back, holding his intense stare. "But I haven't changed my mind at all."

～

MAXIM WATCHED, incredulous, as Tansy flounced off his lap as if he were a raging fire, flipping her gown and petticoats back into place as if he hadn't just made love to her. As if he hadn't just spent inside her.

As if she weren't his.

This was not acceptable.

Grimly, he tucked his cock back inside his trousers and refastened them, though not without taking note of the smear of blood—Tansy's blood, the sign she'd been a virgin instead of the experienced woman he had wrongly supposed.

He knew a pang of regret. Not that he had taken her, but the manner in which he had. On a goddamned chair.

"Of course you have changed your mind," he told her implacably, rising to his full height.

"No," she told him calmly, denying him as she smoothed down her gown and tucked an errant lock of brown hair behind her ear. "What happened doesn't affect my position on the matter of becoming your whore."

For a moment, Maxim could do nothing but stare at her. She was jesting. Surely.

"Not my whore, damn you," he countered, his anger rising. "My woman. There is a distinct difference."

A massive one, though she remained unwilling to acknowledge it.

"Your kept woman," she said dispassionately, her lip curling. "This can never happen again. It was a mistake, truly. I was overwrought and seeking comfort, and you—"

"And I took your maidenhead," he interrupted, following

her as she crossed the room, daring to present him with her back.

No one turned their back upon the King of Varros.

No one except her, it would seem. His spitfire with the daring of a hundred men and the most outrageously stubborn streak he'd ever known in anyone.

"It doesn't signify," she said over her shoulder.

As if she gave herself to a man regularly without consequence. As if what had just transpired between them meant nothing to her, when it had meant every damned thing to him.

She was hastening to the door now, as if she intended to leave.

After she had just given him the most intense orgasm he could recall. After she had ridden him to within an inch of madness. He took longer strides, catching her before she could go with a hand on her elbow.

"Wait, Tansy."

"I must return before my absence is noted," she said, attempting to shrug free of his hold.

"You will turn and face me," he ground out, his pride stinging.

"I don't want to look at you just now." She kept her face carefully averted. "Release me, if you please."

"Turn and look at your king," he ordered.

Because, damn it, that was who he was, lest she forget. Varros was a small, inconsequential island kingdom without the might and vast wealth of England. It wasn't as large or as prosperous as Boritania had been in better days, before the reign of Gustavson had ruined the kingdom. But he would still be her king, and he wished to remind her of that fact if it would keep her where he wanted her.

Here. With him, where she belonged.

Her shoulders stiffened, and she hesitated. For a breath, he feared she would refuse to face him. But then she spun, her mouth swollen and dark from his kisses, her hair mussed, the pink rasp of his stubble on her creamy throat. And all he could think about, God help him, was the fact that he had been her first and he intended to be her only. That even now, his seed was inside her.

She curtsied.

It was a mocking curtsy, her expression serene, her eyes—where all her fire hid—burning into him. "As it pleases Your Majesty."

He clenched his jaw. "Do you imagine that after you gave yourself to me, I'll allow you to run off into the night alone?"

She rose, regal and elegant, the prim and proper Lady Tansy once more. "How else am I to return? I intend to go the way I came."

He crossed his arms over his chest. "I forbid it."

Her chin went up. "I didn't ask your permission."

Vexing woman. He wanted to kiss her and to throw her over his shoulder and carry her to his bed and keep her there for the next decade at least.

But he couldn't do that. Not yet.

"You are under my protection," he told her with a calm he didn't feel.

"As I've already informed you, I'll not be your mistress."

His patience snapped. "You are my woman," he ground out. "Your mind may not accept it, but your body betrays you. In time, you'll accustom yourself to the notion."

"The kept woman of a king is still a kept woman," she said quietly, sadly. "And the princess who will be your queen is like a sister to me. I could never take her husband to my bed after you're wed. You can demand it of me, but I will sooner be locked away in a prison."

Her cursed loyalty to Princess Anastasia was a thorn in his side. But he could see that she intended to fight him on the matter, despite everything that had just passed between them. Or perhaps because of it. Although she clung to her allegiance, when she had been in his arms, she had revealed to the both of them how very susceptible she was to him. Her desire for him had supplanted her constancy to the princess. It would do so again, of that he was certain. There was no mistaking the fire between them.

But he didn't need to win her over this night. There was the matter of where the princess was being kept and the extent of her injuries, to say nothing of finding a means of getting Tansy safely back inside the town house. He had more important concerns, though he deplored the thought of anything other than taking Tansy to bed with him and making her forget her every concern with kisses that sought to soothe the roughness of their first coupling.

Next time, he vowed he would woo her. He would seduce her until she no longer had the capacity to think, let alone fret over her misplaced loyalties. Her fidelity would be to him instead of to Princess Anastasia.

He unfolded his arms with great reluctance, relaxing his posture.

"You have ample time before we arrive in Varros," he reminded them both. "Your mind will alter before then."

He wouldn't stop until it did.

He had fought a war that had raged on for years, all in the name of gaining what was his by right. Tansy was no different from his kingdom. She belonged to him, and he would lay siege until she accepted it.

Because no one kept King Maxim of Varros from what he wanted, and what he wanted with a ferocity that far surpassed any hunger he'd once had for the throne that had

been   denied   him—was   the   solemn   lady-in-waiting
before him.

"It won't," she argued, persistent in her defiance.

He inclined his head. "It will be my greatest pleasure to prove you wrong, my lady. Now, come with me, and I'll see you safely returned for the evening."

CHAPTER 11

*M*axim was in a foul mood.

Nando was missing. Tansy had left him the night before after once more refusing his offer, and he'd yet to see her today, caught up in one troublesome matter after the next. His betrothed had been wounded and was being held somewhere in London by another man. And he'd spent the better portion of the day hunting that man down like the mongrel he doubtlessly was.

All he wanted to do was go to Tansy. To make love to her properly as he should have done last night. To kiss every delectable inch of her body until all the stubbornness and defiance melted away.

Instead, he was following Archer Tierney through London like a wraith. At last, his quarry was within sight. Within reach. With a hand to the Venetian blinds on the window, he peeked into the darkness, spying the man he strongly suspected was bedding his future wife. Strangely, it was a circumstance that nettled his sense of duty and little else. He didn't truly care what Princess Anastasia did after she gave him an heir, but the heir damn well had to be his blood, of his line, and not another man's whelp. He couldn't risk placing the kingdom in peril. There would be no more false claims to the throne of Varros.

The carriage slowed just before the shadowy figure, and Maxim leaned forward, opening the door.

"Get in," he growled at Tierney.

"Not in need of a ride this evening, old chap," the Englishman said politely, as if they were acquaintances passing in the street. "Thank you all the same."

Surely he didn't believe he'd been given a request. This was no favor Maxim was doing him out of the generosity in his heart. He needed to speak with Tierney, and Maxim didn't ask permission. He gave demands.

But Tierney was moving to avoid him, as if he fully expected to carry on his way uninterrupted. Maxim whistled to Felix, who jumped down from the rear of the carriage. His bodyguard stopped on the pavements before Tierney, pistol pointed at the other man's head.

"Halt," Felix ordered coldly.

That certainly gave the bastard pause.

"There seems to be some sort of mistake afoot," Tierney said. "I don't want any trouble."

That made two of them. But Maxim had a missing betrothed, and he needed to know where the hell she was and what had happened. The danger rose by the hour, it seemed.

"Take your hand from your coat," Maxim ordered him, for he wasn't about to meet his end at the hand of an Englishman. "Slowly."

"Who the bloody hell are you?" Tierney demanded.

"I'm King Maximilian of Varros," he said coldly. "Tell me, just what have you been doing with my future queen, Mr. Tierney?"

"What is this about?" Tierney asked, voice hoarse.

Poor fellow. That wasn't going to be the way of it. He would learn soon enough.

"Get in the carriage," he said calmly, "and we'll talk."

"Hand out of your coat," Felix commanded, repeating Maxim's order.

But Tierney didn't appear to be inclined to comply.

"Do you want to die today, Tierney?" Maxim asked.

"I reckon not." At last, Tierney withdrew his hand from his greatcoat, raising both arms, palms outward, to show his lack of armament.

"Excellent choice." Maxim turned to his bodyguard. "Felix, disarm him."

Felix stepped forward, neatly removing a secreted pistol and two blades from his person before kneeling and swiftly withdrawing a third blade from its sheath hidden in Tierney's boot.

His task complete, Felix stood, nodding toward the carriage. "Get in."

Tierney complied with obvious reluctance, stepping up and into the carriage. Felix slammed the door at his back. Within moments, the carriage sprang back into motion, Tierney seated across from him, the glow of the carriage lamp illuminating his face.

He looked ordinary enough. Hardly menacing. Maxim reckoned he could snap him in two.

"What do you want from me?" Tierney asked.

"I want to know where my betrothed is," Maxim said calmly. "Her lady-in-waiting told me that you have her."

The other man held his gaze, unflinching. "She is safe."

Not truly an answer. Had he expected one? Smug bastard.

"And what of her brother?" he asked next, needing to know.

Princess Anastasia had been tasked with finding Prince

Theodoric and convincing him to join their mutual cause, not chasing after Englishmen.

"You know about her brother?" Tierney asked carefully, clearly knowing far more than he revealed.

"Of course I do," Maxim told him curtly. "I learned from Gustavson himself that the lost prince was in London."

"You call him the lost prince. I understand he was exiled."

Exiled by a usurper, a pretender to the throne.

Maxim shrugged. "The means matter not. Have you found him?"

Comprehension dawned on Tierney's countenance. "*You're* the reason she sought me out to find her brother."

Maxim drummed his fingers on his thigh, not bothering to disguise his dislike of the other man. "I was told you were the best. Clearly, I was misadvised."

"I've found him," Tierney said evenly. "However, he's made it more than apparent that he had no wish to be found."

Hope rose, searing in its intensity. He had fought too hard to allow the exiled prince's reticence to ruin his plan. He needed to find the princess, and he needed to speak with Prince Theodoric. If Princess Anastasia couldn't persuade him to join in their cause, Maxim believed he could.

"Tell me, where is Princess Anastasia?" he demanded again.

"She's safe," Tierney repeated.

Damn the man.

"According to whom? *You*, Tierney?"

"What do you want?" the other man asked, as if he had the right to question him.

"I want Theodoric St. George. You've been paid a handsome sum to deliver him to me."

And it would appear that he had entangled himself romantically with the princess instead. There was no denying the possessive note in Tierney's voice when he spoke of Princess Anastasia.

"The gems belonged to the princess's mother, not to you," Tierney countered, "and moreover, they've been returned to her. I'll accept no payment for my services."

The cheek of the man astounded him.

Maxim raised a brow. "And why would that be, I wonder? Could it also have something to do with the reason the princess failed to return to her bedchamber last night?"

"If you are insinuating that something untoward has happened between the princess and me, you're wrong. She was wounded. That is the reason she didn't return. Did her lady-in-waiting not tell you that?"

Tierney was calm and poised. But he was lying; Maxim was certain of it.

"I'll ask you the same question I asked her," he continued, undeterred. "Do you think me stupid?"

Tierney gave him an insolent shrug. "I'm sure I couldn't say."

The man needed to be reminded of his place.

"I wasn't in favor of having you killed as Felix wanted," he said slowly, "but I may change my mind yet."

"I invite him to try."

"Felix is my most highly trained assassin," Maxim warned. "No one can slit a man's throat as quickly and quietly."

"If your intention is to kill me, then have done with it," Tierney said with a fool's defiance. "As we speak, the princess's uncle is conspiring to have her murdered. He tried once, but fortunately I was there to shoot the bastard dead before he could do more than wound her arm. If you want a *living* wife, you may wish to consider that."

Maxim's blood went cold. It was as he had feared, then. But it was impossible to know if the assassin who had tried to harm Princess Anastasia had been hired by her uncle or one of his own enemies.

"How do you know Gustavson was behind the attack?" he asked.

"I can't be certain," Tierney admitted. "But when my men gathered the body, they found Boritanian coins on him. He wasn't known to me or my men. Nor was he a common footpad. He didn't attempt to steal anything. His intent was to wound the princess, and his blade was mere inches from her heart. There is only one Boritanian with the motive and the means to assassinate the princess in London, and it's her uncle."

Boritanian coins were not necessarily the best indicator. The men who had come for him had worn Boritanian colors. Still, he didn't wish to entrust more information than was necessary to Tierney.

He balled his gloved hands into fists. "I don't disagree."

"The princess was escaping from her uncle's town house using her bedchamber window," Tierney added, "by climbing a tree. A physician tended to her wound, but I feared she would cause further harm if she tried to exert herself too soon after the injury occurred. I sent word to her lady-in-waiting that the princess would remain with me in the hopes that her wound would heal well enough that she could safely return. However, given the fact that her uncle wishes her dead, there is ample reason for her to remain where she is, beyond her uncle's reach."

"If all this is true, then what were you doing this evening?" he asked sharply.

"You had me followed," Tierney said baldly.

"Naturally," Maxim admitted with ease. "Princess Anastasia's lady-in-waiting is loyal to a fault, and I wasn't certain I could trust her. I had to see for myself what you were about.

Why were you going to the town house tonight, armed as you were?"

"The princess was deeply concerned for her lady-in-waiting's welfare. My intent was to liberate Lady Tansy and bring her to my home, where she would be far more protected than in her current location."

Ye gods, the man was bold. And stupid.

"You intended to kidnap a princess and her lady-in-waiting."

"Not the princess," Tierney denied. "But her lady-in-waiting, perhaps. Only if she resisted."

The mere notion of Tansy falling into the Englishman's clutches made him long to roar with rage. Tansy was his, damn it. He alone would protect her.

"You're an idiot, Mr. Tierney," he said, feeling vicious.

"So it would seem, considering I've been captured by you."

"I don't like you, Tierney," Maxim growled. "You're an insolent Englishman, and I ought to have Felix slit you from gut to gullet."

"Felix isn't in this carriage. I could kill you with my bare hands before he even knew anything was amiss."

A muscle in Maxim's jaw began ticking, so tightly was he grinding his molars. "I fear you underestimate me, English puppy. I'd snap you like a twig and use your bones to pick my teeth."

Tierney had the effrontery to laugh. "If it pleases you to imagine you could best me, then by all means, do so."

More silence descended, their glares clashing as the carriage swayed on, bouncing over a rut in the road.

"I've a bargain to offer if you wish to hear it," Tierney offered at last.

Maxim was a king. He didn't need to make bargains with

HOW TO LOVE A DANGEROUS ROGUE

bastards. But he was also running out of time to accomplish everything that needed to be done in London.

Grimly, he nodded. "Go on then, Englishman. Say it."

"You want Theodoric St. George, do you not?" Tierney asked. "I believe I can deliver him."

～

TANSY WOKE with a strangled cry in her throat on the cot in Princess Anastasia's bedroom, shaking and covered in sweat. The dream had been terrible. She had been dreaming of *him*, on the battlefield. Covered in blood, an enemy army bearing down on him. And yet, he had been standing alone and fearless, prepared to fight to the death. The anguish in her heart remained, as if it had been real, a deep and vicious ache she couldn't seem to escape.

Maxim.

No, she did not dare think of him thus.

Her eyes fluttered closed, anguish rushing over her.

She must think of him as King Maximilian. As the sovereign of the kingdom of Varros. As the man who would marry Princess Anastasia.

Not as the man who had kissed her with exquisite tenderness. Who had held her in his arms and brought her to life. Who had taken her innocence.

Breathing harshly, she fell back against the bedclothes, clapping a hand over her eyes, as if doing so might ward off the memories rushing over her from two nights ago. But nothing could. Even now, her body tingled with awareness. She was still sore in places she hadn't known it was possible to be sore. Delicate places. Places that reminded her just how wondrous it had felt to have him inside her.

But the most frightening discovery of all that she had

made during the lonely daylight hours yesterday? She loved him.

She had fallen in love with King Maximilian, a man who could never be hers. And she had committed the ultimate betrayal of Princess Anastasia, the woman to whom she owed everything. Her friend, the sister she'd never had. The one steadfast part of a life that had been ravaged by loss and abandonment and upheaval. Her only family.

How could she have done it?

Try as she might to tell herself that she had been overwhelmed by concern, that she hadn't been thinking properly, she knew that she had been motivated by more than fear. She had wanted the king. Had wanted him more than she had ever wanted anything. Even knowing he could never be hers, that she was making a great mistake in allowing him to make love to her, she had done so because she had been selfish.

She would have to confess to Princess Anastasia when she returned.

Tansy sat up, pressing a fist to her mouth to stifle her worried sob.

If she would return.

There hadn't been further word. It had been too dangerous.

The morning was rife with gloom, rain spattering on the windows, the room lit by the meager strains of light seeping from behind the curtains. After spending the previous day in a state of constant fear of discovery from the guards, and then staying awake most of the night hoping the princess would return, she must have finally fallen asleep.

A knock sounded at the door, startling her.

"Lady Tansy."

She recognized the low, deep growl instantly.

"Just a moment, please," she called.

What was he doing here at this early hour? She shot from

the cot, clad in nothing more than her chemise. With trembling hands, she rushed to don a petticoat and gown.

The door opened suddenly, the king shouldering his way inside, his massive form instantly seeming to take up all the space in the room. He was so large and powerful. This morning, there was a new air of intensity about him, his expression drawn and tight. Gone was the passionate lover of two nights before.

How to greet him? Perhaps he had taken her at her word and decided he no longer wished to pursue her as his mistress. The knife's edge of disappointment came with a corresponding arrow of guilt. That was what she wanted, she reminded herself firmly, his acceptance.

"Your Majesty." She dipped into a curtsy, clinging to formality.

The door had snapped smartly closed at his back, and he was striding across the chamber with great determination, his gleaming boots eating up the distance separating them. He caught her arm in a firm but gentle enough grasp, tugging her to the window.

"Come."

"Is anything amiss?" she asked, confused.

Her heart leapt as the obvious occurred to her. Had something happened to Princess Anastasia?

"I wish to see you in the light, and it's damnably dark in here," he muttered, hauling her behind him as he swept aside the window dressing with one haphazardly flung arm.

The sun was nowhere to be found, the day beyond distinctly gray. But a faint light fell over the two of them, illuminating the scar near his eye and reminding her of the dream that had jarred her from sleep, not so far removed from the life he had lived. He was known as the warrior king. He had earned his throne on the battlefield, proving his might and right, facing mortal danger.

She shivered.

Maxim caught her chin, tilting her face toward the scant light, studying her, his brows drawn together. "Are you hurt?"

His touch made a strange, liquid sensation pool low in her belly.

"Of course not," she reassured him. "Why do you ask?"

"You were trembling."

He had noticed.

She swallowed hard against a rush of longing. "It was nothing."

"It was *something*." His frown was ferocious, his gaze traveling over her as if searching for evidence that she had been somehow hurt or wounded. "I came to you as soon as I dared."

To her. A glowing warmth pervaded her at his words. And then it was chased quickly by guilt and duty. How dare she allow herself to feel joy from his pursuit of her? She had no right. He was not, could never be, hers. He belonged to his kingdom and, soon, to Princess Anastasia. Never to Tansy.

"You should go to your betrothed, not to me," she told him, seeking to put some necessary distance between them. "Have you word of the princess?"

His lips twisted into a cruel smile. "She is well enough, from what I'm told. It is you I'm concerned about most. From this morning on, my men will guard this chamber. If you need anything, call for them and they'll reach me forthwith. Do not hesitate. Indeed, it's imperative that you notify me immediately if anything untoward is happening."

There was an urgency in his voice, in his countenance, that she didn't like.

Tansy frowned, searching his gaze. "What are you not telling me?"

He swallowed hard, and she tracked the bob of his Adam's apple. "There is danger."

She might have scoffed had she not been so thoroughly upended by his unexpected appearance and concern. "There is always danger, is there not? It is inherent to the roles we play, this evil world in which we live."

He exhaled, the sound sharp in the morning stillness. "This is a different danger entirely. Do you understand my meaning? And I want you...nay, I *need* you safe."

A new wave of fear swept over her. "I pray you would be honest with me, Your Majesty."

"By God," he bit out. "You are to call me Maxim."

"But you are to be my king," she reminded him, repeating his words from the night she had sought him out.

The night he had taken her.

The night that had changed everything.

And yet, the night that had also changed nothing. For while her feelings for King Maximilian had altered whole-heartedly, her ability to embrace those feelings had not. She was still merely Tansy Francis, the lady-in-waiting of Princess Anastasia St. George of Boritania. She was the orphan who had been taken in by the royal family. She owed her friend everything, most of all, her loyalty.

Loyalty which she had torn asunder two nights past.

"I am your king," he agreed solemnly, "but you are my true queen. I want you with me, at my side. In my bed."

His words jolted her. For a moment, her foolish heart dared to believe and hope.

And then she understood that he was offering her a position instead of a marriage. He wished for her to be something she could never be. And her hope shattered along with her foolish heart.

"I can only be your queen if we are joined in holy matrimony as husband and wife," she informed him. "And you are marrying another. Understandably, Your Majesty. I am but a humble orphan cast upon the benevolence of the royal St. George family."

"Tansy—"

"Are you not marrying Princess Anastasia?" she demanded, her voice unusually high, her emotions rising, beyond her control. She was making a fool of herself and she did not like it, but neither could she rein in her reaction. Too much had happened. She loved Maxim. The King of Varros.

A man forever beyond her reach for so very many reasons.

"You know that I am marrying the princess." His head dipped, a heavy sigh falling from his sensual lips. His dark gaze burned into hers. "Some circumstances are beyond my control. I am acting in the best interest of my kingdom. I've no choice to do anything less."

Of course. She understood, even if the knowledge was akin to a blade between her ribs, rendering each breath painful. Even if tears she refused to shed pricked her eyes. She was not free to live the life of her choosing; her future had been decided for her, from the time her parents had both died and she had been given into the care of the Royal House of St. George.

Just as Maxim's had been decided for him. He had been born to the throne; the blood of kings flowed through his veins. She was a mere lady, her claim to nobility limited. Her father had been neither wealthy nor powerful, and her mother had been a merchant's daughter.

She was, by comparison, no one. She understood the disparity between them. She always had, but it had never felt greater than in this moment, his eyes searing hers with such tender urgency, words she would have otherwise welcomed falling from his lips. There could be no future for them. She could never live with being his mistress, and he could never marry her.

"I accept that you are bound by your duty to your people," she told the king earnestly. "You must extend me the same courtesy."

"I'm a king. The weight of my kingdom, the future of its people, rests upon my shoulders."

His voice was low and soft, yet undeniably burdened with the heavy weight of responsibility. She wanted to kiss him. To fold her arms around him, to bury her face in his throat and inhale the decadent masculine scent of his soap and musk and leather. To hold him tightly, to lead him to the cot she had so recently vacated.

None of those things could happen.

"I understand, Your Majesty," she said simply.

"No," he bit out, shaking his head. "You don't. Damn it, woman, heed me. There is danger afoot. I need to know you will be safe. I need you to understand that there are men who would do you great bodily harm."

"Why?" Her brows drew together as she searched his gaze for an answer, trying to understand what had changed, why this difference had been brought about within him. "Nothing has changed, has it? Is the plan the same?"

His jaw tensed. "The plan remains the same. The only alteration is in the danger. The man who wounded the princess intended to kill her. He was an assassin either sent from King Gustavson or from one of my own enemies."

One of his own enemies? This was the first occasion upon which she had heard of such a possibility. She had believed his reign over Varros had been solidified by his victory in the Great War.

Her frown deepened. "But you are the celebrated King Maximilian. What enemies do you have, after rescuing

Varros from ruin? Your victories in battle are legendary. You have changed everything for your people."

Maxim's nostrils flared, his smile turning tight, almost feral. "My uncle has supporters who linger like vermin. There will never be a day that I do not have to fear that someone will be waiting, with either a bullet or a blade or poison or something else, equally capable of bringing me low."

She couldn't contain her gasp, pressing a hand to her heart. "But you are the king."

His countenance was fashioned of granite. "Even a king is a mere mortal. No one knows that better than the enemies of the king, and God knows I have enemies just as any other man. More enemies, in fact. My position is not as secure as I would prefer. Coming to London has taught me as much. Marrying the princess and bringing Prince Theodoric back to power will benefit Varros, but it will also help to solidify my power. With Boritania as a trusted ally, my detractors will be far less likely to make attempts on my life."

For the first time, it occurred to Tansy that Maxim's betrothal and marriage to Princess Anastasia was rooted in so much more than she had ever supposed. He was seeking to improve his own position, yes. But he was also apparently in danger, and marrying someone connected to another sovereign in the region would leave Varros in a better position of stability, particularly if he had heirs, should he die.

That brutal realization, coupled with his words, sent icy tendrils of fear through her.

She swallowed hard, trying to understand. "What else has happened? Has someone tried to do you harm? Is that why you feared that something had happened to me?"

If possible, his expression closed even more. "You needn't concern yourself with the details."

She scoffed, frustrated with him, loving him, hating him. At an impasse.

"Because I am a woman?" she demanded. "If so, I can assure you that I am more than capable of understanding such complexities as danger and trepidation."

"Because you are *my* woman," he countered fiercely, "and I don't want to fill your heart with ugliness and fear. I want you to remain as you are."

Too late for that, she longed to tell him, and not without bitterness. She had been complacent enough with her life and her role in the past. But her involvement with him had changed things. Had changed everything. Had changed her, and—heaven help her—had changed her heart forever. And she couldn't quite banish the warmth pooling inside her at his possessive pronouncement that she was his woman, even if she knew she could never truly be.

"You are in danger, Princess Anastasia has been wounded, and you believe I'm in danger as well," she said instead. "That is the reason for the guards."

"I need to make certain you're protected," he said sternly, frowning down at her. "Until you're in my court at home in Varros, this is the best I can do."

She nodded, a sudden rush of tenderness overwhelming her. He was an arrogant, cold man in many senses, but with her, he was caring in a way she had never expected him to be. "Thank you."

"Don't thank me." A muscle tensed in his jaw beneath the dark shadow of his stubble. He looked forbidding and fearsome. "It's my duty to protect you. I wish I could do more, but with you being here guarded by Gustavson's men and the princess's position being so damned precarious, my hands are tied. Promise me that you will take great care with yourself and that you'll go to my guards should anything happen."

"I promise."

He was always somber, a man clearly haunted by his past and the years he had spent waging war, but there was no denying how serious he was now. Maxim reached for her then, drawing her against his big body, the warmth and strength of him radiating into her. Despite herself, Tansy twined her arms around him, holding him close. He was in danger as well, and although he hadn't provided much detail, she hated the notion of anything befalling him. He nuzzled her temple, his breath falling hotly over her ear.

"I need you safe, spitfire."

She inhaled deeply of his scent, wishing their circumstances were not so hopeless, not daring to speak. For if she did, it would be to tell him that she needed him safe too, that she loved him, and those were words she had no right to speak.

CHAPTER 12

*H*e shouldn't have revealed such weakness to her.

Maxim regretted the admission the moment it left his lips, not because it wasn't true. For he did need Tansy. Needed her so much it terrified him. *Him*, a man who hadn't known fear on the battlefield even with death all but imminent.

But she was warm and soft and sweet-scented in his arms, and he may have been born to be king, but he was also man. Fallible, weak, susceptible man. Far too fallible where she was concerned.

No, he regretted his admission because he understood what it meant. He hadn't known this deep, inexorable pull to anyone since Mina, and if he were brutally honest with himself, he would acknowledge that not even his feelings for Mina had been as strong as this all-consuming desire and deep, abiding...ye gods, he didn't even have a name for it. His mind struggled to form a word, but he could find nothing to encompass all that he felt for Lady Tansy Francis. It was vast and frightening.

She turned her face toward him, and there was a look of such tenderness in her eyes, tenderness that was all for him. Tenderness that melted all the hard angles inside him into something molten and smooth. And then she cupped his cheek, the soft warmth of her skin setting him alight, and her lips angled over his. Tansy kissed him sweetly, tentatively at first and then with greater determination. A bolt of desire shot through him, making his cock instantly hard.

All his good intentions, his worries, were burned to ash. Nothing that wasn't her mouth, her lush body, existed to him. He was lost in her, on fire for her, his need for her only increasing with every furious pump of his heart. His hands moved with a will of their own, molding to her waist, caressing. He shouldn't be here with her now like this, inviting danger when there was already a perilous amount surrounding them.

Enough to drown in.

And yet, how could he be anywhere else? How could he not take her into his arms and carry her across the room to where the bed was still generously stuffed with blankets and pillows beneath the counterpane to resemble the missing princess?

He had to. Like his quest to regain the throne, Tansy had become a part of him, not so different from blood and bone. His booted strides were taking them across the chamber, their lips still fused. He kissed her like she was air and water and every other requirement of life in one. He kissed her like he was going to battle and feared he would never return—a kiss to last an eternity.

Kissed her and carried her to the bed, showing her wordlessly that she was his. That she meant far more to him than he had ever dared to imagine she could. That the flames burning hotly between them were inevitable. His legs met with the edge of the bed and he began lowering her to the mattress, intending to join her there.

But she broke the kiss, her breathing harsh, her lips painted dark from his mouth on hers. "Not in her bed. We can't."

He growled, staying himself mid-motion. "Why not? We made use of it previously."

"We shouldn't have. I wasn't thinking properly."

But she was now? Clearly, he would need to remedy that problem.

Maxim sighed. "Where, then?"

He would take her on the floor if necessary.

A terrible silence descended during which he feared she would deny him, deny them both what they so obviously wanted. But then she spoke, so quietly he could scarcely hear her past the blood rushing in his ears.

"My cot."

He looked around furiously, a man possessed by the need to be inside his woman, and spied the small, portable bed in a corner of the room. Very small. By God, the frame looked as if it might bend and break beneath a strong wind.

He frowned. "I'll never fit on there."

She stiffened in his arms. "We shouldn't."

Not the words he wanted to hear.

So he kissed her again. Held her glorious weight in his arms and devoured her mouth until she went soft and pliant again. Until his ravenous cock was straining harder than ever against the fall of his trousers. Until she made a breathy sound of surrender that told him she had forgotten her objections. He began lowering her back to the bed, because he had taken her in a chair as if she were no better than a common strumpet, and because he wanted to pleasure her as she deserved, in the greatest comfort this damned prison of a chamber would afford them.

But she stiffened again, tearing her mouth from his. "Maxim."

There was protest in her voice and in the stubborn set of her jaw. He kissed her there, nuzzling her silken skin and wishing he had her in his bedchamber at home in Varros. His bed had been built specifically for him, the size immense. How beautiful she would look in his sheets, naked and his. Yes, he would have her there and everywhere else he could.

"Not in her bed," she repeated. "We can't."

Damn it.

He groaned and lifted his head, thwarted lust making his voice low and raspy. "Not the cot, spitfire. I'll break it, and then how will we explain that to the guards?"

She nodded. "You are very large."

His chest puffed up with pride. He couldn't help it.

She caressed his cheek. "The floor? We can spread some counterpanes."

He kissed her palm, then couldn't resist running his tongue along the lined surface, tasting her. "It will have to do until I have you where I want you."

He could have cursed himself for mentioning the future, when he wanted to keep her agile mind very much in the present. So he kissed her again before she could further ponder what he'd said or find new reasons why they shouldn't make love.

He gave her ravishing kisses, hard and swift and deep and passionate kisses. Kisses that he intended to banish every modicum of resistance in her body. All the loyalty that belonged to anyone other than him, too.

Maxim walked toward the fireplace and deposited her gently in a chair. She looked wide-eyed and dazed, thoroughly kissed, and deliciously beddable. He paused for a moment, even as lust licked through him, and stared at the vision she presented.

His.

New pride rose inside him, along with another feeling that was far more than lust. He cupped her cheek and kissed her again for good measure and then reluctantly turned away to retrieve some coverlets from the abandoned bed she had decreed they couldn't make use of.

Anything to please her.

He scooped up as much of it as he could in his arms and turned back to her, feeling every inch the triumphant warrior about to claim his prize. Sweet, gray-eyed, devoted, beautiful, stubborn Tansy, who possessed a fouler vocabulary than some men he knew. The corner of his lips tugged up as he remembered her Boritanian curse the day he had first come to the town house and found her alone.

May God rot your cock.

"You're smiling," she said, as if his levity were a thing of wonder.

And perhaps it was.

Maxim couldn't recall the last time he'd felt so damned content.

"I was hoping you aren't wishing for any deities to curse a certain portion of my anatomy now that you've enjoyed it for yourself," he confessed softly, teasingly.

There was a strange lightness within him now that had no business lingering. A dizzying glow that tempted him mightily to believe in fanciful notions he'd long thought nothing more than blatant falsehoods.

Happiness.

Love.

Hope.

All emotions he'd known once. Emotions he'd vowed never to allow himself again after they had been so ruthlessly snatched away. Emotions he had no right to entertain in his present position. But he couldn't help himself as he spread the blankets before the fire.

Tansy had risen, her fingers chasing his, delicate and fine-boned in his massive paws. "Let me."

"No." Here was another rare indulgence, the ability to do something for someone else. Ordinarily, everyone else did for him. Servants, privy council, even the fawning courtiers and the men who had fought at his side. He brought her hand to his lips for a reverent kiss, then her wrist, holding her gaze. "Allow me. I want to."

Another admission. It seemed he was full of them today.

The sound of footsteps in the hall beyond shook them both from their idyll. Her brow furrowed, and she snatched her hand away, a look of wild fear entering her eyes that he'd give his very life to erase.

"We shouldn't," she said again quietly, catching her lip between her teeth. "If they suspect…"

"To hell with them," he snarled, feeling irrationally blood-thirsty after the intrusion upon this rare moment of peace. "I'll kill them all with my bare hands."

"And where would that leave Varros?" she asked, shaking her head. "You don't need to start a war."

But starting a war was precisely why he had come to England. It was why he was marrying the princess he didn't want. Because he needed to remove Gustavson from the throne. However, he didn't intend to start the war by slaying all the usurper king's guards.

"They'll not dare to interrupt," he reassured her, grimly resuming the task of positioning the bedclothes on the floor.

Maxim was careful not to tell her why. He didn't reckon she would approve of his threatening the guards.

"And why not?" she asked, far too perceptive as always. "Have you done something, Maxim?"

A new smile was curving his lips. He liked that she was

calling him by his given name. He liked, too, that she had returned his kisses with equal ardor, sucking on his tongue and kissing him frantically, her small hands clutching at his shoulders and grasping at his coat as if she intended to tear it to shreds. He had hoped she might. The less clothing he was wearing in Tansy's presence, the better.

"I'm the King of Varros," he said simply instead of elaborating, plumping a feather pillow as if he were an accomplished chambermaid. "They'll not dare to open the door after I've warned them against it."

He *was* the king, but on the battlefield, he'd had to attend himself in many ways. He hadn't grown to manhood as a spoiled, cosseted royal. He'd come of age fighting for what was his, facing death without blinking. He felt more at home marching, on his aching knees, bedding down on the floor as he'd done for countless cold, dark winter's nights, than he did luxuriating in the riches of his kingdom.

He felt more at home with Tansy than he ever had with anyone. Even here, in this stolen fragment of the day, with the fear of discovery looming over them and the somber specter of the future ominous before them.

"I suspect you've warned them with more than words," Tansy said, on her knees at his side, smoothing the blankets with quick, efficient motions.

He realized that it was a task she had conducted many times, and that she was little more than a servant, waiting upon the whims of the disappearing Princess Anastasia. Anger coursed through him, mingling with the lust. The urge to demand that she cease acting as the princess's lady-in-waiting struck him strongly. He almost blurted the order, as he would have to any soldier on the battlefield. But he held his tongue, knowing that it would only heighten Tansy's determination to continue. He admired her defiance. It repelled him and enthralled him all at once.

"Perhaps," he allowed then, studying her face, the hints of gold and red hiding in her mahogany locks. "Take down your hair."

His boldness took her by surprise. Fine brows arched.

"Please," he added gruffly. "I wish to see it unbound."

"It is plain hair, no curl," she protested. "The color of mud."

Mud? Sacrilege. He'd seen more than his share of mud, and her beautiful tresses bore no comparison.

"It's glorious," he countered firmly, wondering if it was possible that she didn't know. If her humility kept her from seeing her true beauty. "There are hints of gold and red hidden within it when the light catches. I have dreamt of running my fingers through it."

He already knew it would be decadently soft. But he wondered how long it was. Wondered what it would look like draped over a pillow, wrapped around his fist.

"You have?"

Her hesitant question made him want her even more. She was far too humble, his spitfire. She'd been forced to hide in the shadow of a princess, but she had been born to be a true queen. How he wished, with a ferocity that would have knocked him to his knees had he not already been upon them, that he could make her his. That he could marry her in truth.

"I have," he confirmed.

They faced each other, on their knees, the world beyond this chamber desperately uncertain. Danger, wars, unwanted marriages, assassins, wrongful kings, exiled princes, guards. None of it mattered.

Holding his gaze, Tansy reached for the pins holding her hair in its tidy chignon. One by one, she pulled, her eyes never leaving his. Fat tendrils spilled down her shoulders and back. And ye gods, it was longer than he had supposed.

Thicker and richer. He reached for a handful that had fallen over her right breast, but his greedy hand cupped, weighing the fullness, finding her nipple hard and demanding beneath the layers of her garments and hair.

Fuck.

He had never surrendered on a field of battle. Not once in all the years of the Great War.

But he was surrendering now.

Surrendering to this small, mysterious woman with the fortitude of an entire cavalry brigade.

"Softer than I imagined," he murmured, realizing that his hand trembled.

Because he understood the gift Tansy was giving him, not just herself, not just her body, but a complete refutation of the marrow-deep loyalty she harbored for her princess. She was a woman of vast principle. He knew this. But for him, she was willing to sacrifice her own beliefs, her loyalty, everything.

And it wasn't because he was king.

Other women had thrown themselves at him after he had taken the throne. Their avarice had been reflected in their glittering gazes, a lust for not just himself but the power he possessed. He hadn't bedded a one of them.

The last pin was removed. Even this revelation was executed with typical Tansy care. The hairpins were laid in a tidy pile for easy retrieval later, just off the blankets.

"Will you let me tend you?" she asked.

He might have thought it the question of a servant but for the tone in her voice, the longing in her eyes. Maxim swallowed hard, feeling small for the first time in his life.

He nodded, relinquishing his hold on her breast, the cool, silken strands of her hair. "How would you have me?"

She cocked her head, practical even in seduction, and the

urge to kiss her thundered through him. "Sit, I think. If it pleases you to do so, of course."

He was damned glad she hadn't called him *Your Majesty*. He might have lost control and pinned her to the floor, lifting up her skirts and burying his face in her cunny until she forgot all sense of formality and covered him in her sweet, dripping dew.

But he wanted to prolong this. They had time. He needed this time. It might be the last they had together before the inevitable, long journey to Varros.

So he gave her what she wished, settling on his arse, legs stretched before him. "Thus?"

"Yes." She moved to his boots.

He wanted to tell her not to remove them, that it was beneath her.

But she glanced up at him shyly as she settled there. "Please. I want to."

And damn it all to hell. He couldn't speak past the longing clogging his throat. She *wanted* to attend him. No one had done something for him because they wanted to in as long as he could recall. He inclined his head.

Another shy smile that settled behind his breastbone in a painful ache. And then her nimble fingers were at work, removing the boots with deft, efficient motions. He'd never in his life been incited by the mere act of removing his boots, but his cock was harder than iron by the time she had completed her task.

"Come here," he said gruffly, hauling her into his lap without waiting for her response.

She was soft and womanly, her curves melting against him, her hands settling on his shoulders. Her lips came down on his. Greedy, hungry. He gave her his tongue, and she sucked on it as if she couldn't get enough of him. All the pent-up longing exploded between them like fireworks careening into the night sky, booming and sparkling. In a flurry of movement, they divested each other of garments. Cravat, coat. Chemise, petticoats. Stockings, trousers, shirt.

Until there was nothing remaining but bare skin and Tansy was stretched beneath him on the soft nest of blankets he'd arranged for them, her unbound hair lustrous as it fanned over the feather pillow. Maxim settled between her thighs, spreading them wide with two flattened palms on either side, opening her to him. Pink, glistening folds greeted him, the taunt of her pouty little bud. He was going to lick and suck and fuck her until she forgot all the reasons why she was so determined to resist the inevitability of them together.

He was a starving man, and Tansy was the feast.

~

HIS TONGUE.

Oh heavens, his *tongue*.

Tansy squirmed. She should be embarrassed. Ashamed. But Maxim's handsome face was buried between her legs, and his mouth was performing wondrous feats upon her most sensitive places. It was difficult to form thought, let alone castigate herself. Instead, she surrendered, promising herself this would be the final time. That she would take the memory of these stolen moments and it would last her the rest of her life.

He licked up her center, his clever tongue playing over the nub of flesh her fingers found late at night when she was alone. And oh, how delicious it was. Beyond her most feverish imaginings. She had read about such acts, of course. But nothing could compare to the wicked glide of him over her. When his lips closed over her and he gave a hearty suck, she feared her head might fly from her body. The sound that escaped her was too loud.

He looked up, his lips wet with her essence. "Hush, sweeting. A bit quieter."

He was right. She had no wish to bring the guards upon them.

"It's so…" Her words trailed off as she failed to explain. So she pressed the back of her hand to her mouth instead, hoping to muffle any more inadvertent noises.

The smile he gave her was beautiful. "You like my mouth on you, don't you?"

She nodded, her sex aching for him to continue his merciless torture.

"Good," he said with his characteristic firmness. "When we're in Varros, I'm going to lick your cunny every day."

She might have protested—she had no intention of being intimate with him after today. And she most certainly would not lie with him when he was married to another. But then, his head lowered and his tongue went to work making her mindless again, and she surrendered herself to the exquisite sensations.

He hooked her knees over his shoulders, his big hands cupping her bottom, and held her to him, ravishing her until she was gasping and sounds were emerging from her throat that refused to be contained. She stuffed her fist against her mouth to keep from crying out as he sank his tongue deep inside her. His fingers replaced his tongue, thrusting into her in a mimicry of lovemaking, moving in a way that inspired an exquisite quake of sensation to overcome her. He licked and sucked her bud, fingers probing, filling, driving her to the heights of madness and beyond.

Her release seized her suddenly, and she bit down hard on her knuckles to keep from crying out as wave after wave of delirious pleasure washed over her, radiating outward. He didn't stop until he had drawn the last of it from her. Until she was limp and throbbing and gasping for breath, her heart pounding and her body glowing.

Slowly, tenderly, he lowered her legs, caressing them with his strong, battle-callused hands. He made a growl low in his throat, as if he too were out of his mind with ecstasy, and all from the act of pleasuring her. He dotted kisses over her hip bone, her stomach, the curve of one breast. His mouth closed over a nipple, sucking hard, and her body arched instinctively into him, her hips fitting snugly around his big frame. She couldn't resist touching him then, and once her hands began to move, they were everywhere. Over his shoulders, the hard plane of his back, following his spine. Higher, to his nape, the soft tickle of his hair falling over her skin.

His eyes met hers as he moved to her other breast, his tongue flicking the tight, pink tip, back and forth.

"Oh," she said, a sigh of wonderment that he could make her feel so wonderfully, deliciously alive.

Everywhere.

He caught her nipple in his teeth, delivering a sharp little bite that sent an arrow of heat directly to her core, and then he chased the sting with a reverent kiss. "So beautiful. So perfect."

She was far from perfect, and she had never considered herself beautiful. But he made her feel both those things, so she didn't argue. Instead, she savored him as he kissed a path to her collarbone, his lips finding a place at the base of her throat that she had never known was so sensitive. His fingers dipped into her sex again, stroking, as he leveraged himself on a forearm and rasped her skin with his stubble.

"Tansy," he murmured into her ear. "My Tansy. Tell me what you want."

A small moan fell from her lips, all she could manage.

How dare he expect words from her? But that was Maxim. *Her* Maxim, if only for these precious, stolen minutes.

He gently bit her earlobe, strumming over her bud. "Tell me."

Demanding. Always demanding. And arrogant and yet so tender.

She wanted to give him everything.

Tansy kissed his cheek. Kissed the scar from the enemy soldier's blade. "I want you inside me."

"Yes," he said, the word almost hissed from him, laden with such victory.

As if he had just conquered a kingdom.

And then he was there, his cock hard and demanding at her entrance. His lips dusted over her cheek. "Relax, my darling."

He said the words in her native tongue, and the last of any restraint she possessed was shattered. She held him to her, undulating her hips, welcoming him inside her. His mouth found hers as he pressed, a shallow thrust to allow her to adjust to the intrusion. He was so impossibly large. She hadn't forgotten, and there was a twinge of pain as he moved again. His touch was there, fluttering over her nub, inciting more sparks of desire. Chasing any discomfort. Another thrust, and he was inside her to the hilt.

They were pressed together, hip bone to hip bone, her breasts crushed to his muscled chest, and she was so deliciously full of him. He remained still for a moment, kissing her jaw, her eyebrow, the corner of her lips.

"How does it feel?" he asked softly, solicitously.

Such concern for her.

She sifted her fingers through his black hair, through the silver strands at his temple, loving him so fiercely that she thought she might never recover from it.

"Wonderful," she managed.

He took her mouth then, the kiss deep and drugging, and she tasted herself. Tasted passion and Maxim and the forbidden. He made love to her slowly, so slowly, taking such care. Too much care. She told him so with her nails on his shoulders, with her legs wrapped around him. With her tongue in his mouth.

He growled and gave her what she wanted, moving faster, harder, thrusting in and out of her until they were both breathless, careful to swallow each other's sounds. Lost in the moment, in their bodies, in the way they fit together, in the endless pleasure. She never wanted it to end.

It had to end.

It would end.

But then he sucked on her lower lip and his knowing fingers whorled over her bud with greater pressure, and the bliss of it all was too much. She clamped down hard on him, her second peak every bit as explosive as the first. He sank into her, his hands finding hers, lacing their fingers together. He pinned them over her head on the layers of counterpanes, holding her there as he lavished fast, intense strokes upon her, his cock gliding in and out, his mouth fastened to hers as if it would forever live there.

He stiffened above her, pounding into her one last time before he groaned into her kiss and the hot rush of his seed flooded her. The kiss turned sweeter, less frantic, and at last the tension seeped from his big body and he laid his head on her shoulder, breathing as hard as she was.

Tansy pressed another kiss to his scar.

She had never loved him more.

CHAPTER 13

*T*he first sight that greeted him was his brother's bare arse. The second was a pair of breasts covered in something that looked alarmingly like trifle, the avid tongue of another woman licking the syllabub layer away.

Maxim clamped a shielding hand over his eyes and averted his gaze to the floor. "Damn it, Nando."

He had scoured half of London after reluctantly leaving Tansy earlier, intent upon finding his brother. Half fearing he would discover an assassin had claimed his life.

As it turned out, he needn't have been so consumed with fear.

It wasn't an assassin that had claimed Nando. Rather, it was cunny.

No fewer than three of the illustrious brothel's women of the night surrounded his brother, who was lying prone in nary a stitch, red welts on his arse that had undoubtedly been left there by the riding crop one of the women held.

"Is that you, brother?" came Nando's muffled query,

sounding lazy and, if he knew his brother, thoroughly soused.

By God.

Nettled, Maxim removed his hand, facing the grim picture of debauchery before him. Had he thought there were only three women? Clearly, he had miscounted. For there were also two women making use of a strange chair on the opposite end of the chamber, one behind the other.

"Slower or faster, Nando?" cooed the woman at the rear, thrusting her hips slowly and giving her bottom a shake, undoubtedly for his brother's benefit.

"Not at all," Maxim interrupted sharply.

There were some aspects of his brother's depravities that he hadn't ever wished to know. He'd heard whispers, of course. Nando had the face of an angel and the appetite of the devil, it was said. Maxim had never stopped to ponder the implications for overly long.

The generously endowed brunette didn't appear at all concerned by Maxim's order. She cupped the blonde's breasts, giving her nipples a pinch that made the other woman moan in what sounded very much like feigned enjoyment to Maxim's ears.

"Faster," Nando directed, as if Maxim hadn't spoken. "Mademoiselle Jeanette likes when you're rough."

"Nando," Maxim gritted out, repelled by the den of sin before him.

"You're still here, then?" Nando drawled without turning away from the spectacle he was apparently directing. "I thought you'd be too shocked to stay. I've paid the ladies for another hour, Maxim. Won't you come back then?"

Likely, *he* had paid the ladies for another hour of entertainments for his ne'er-do-well brother, and not the other way around.

"They'll thank you for the extra hour to themselves," he snapped curtly. "Mademoiselles, I'll thank you to dress yourselves and take your leave whilst I speak with my brother."

"Coin's already been spent," said one of the women lounging on the bed.

"You'll not be getting it back," added the red-haired harlot bearing the riding crop.

"Keep the coin," he ground out. "It's yours."

"See here," Nando exclaimed, sounding indignant, finally craning his neck in Maxim's direction. "You can't send away my goddesses, Maxim. I've paid for them. And Mademoiselle Jeanette hasn't come yet."

From the looks of her, she wasn't about to either. Any noises of enjoyment she was making had purely been to titillate his dolt of a brother.

Assassins were trying to kill Maxim and Princess Anastasia. The danger had never been more heightened. And Nando had spent the last few days frolicking with women of ill repute as if he hadn't a care in the world. But then, this was his scapegrace brother. There *were* no worldly cares for Nando.

"Get. Out," he commanded the strumpets succinctly. Not unkindly, for they had been paid for their presence and their efforts. They weren't at fault for his brother's insatiable capacity for iniquity.

And stupidity.

At the new edge of steel in his voice, the women leapt into action, disengaging from one another and hastening to don dressing gowns. Impassively, he wondered whether the one who had been covered in trifle had managed to wipe herself clean before attending to her dubious modesty.

"Maxim," Nando complained.

"Cover yourself," he commanded his brother crisply. "The last thing I wish to see is your hairy arse, and covered in lashes, no less."

"My goddesses told me I was being a very bad lad and that I needed to be punished."

Just how sotted was his brother?

One of the ladies tittered and then emitted a hiccup.

How sotted were they all?

The room, now that he thought upon it, stank of spirits and sexual congress. He swallowed back the urge to gag. After the tender passion he'd shared earlier with Tansy, this sordid spectacle was all the more repugnant to him.

"Be gone," he repeated thunderously to the ladies.

He waited as they sauntered from the chamber, some more unsteady on their bare feet than others. When the door had finally closed on the last of them, he turned back to Nando, gratified to discover his brother had at least possessed the decency to cover himself and sit up in the mound of pillows he'd been inhabiting.

"Do you know," Maxim began, his voice vibrating with suppressed rage and concern, "how worried I've been about you?"

"Worried about me?" Nando raised his brows. "Why should you be? You told me no more married women. I would've thought you'd be pleased I've followed your edicts."

Maxim had never wanted to cuff his brother more. He clenched his hands into fists at his sides and cast a look around the room for signs of his brother's garments. It didn't take long to discover them draped over various pieces of furniture, likely flung wherever he had discarded them.

"I'm not in the mood for your games, Nando," he said curtly, using a calming, rhythmic march to pace down one length of the chamber in an effort to cool his rising ire and the fit that was never far behind moments of great upheaval and upset.

He had been damned distressed when he had learned

Tansy was potentially at peril as well. The sole motivating force that had kept him going was the need to see her as safely protected as possible. And then, when he'd seen her, he'd fallen into the abyss of desire.

Now that he had located Nando and the necessity of his retaining his wits had faded, he was losing control. It was likely the combination of fear and fury. His heart was galloping faster than a spooked horse.

"Maxim?" Nando's voice reached him, as if from the other side of a tunnel. "You're not having one of your spells, are you?"

Some of the jocular air had faded, and in its place was concern. Maxim attempted to concentrate on his brother's tone, his safety, his presence. He tried to tell himself that Tansy was being guarded by his best men. That no harm would befall her.

But then he thought of Mina.

Of Mina's battered, bruised face, her broken, lifeless body.

And everything inside him seized.

A sound escaped him that was more animal than human. He hated this wretched weakness. Hated the memories. Hated the bastards who had killed his wife so many years ago, the enemy soldiers who had captured her and paraded her around like spoils of war before killing her.

Hated the thought that he could ever again be responsible for such a horrific, brutal attack.

Breathe, damn it, he told himself, pacing, pacing.

He'd intended to fetch his brother's clothing, but now he was two-and-twenty and he was rolling over the body of the woman he loved, left battered and bloodied on the ground as if she hadn't been someone precious. Someone beautiful and vivacious and filled with life. Someone so very loved and innocent. A wife and a sister, a daughter, and a friend, a soon-to-be-mother.

A hand clamped on his shoulder, and Maxim gave a violent cry, wrenching away. For a moment, he was trapped between two worlds, the past and the present. He could smell the burning fires, the scorched earth, the unmistakable scents of blood and death.

"Maxim, brother."

Nando's voice. Calming. Soothing. Emerging from the fiery hells that had engulfed his mind.

Maxim choked in a breath, his chest as tight as if he had just run a great distance.

"We'll march together," Nando added.

And then it was his brother's face and not Mina's. It was Nando, stupid, boyish, careless Nando who was challenged to duels and who bedded five women at one time and asked one to eat syllabub off the other's bubbies.

Maxim nodded, sucking in a struggling breath. Sanity was gradually returning to him as they struck up a familiar pace together, walking up and down the length of the den of sin. Nando had thrown on some trousers and haphazardly stuffed a shirt over his head. Thank Christ for that.

"Has something happened?" Nando asked. "Tell me when you're ready."

He sounded remarkably lucid, perhaps pulled from the depths of his stupor by Maxim's own madness. Here was a reminder that he might judge his brother for his faults, but Nando never judged Maxim for his.

He swallowed hard. "I was worried."

"You're always worried, brother."

Pace, pace, pace. The measured steps restored his mind to a sense of order amidst chaos. His thoughts were no longer muddled. The past was not before him, even if he would never forget the way he had last seen Mina. Even if he would never forgive himself for the role he'd played in her death.

"The princess has been wounded," he managed at last. "There are assassins afoot. And her lady-in-waiting is in danger as well."

"Lady Tansy? I wouldn't be averse to offering her my most sincere protection."

Nando didn't protect women from murderous villains. He bedded them. And the only man in Tansy's bed was going to be Maxim.

He stiffened, disliking his brother's continued interest in her. "You needn't concern yourself with her. I've seen to her protection with some of my guards."

But would it be enough? The fear was there, heavy and hot, lodged in his stomach like a stone that would not be removed.

"What is that edge I hear in your voice, brother?" Nando asked smoothly as they continued their march.

Slow and steady. His heart was resuming a more normal pace. The madness had almost entirely faded.

"I don't know what you're speaking of," he lied, for he had no wish to examine the complexities of the emotions he felt concerning Tansy here and now, in this den of iniquity.

It felt wrong.

"You forget how well I know you," Nando persisted.

Damn him. His brother was a ne'er-do-well, but he also knew Maxim better than anyone else. It was the primary reason he was here in London with him. That, and Maxim feared the trouble Nando would make for himself in his absence.

He sighed heavily. "Lady Tansy is under my protection."

It was all he would allow himself to reveal.

But Nando understood the implications.

He turned to Maxim, his countenance lined with surprise. "You've taken the lady-in-waiting of your future queen as your mistress?"

He very much disliked the term *mistress*. His ears burned.

"She is mine," was all he said curtly, looking away from the questions in his brother's curious stare.

They continued their march, down another length of the chamber.

"What of Lucinda?" His brother wanted to know.

Lucinda was a distant memory. A kindhearted widow of gentle persuasion who had warmed his bed.

"I'll be cutting ties with her when we return to Varros," he said.

Nando whistled through his teeth. "And yet you barge into my chamber and chase away my goddesses."

"I interrupted an orgy," he countered, and not without disapproval. "And the women whose company you were keeping were paid to do so. They're not goddesses, Nando. They're prostitutes."

"Does the princess know you're bedding her lady-in-waiting?" his brother asked slyly.

Maxim halted, turning to face Nando, a snarl on his lips. "You'll not speak of Lady Tansy with such disrespect."

"Apologies." Nando flashed him a crooked grin that reminded Maxim his brother had been drinking heavily whilst cavorting with his *goddesses*. "The disrespect was aimed at you, not at the lady."

He ground his molars. "She will have a place of honor in my court."

"As she tends to your wife like a servant."

It wasn't a concern he hadn't already thought of himself. He hated the notion of Tansy being relegated to the periphery of his life when he wanted nothing more than for her to be at his side. But the observation was even more unwanted when Nando issued it in his superior tone.

He stopped marching. "It is none of your affair."

Nando paused as well, spinning to face him, wearing a familiar, mulish expression. "And yet it is your affair if I'm conducting myself discreetly with my English goddesses?"

Maxim suppressed a groan of irritation. "Prostitutes."

"Goddesses."

They glared at each other, at an impasse.

"I am your king," he reminded Nando firmly. "Everything you do is my affair. Particularly when you are endangering yourself for the sake of your prick."

It was crude, but Maxim was feeling harsh. Sharp as a blade.

Nando crossed his arms over his chest. "I fail to see the difference between us. Indeed, if anything, your conduct is worse than mine. You are about to marry your queen, and yet you've been secretly bedding her lady-in-waiting, with every intention of keeping her as your mistress."

"My woman," he bit out.

"Mistress," his brother hissed insolently. "Whilst I'm the prince with nothing to do. You won't trust me with any information, save your fits, and I only know about them because you had one before me and couldn't hide it. Meanwhile, Felix knows all, and I'm left in the dark. What am I to do but keep myself out of trouble as you commanded me?"

"Hiding yourself away without telling me where you've gone and fucking five harlots at one time isn't keeping yourself out of trouble," he roared.

Although, the moment his burst of anger left him, he couldn't deny that his brother's words affected him. He didn't entrust Nando with much, aside from helping to calm him if he was near when one of his spells began. Could it be possible that his scapegrace brother wanted more responsibility? If so, lying abed in a whorehouse all day was certainly not the way to persuade Maxim he ought to share some of his burdens with him.

"I only have one cock. How do you think I was fucking five of them at once?" Nando asked, grinning.

Maxim heaved a sigh, unclenching and clenching his fists at his sides. "I don't want to think about what you do with your prick or how you manage it. I've seen more than I ever wished to see today. All I'm saying is that I need you close. I need you safe. I need you to not be challenged to a duel at dawn or at the mercy of some assassin's blade." Another sigh, and then some of the harshness inside him faded. "I need you, brother. You're the only family I have left."

"You need me?" Nando raised a brow, his expression turning suspicious, as if he didn't believe him.

Was he such a damned ogre, then?

Maxim nodded, the motion jerky, emotion roiling inside him. Emotion he didn't want. "I do."

Nando's look turned sly. "I can help to guard Lady Tansy if you like."

"No, you damned well can't," he growled.

It wasn't that he didn't trust his brother not to force his attentions upon her; he knew that Nando was a rakehell, but he was also a man of principle. Seduction was a sport to him. But neither did he relish the prospect of his Tansy being flirted with by his beautiful younger brother. Maxim was all too aware of his battle-scarred visage, the twin patches of silver at his temples, his unruly, almost barbaric size. To say nothing of his age, forty compared to Nando's youthful thirty, a man far more of an age with Tansy than he was himself.

Nando tucked his chin and raised a brow, pressing a hand to his heart like a lovestruck courtier. "Could it be that the mighty king considers his wayward younger brother competition?"

"No."

Yes. And may God rot his cock, to borrow Tansy's stinging curse.

"Hmm," Nando said, sounding unconvinced.

Maxim grunted. "She is mine to protect."

Mine to kiss, mine to hold, mine to love.

The last thought struck him with the force of a blow. Love? He didn't. Couldn't.

Could he? Did he?

"Is the lady in agreement?" his brother asked sagely, piercing the confused questions muddling Maxim's mind, the emotions warring with each other.

"Of course she is," he lied smoothly.

"She seems terribly loyal to Princess Anastasia," Nando pointed out, stroking his jaw now. "One of the Boritanian courtiers told me that it was widely claimed Lady Tansy would forfeit her life for the princess, so steadfast is her loyalty."

"She is loyal," he agreed.

To a fault. And he hated it and admired it all at once. He wanted to be the sole recipient of that devotion. The princess could find another to take Tansy's place.

"Have you bribed her?" Nando's tone was curious.

"Hell and damnation, Nando. Do you think I can't attract the attentions of a lady in my own right, without need to lure her with the promise of baubles and gold?"

His brother shrugged. "I've never witnessed you wooing a lady before. If anything, it was Lucinda who seduced you. Lady Tansy doesn't seem such a bold sort."

She wasn't. Not until one grew to know her better. And Maxim *had* grown to know her. He knew her very well indeed. He would like to know her better still. But there was time aplenty for that.

"She is different," he said quietly, the revelation torn from him.

Startling him as much as it appeared to surprise his brother.

"Different," Nando repeated. "Different from Lucinda?"

He didn't want to admit the truth, and yet to keep it within seemed a base insult to Tansy. "Different from every other woman."

He heard his brother's sharp inhalation and saw the shock in his expression. "Even Mina?"

Maxim was silent for a few moments, considering his words with great care. "I will always love Mina. Nothing and no one can change that. But neither can I deny what I feel for Lady Tansy."

"You love her," Nando breathed, understanding dawning on his expressive face.

He swallowed hard. "I'll not put a name to it. Everything is new and we are in a strange and foreign land, so much danger swirling around us. It's not the time to be fanciful."

"Fanciful," his brother repeated, lips twitching as if he were valiantly attempting to suppress his mirth after hearing the world's greatest sally.

"What is so amusing?" he demanded, though he suspected he already knew the answer.

"The impenetrable King Maximilian, in love." Nando shook his head ruefully. "But not with his bride."

Maxim's lip curled. "You know why I have to marry Princess Anastasia."

"For the good of the kingdom," his brother said instantly.

Likely, those words had been emblazoned upon Nando's mind, for Maxim had repeated them often enough. It was what he had been taught, from the time he'd been a lad.

Every action he had undertaken had been in the name of Varros, her people, the future of the kingdom, regaining the throne. Every privation, every battle, every wound, all those desperate years of war. The death, the destruction, the agony, the loss. All had been in the name of Varros. His own father had planted the seed in Maxim long ago, and Maxim had carried on the tradition.

He nodded. "For the kingdom. I haven't any other choice."

Nando cocked his head. "What if you did have another choice? What if you could have whatever you wanted? If you could marry Lady Tansy instead of Princess Anastasia? Would you do it?"

Maxim didn't answer that question. It didn't signify. Because the King of Varros didn't have the freedom to do as he wished, whether that meant bedding five goddesses for days or making the woman he truly wanted his wife. There was only duty, obligation, and alliances.

"Finish dressing yourself," he told his brother quietly. "I'll be waiting for you in the carriage. But be warned. If you don't emerge in a quarter hour, I'll come looking for you, and you won't like the consequences."

$\sim$

"YOU SHOULD EAT, YOUR HIGHNESS," Tansy urged Princess Anastasia, once more at home in her role of dutiful lady-in-waiting.

Only, the role no longer felt like home. It felt hollow and desperately wrong. And her every interaction with the princess felt like a betrayal in itself for what she was keeping from her.

Days had passed. Days fraught with tension, fear, and loneliness. With longing for Maxim, too. But since they had last parted, she'd had nothing from him, save curt missives delivered by servants. Inquiries into her welfare. Into the princess's welfare. Tansy had answered with a shaking hand each time, taking great care with what she revealed, lest one of the guards open her note and read it before sending it on its way. No tenderness. No caring words. No hint of the intimacies they had shared.

Tenderness and love were not hers to give Maxim anyway. He could never be hers, regardless of how deeply her reckless heart longed for it to be otherwise.

Finally, Princess Anastasia had been well enough to return.

Her prayers had been answered. Tansy had rejoiced when her dear friend had tumbled over the window casement in the darkest depths of the night two evenings before. But she had also begun to dread most fervently the moment that would come when she had to unburden herself to the princess and reveal what she had done. A moment that came closer with every passing minute, for she had decided that today must be the day. She could keep the truth to herself no longer.

The princess stood at the window, staring down at the rain-drenched world below.

"I'm not hungry," she told Tansy after a lengthy silence, refusing to turn and face her.

Her friend had been most unlike herself since her return. Tansy had noted the difference at once. Initially, she had assumed she had been weary, but despite two nights of rest, Princess Anastasia remained listless and quiet. Almost sullen, her mien funereal.

Had she guessed at the truth of what had happened between Tansy and Maxim in her absence? Her heart beat faster at the thought.

"But you must eat, regardless," Tansy urged. "You haven't taken a thing since supper last night, and it is afternoon.

King Maximilian will be calling soon."

King Maximilian. How wrong that name felt, the pretense of formality after he had come to mean so much to her. After they had been as close as a man and woman could be.

Princess Anastasia released a heavy sigh. "What does King Maximilian's visit have to do with eating?"

Heat suffused her cheeks. She mustn't think of those forbidden intimacies. Nor must she think of Maxim as anything other than the king. A stranger. A man who would soon be the husband of another.

"It wouldn't do for you to swoon," Tansy forced out, struggling to be mindful of her duties amidst her conflicted emotions. "You must have at least a bit of tea and toast, Your Royal Highness."

"Call me Stasia," the princess said suddenly, whirling to face her. "I find the title is too heavy a mantle to carry on my shoulders at present, and you are like a sister to me. Let us cease with formality."

The guilt that had been threatening to swallow her whole ever since the day she had first allowed herself to succumb to Maxim came back with a vengeance. Tansy had done her best to stay busy with tasks, but she had no choice but to attend her friend now. The princess had managed to persuade her brother the exiled prince to aid Maxim in his cause. There was no longer a need to linger in London. The betrothal would be announced today.

Which was why Tansy needed to reveal the truth.

She bowed her head now, for she could no longer hold her friend's gaze, knowing what she had done. Knowing the boundaries she had crossed, the loyalty she had so swiftly shattered. All for the sake of a man she could never have.

"I couldn't presume to do so," she denied quietly.

"You can," the princess countered, her tone firm. "I

186

consider you a sister, a friend. The only friend I have. And I am weary, so very weary, of being a princess."

Sweet Deus. It was unbearable. She had to confess what she had done. The consequences were hers to bear. If Princess Anastasia banished her, the fault was no one's, save Tansy's.

"It is not wise of you to think me your friend, Your Royal Highness," Tansy warned, keeping her gaze lowered.

"Because you're my lady-in-waiting?" the princess asked. "Don't be silly. You have been at my side since before my mother's death, a lady in your own right."

"From a House that is impoverished." Tansy paused, lifting her head at last. "No better than an orphan."

And for all the princess's generosity, look at how Tansy repaid her. Shame washed over her.

"The circumstances of our birth should not define us," Princess Anastasia said firmly.

"And yet, they must," Tansy told her sadly. "I will never be your equal, Your Royal Highness. Nor would I presume to act as such."

"I am sick to death of my royal bloodlines," the princess snapped. "What have they dealt me, other than misery and despair? They have robbed every happiness from my life. Call me Stasia, or do not speak to me at all."

"Your Royal—"

"No!" Princess Anastasia cried out in most unusual fashion, interrupting. "No more. I'll not have it." Tears were streaming furiously down her cheeks, and she dashed at them with the back of her hand. "I don't want to be a princess. I want to renounce my blood. To surrender the title and live the life I was meant to lead."

"You mustn't say such things." Tansy moved to her, offering a soothing pat on the shoulder, wondering at her friend's sudden disquiet. "You are overset."

"Call me Stasia," the princess demanded.

She had to reveal the truth. Now. She couldn't wait another moment longer.

"I cannot," she admitted. "I'm not worthy of the privilege. For I have betrayed you."

"Betrayed me?" Princess Anastasia's brows drew together, a question in her eyes that Tansy had no wish to answer. "How?"

Tears glistened in Tansy's eyes, burning until she blinked and they trailed down her cheeks in warm rivulets, the result of her betrayal. "I've fallen in love with King Maximilian."

"In love with him?"

Tansy closed her eyes, too anguished to hold the princess's gaze. To look at her, for fear of the disgust and loathing she would see reflected there. All of which would be so richly deserved.

She had betrayed her in the worst possible way, and more than once, in thought, word, and deed.

"Yes," she whispered, hating herself.

Hating her answer.

Loving Maxim anyway.

"Oh, Tansy." The princess's voice held a note of sympathy. "When did this happen? How?"

Not fury, then, as she had feared. There was no betrayal to be heard. Instead, there was a tone of calm understanding. Of sad acceptance.

Tansy dared to open her eyes, forcing herself to meet her friend's searching stare. "I'm not sure when or how. We've spent an inordinate amount of time together during your absence, and I...he...we..."

Her fumbling explanation trailed off, her cheeks going hot with the bitter sting of embarrassment. How could she possibly reveal to the princess that she had been intimate with her future husband? And not just once either. The words refused to emerge. She swallowed hard against a rising lump in her throat.

"I understand," Princess Anastasia said, shocking her.

Tansy's brows rose. "You do?"

Her friend gave her a forlorn smile, eyes glistening with unshed tears. "I've fallen in love with Archer Tierney."

She had known, of course, that Princess Anastasia intended to give herself to him. But she had never imagined she would also surrender her heart. What a muddled mess they both found themselves in, loving men they could not claim as their own.

"What do you intend to do?" Tansy asked, understanding all too well the fraught emotions on her friend's countenance, for it reflected the heaviness swirling in her own heart.

"What I must do," the princess said firmly, even as her ice-blue eyes filled with tears.

"You're going to marry King Maximilian," Tansy said, the words like knives cutting away at her tender skin. Straight to the marrow of her.

Princess Anastasia nodded, grim determination etched on her lovely face. "I haven't any other choice."

"I understand if you want to dismiss me from my position," Tansy hastened to add. "Regardless of your feelings for Mr. Tierney, what I've done is unconscionable. It never should have happened."

The princess's brow furrowed. "It is more than love, then, that has passed between you and the king."

It was a statement rather than a question.

She took a deep breath, knowing that she had to be completely honest, even if she didn't want to admit the depths of her betrayal to her closest friend. "It was more," she confirmed needlessly.

I could be carrying his child.

It was a thought that had occurred to Tansy in the lonely quiet that had fallen after Maxim's departure, when she had been swimming in the depths of misery and despair, hating herself for what she'd done, longing for him just the same. She had considered what she would have to do should that prove the outcome of her reckless affair. But these were worries she would consider later, if they became necessary. And so she kept the final confession to herself.

"And he didn't force himself upon you?" Princess Anastasia asked, echoing the question she had posed before.

"He would never do so," she said, for she had no doubt of the veracity of her statement.

Maxim would never harm a woman. She trusted him implicitly. With her body, with her heart.

The princess gave her a long, searching look, as if she wasn't certain she should believe Tansy's claim. Until, at last apparently satisfied, she nodded. "Good. I couldn't live with myself if something had happened to you while I was gone. You're too precious to me."

Tansy gaped. "How can I be precious to you after what I've done? I've committed the greatest sin against you. You should be sending me far from you, far from the king. I don't deserve your concern or your understanding."

"You know that I don't care for him," Princess Anastasia said quietly. "I'm not in love with him. He could bed a hundred other women, and it wouldn't affect me. The love I have for Archer is bigger and stronger than anything. And if you are happy with the king, that is a great consolation to me."

"I can't be happy with him." She shook her head. "He's marrying you."

Princess Anastasia nodded. "It isn't uncommon, particularly in arranged marriages, for the husband and wife to seek happiness beyond their union. I don't love the king, and I don't want to marry him. But if I haven't a choice in who I wed, then should I not at least have the chance to find my own contentedness? And should not the king find his own as well? But more than that for you, my dearest friend. You deserve happiness too."

Tansy was certain she was misunderstanding the princess. "Are you telling me you want me to be the king's mistress?"

"If you love him, as you say. And if it is what you want."

Tansy reeled. She had anticipated many reactions from Princess Anastasia—had dreaded them all. And yet, she had never expected calm acceptance among them.

"Why?" she asked. "Why would you wish for such a thing?"

"Because I can never truly find happiness myself," she said. "Not living in Varros, not as any man's wife, save Archer's. I cannot have what I want, but you can."

"No," she denied. "Not as his mistress. Not when I'm betraying you."

"It wouldn't be a betrayal if I sanction it."

"I couldn't forgive myself," she insisted. "I won't do it, Your Highness. Not even if you demand it of me."

"I would never make such a demand." Princess Anastasia placed a soothing hand on her arm. "You needn't fear on that account, Tansy. But if you expect me to dismiss you for following your heart, you're sorely mistaken. Indeed, it would be dreadfully hypocritical of me after I've just followed my own, even if doing so has left mine irreparably broken."

Tansy swallowed hard against a rush of emotion, knowing all too well how her friend felt. There was a certain, imprecise agony in loving a person who could never be one's own.

She took a deep breath and forced a reassuring smile she

didn't feel, for that was her duty. "Your heart will heal. Given time and distance, it will be whole again."

The princess gave her a rueful smile. "How I wish that you were right, dear friend."

And Tansy couldn't argue the matter. For she wished the same.

CHAPTER 14

"You don't want to marry her," Nando observed needlessly as their carriage rattled over the rutted London road, splashing through the incessant rain that seemed intent upon drowning the land.

The weather was a mirror to his soul, Maxim thought with uncharacteristic whimsy. Word had reached him that Princess Anastasia had found her brother Prince Theodoric and convinced him to join their cause. At last. She had also recovered from her wounds sufficiently enough so that she could return to the town house where Lady Tansy kept her vigil. And miraculously, there had been a sudden halt in further attempts on his life.

Which meant that, for now, Maxim and his men had managed to kill every bastard sent to spill his blood. He had no doubt there would be more.

It also meant that the time to formally announce his betrothal to the princess had come.

"As we discussed, whether I want to marry the princess is a moot point," he said, drumming his fingers on his knees.

His cravat was too tight. It felt like a noose.

"Why moot?" Nando asked.

Maxim hissed out an irritated sigh and pinned his brother with a glare. "I should have left you in the brothel."

Nando gave him a beatific grin. "Yes, you should have. My goddesses miss me, I have no doubt."

"Your goddesses are servicing other patrons," he pointed out.

Nando sighed dramatically. "I could bring them back to Varros with me."

"Try it, and I'll throw you overboard," Maxim warned.

His brother grumbled something unintelligible.

Maxim made a shoving gesture. "Splash."

"You love me too much to kill me," Nando said confidently.

Maxim raised a brow, impassive. "Believe what you wish."

His brother snorted. "I suppose I don't need to bring all five. I might settle for three."

"You might settle at the bottom of the sea."

Nando sighed. "Someone is feeling murderous today."

Yes, he damned well was. Maxim inserted a finger between his cravat and his throat, attempting to make the blasted knot loosen. To no avail. He was going to choke before he reached his prospective bride's side.

"I'm feeling like a man about to announce his impending doom," he muttered.

Because, as his irritating brother had announced, he didn't want to marry Princess Anastasia. But wants and needs were two different beasts entirely. And kings could not choose wants when needs were far more important to the future of the kingdom.

"You're the King of Varros. Can you not choose the woman who will be your queen?"

Only reckless, aimless, lighthearted Nando would view his circumstances in such a way.

Maxim gave his cravat another vicious tug. "I *have* chosen her. That is why we are announcing the betrothal today."

But he couldn't lie to himself. Nando's question returned to him. *If you could marry Lady Tansy instead of Princess Anastasia, would you do it?*

Yes. If he had the power to choose a bride, he would choose Tansy.

His prim spitfire who secretly read wicked books and defied him at every turn. Ye gods, how he had missed her these last few days. It had required all the resolve he possessed to keep his distance and relegate himself to tersely worded missives and reports from the guards he had sent to the town house. He had hoped the time and distance would make the unsettling feelings inside him relent.

They hadn't.

"And after the betrothal is announced, how soon are we to return to Varros?" Nando asked, frowning. "I find I've rather begun to like it here in England."

"As soon as possible. Felix is making the arrangements. I need to have Princess Anastasia and Lady Tansy far from Gustavson's guards before we send our men to Boritanian shores to unite with the rebel forces."

"That's wise of you," Nando said solemnly, his customary humor absent.

Maxim had entrusted his brother with the full details of his plan of battle. It hadn't occurred to him, until their clash at the brothel, that Nando secretly longed for a more meaningful role in the monarchy. He had always assumed his younger brother was content to indulge in women and drink, freed of the shackles of responsibility.

"Thank you," he said simply. "The safety of the women is

of utmost importance. There's also the matter of Princess Anastasia's two sisters, who remain in the August Palace in Boritania."

He had yet to settle upon a means of freeing them from their uncle's tyrannical rule. It was a matter he intended to discuss with Prince Theodoric forthwith.

"Do you think Gustavson will harm them?" Nando asked shrewdly.

Maxim clenched his jaw. "It is a possibility. We'll need to tread lightly."

The carriage slowed. His cravat tightened again. He was grateful for Nando's presence, for his support. Already, his chest felt as if a boulder had been laid upon it. He didn't want to do this. Didn't want the finality of a betrothal announcement, nor the potential loss of life that was to come in the war facing them.

But it had to be done.

"We've arrived," Nando said grimly.

He swallowed hard. "So we have."

"It's not too late to change your mind," his brother added gently.

If only.

Maxim shook his head. "I have to marry Princess Anastasia. It is the sole path to prolonged peace, and our people and the people of Boritania need that peace."

"I was talking about the goddesses," Nando said with a grin. "Are you certain I can't bring three of them along with me to Varros?"

"Nando," he growled warningly.

His brother shrugged. "A fellow can ask."

"Or a fellow can hold his tongue if he wants to keep it."

"Always threatening your poor brother," Nando grumbled.

He snorted. "Poor brother, indeed."

The carriage doors opened before either of them could say anything more. The time had come.

~

WHEN MAXIM HAD ENTERED the chamber, it was as if he stole all the air from the room. His presence, amidst great pomp and circumstance, was intimidating enough. His massive height, broad shoulders, and muscled frame added to the effect. He was dressed formally in the style of an Englishman, wearing finely tailored trousers and coat, along with an intricately knotted cravat at his throat, and he was so handsome that an ache of raw, unabashed yearning sliced straight through her when he first entered the drawing room.

Their gazes had met only once for the interminable duration of the interview thus far. She'd felt the connection as if he had passed a hand over her bare skin. It had required all her self-possession to keep her features a carefully schooled mask of impassivity. To curtsy and lower her eyes demurely and pretend as if the man she loved, the man who had claimed her body with almost brutal tenderness twice before, was nothing more than a stranger to her.

He was speaking to Princess Anastasia now, their dark heads bent together as they signed the documents making their betrothal official. She hated their proximity to each other. Hated the inevitability of their union. Hated herself for being weak enough to fall in love with a man so beyond her reach.

"Have you ever been to Varros, Lady Tansy?"

The soft question at her side jolted her from her tumultuous thoughts. She turned to Prince Ferdinando, who had joined her on the periphery of the ceremony. It was difficult to believe this golden-haired lothario was Maxim's brother. The two men could not have been more different in appearance or demeanor. Where Maxim was cold and aloof, sometimes harsh, Prince Ferdinando was lighthearted and smoothly charming, always with a ready smile that glinted in his bright-blue eyes. Maxim's black hair and dark eyes, height, and build were in complete contrast to his brother.

"I have not, Your Royal Highness," she said, forcing a polite smile to her lips.

"You will like it there," he pronounced, as if it were a certainty.

Her mouth felt as if it would crack from the strain of her attempts at feigning happiness. "I'm sure you're right, Your Royal Highness."

He leaned nearer, his scent washing over her. It was a pleasant enough scent, unique in some ways and yet not so different from the courtiers intent upon seduction with whom she had crossed paths in Boritania. It was the scent of a man who knew he was attractive and intended to use his appearance to his every advantage. Who enhanced his natural gift in any way he could to lure ladies into his spider's web.

Tansy had heard the rumors, which abounded. Prince Ferdinando was a rakehell to the marrow.

He raised a light brow, his perfect curls falling over his forehead as he shifted ever so slightly to lean nearer to her, almost as if imparting a great secret. "I'm right about most things, Lady Tansy. Given time, you shall see."

He was vain as well.

She bit her lip and held her tongue, returning her gaze to Maxim's broad back as he bent over the documents, his quill moving with swift motions that suggested he hadn't hesitated in signing his name everywhere it was required on the marriage contract that would bind him to the princess.

And so? Had she believed he would? Had she been foolish enough to suppose, even for a wild heartbeat, that he had somehow developed feelings for her to rival hers for him, and that he would choose her over Princess Anastasia? That he would abandon his sense of duty to his kingdom, that he would choose a mere lady-in-waiting over a princess whose position and family wealth were sure to enrich his own power?

What a fool she was for secretly harboring such hopes. Her recklessness knew no bounds.

Nor did her disappointment.

Her eyes stung with the promise of tears. She blinked furiously, averting her gaze, unable to watch as the man she loved bound himself to another.

Suddenly, a handkerchief was before her, snowy white and monogrammed with an N. She could only wonder at the letter. Perhaps the handkerchief belonged to one of his paramours.

"For you, Lady Tansy," the prince said when she hesitated. "Your eyes appear to be watering, my dear. Perhaps you've taken on the same illness as the princess. I do hope it isn't catching."

She had indeed taken on an illness.

An illness called love.

A hopeless illness for which there was no cure.

She snatched the handkerchief from his waiting hand with far less grace than she ought to have used. "Thank you, Your Royal Highness."

"You may call me Nando if you like," he said, keeping his voice low, as if the two of them were alone and engaged in an intimate conversation. "Indeed, I'd prefer it if you would."

The N suddenly made sense. She supposed his irreverence shouldn't come as a surprise, given his reputation.

"Thank you, Your Royal Highness," she repeated crisply, not about to invite informality with him.

Not because she feared she would be susceptible to his

advances, but because she wasn't entirely certain she could trust Prince Ferdinando. He was Maxim's brother, but he exuded such silken allure that his intentions were impossible to define.

"A lady of substance," he said quietly. "I might have known."

She clenched her fingers on the handkerchief, her knuckles aching, and turned to him, curious. "What do you mean?"

"He's taken an interest in you," the prince said calmly.

Her cheeks were instantly hot. She cast a worried glance around to see whether Gustavson's guards were watching. But it seemed that all eyes in the chamber were upon Maxim, Princess Anastasia, and the proxy who had been sent from Boritania in Gustavson's stead to witness the signing of the betrothal contract.

"I don't know of whom you speak," she lied.

"My brother," Prince Ferdinando elaborated.

She swallowed hard, still clutching the handkerchief tightly as she struggled to keep her expression impassive and blank, returning the prince's inquisitive stare. "I'm afraid I don't understand."

The prince gave her a small smile. "Oh, I think you do, my lady."

She looked away, disliking the subterfuge. Heaven knew she had been embroiled in far too many deceptions since her arrival in London, and she disliked every one of them. But her gaze settled upon Maxim's broad back, his bent head. She watched as he passed the quill to Princess Anastasia.

And her heart broke some more.

"It hardly matters," she muttered to the prince at her side, the words intended as a reminder for herself as well. "He is marrying the princess."

"Perhaps."

She shot the prince a look. "There is no uncertainty about it."

"Will you take a walk with me, Lady Tansy?" he invited, shocking her.

"We are witnessing the ceremony," she protested.

"No one will mind if we take the air," he countered, unconcerned. "You are looking frightfully pale. No doubt a turn in the gardens will prove restorative."

She wasn't pale; she was sure of it. If anything, her cheeks were on fire.

"It's raining," she pointed out.

"Misting," Prince Ferdinando countered, offering her his elbow. "Come."

At the opposite end of the chamber, Maxim was leaning nearer to Princess Anastasia's ear, murmuring something to her. The picture they presented was akin to a dagger in Tansy's heart. And suddenly, she couldn't bear to remain another moment, witnessing the grand spectacle.

Impulsively, she placed her hand in the crook of the prince's elbow. "As Your Royal Highness wishes."

The prince whisked them from the drawing room without a single objection from the guards and other courtiers lining the chamber. They passed quietly through the town house. In no time, they reached the double doors that led to the small outdoor courtyard and the privacy beyond.

They didn't even stop for wraps or a hat.

The air was cool and damp beyond the brick walls of the home they'd fled. But she was surprised to discover that the prince was not wrong in his assessment. The rain of the morning had dissipated, giving way to a fine, cold mist.

"You were correct, Your Royal Highness," she observed, trying and failing to keep the bitterness from her voice. "No one noticed our departure."

"And why should they? Those ancient documents they're poring over are undoubtedly scintillating," the prince told her with a teasing air and a rakish grin that revealed a pair of dimples.

His conquests likely sighed over those dimples. Tansy felt distinctly unmoved.

"Indeed," she said, suppressing a shiver as a brisk wind whipped at her gown and they moved down the gravel path together, farther from the windows and door and prying ears and eyes. "I suppose they must be."

"You're cold," Prince Ferdinando said, startling her with his concern. "Take my coat."

"No," she hastened to deny. "It would be dreadfully improper of me to do so."

But he paused on the walk and withdrew from her to shrug from his coat just the same. "I'm known for being improper. No one will be surprised in the slightest."

Another wind blustered past them, and the prince settled his coat over her shoulders as if it were a cape, the warmth of his body seeping into hers. She pulled it around her, grateful for the protection from the mist and chill, even if it was wrong.

"Thank you."

He smiled. "My pleasure, Lady Tansy." He gestured for her to continue along the path. "Shall we?"

She resumed their journey. "Will you tell me the reason for our walk now?"

"Need there be a reason for a gentleman to take in the air with a beautiful lady?" he asked with a flirtatious air.

Tansy gave him a stern look. "I'm hardly beautiful."

His expression turned serious. "You are, though. I can see why my brother is so taken with you."

A strange sensation settled in her stomach at the mentioning of Maxim being taken with her. She reminded herself it didn't mean what she wanted it to mean. He desired her. He was a powerful man who could have whatever and whomever he wanted.

"His Majesty isn't taken with me," she protested.

"Of course he is," Prince Ferdinand said easily. "I know my brother very well. Better than anyone, I should venture to say. I haven't seen him react to a woman this way since his wife."

Wife.

The word almost made her stumble.

She cast the prince a searching glance. "His wife? His Majesty was married before?"

It stood to reason that he could have been; he was forty years old after all. But Tansy had never heard a word to suggest he had been. Rumors abounded concerning his campaigns on the battlefield. His bravery, his fearlessness. But try as she might, she could not recollect a single mentioning of a wife.

"It was many years ago, before Maxim became king. He was young, and so was Mina."

How strange to think of Maxim with a wife. She didn't think she liked it.

"Was theirs a love match?" she asked.

"It was," the prince confirmed quietly. Sadly. "Her death broke his spirit."

Oh. Of course it had.

He had been desperately in love with his wife. With this Mina.

"He hasn't spoken of her," she admitted, wondering at the reason.

Was she too tender a subject? Did he not wish to share her memory? Was Tansy not of sufficient import to merit the mention?

"He doesn't," Prince Ferdinando said. "Mina was killed in the war by enemy soldiers."

Her heart clenched. "Dear heavens."

"She was brutally beaten before she was killed. She married my brother in secret, but somehow, the pretender to the throne's forces found out. When they did, they beat her to death and burned down her home."

"My God." Tansy stopped on the path, overwhelmed by emotion at the revelation.

How Maxim must have suffered. And his poor wife as well, to be beaten and murdered in such brutal fashion. A lump of horror and profound sadness rose in her throat. She swallowed hard.

"I tell you this because I want you to understand my brother," the prince said. "He is not a man who loves or trusts easily. Mina's death changed him, made him hard as stone. It was as if, with her death, he sealed away the part of himself that possessed any vulnerability at all. And yet, despite that, I've never seen him care for a woman as he does for you."

Prince Ferdinando's revelation affected her. How could it not? She had to move. To think. Tansy continued on the path, her thoughts overwhelming.

She had told herself, again and again, that his interest in her was likely nothing more than lust. But oh, how she longed to believe it was more than that. That he could possess tender feelings for her. That he could love her.

No, no, no.

She shook her head, banishing those thoughts, reminding herself that it didn't matter even if Maxim did love her, because he was marrying her best friend. "His Majesty is wedding Princess Anastasia soon. I am the princess's lady-in-waiting, and that is all."

"You are far more than that to Maxim," Prince Ferdinando insisted, following her and catching up easily with his long-legged strides. "And he is more to you as well. I saw it in your eyes as you watched him in the drawing room."

Had she given herself away so easily? It was those stupid, futile tears.

"It doesn't matter if he is more to me, or if I am more to him," she countered stoically.

"It could," Prince Ferdinando said. "If you would both allow it."

Yearning knifed through her, potent and strong, making her knees go weak. But she continued down the path, turning back toward the town house now. The mist was growing more pronounced, a heavy fog descending. The gray, grim day seemed somehow appropriate.

"Surely you know that we cannot," she told him. "We are bound by obligations and duties far larger than the both of us."

"Maxim deserves happiness, Lady Tansy." The prince stopped and looked down at her earnestly, uncharacteristically solemn, taking her hands in his. "You care for him."

She loved him. And quite desperately, too. But she didn't dare say so aloud.

"Your Royal Highness," she protested.

But before she could say anything more, the door to the gardens flew open and Maxim strode toward them on the gravel path, his eyes flashing with fire.

"What is the meaning of this?" he demanded.

～

Nando was holding Tansy's hands.

He was *touching* her.

Maxim stalked toward them, hating how they looked together, Nando towering over Tansy, the contrast of his light hair to her dark. They would make a lovely couple.

205

Nando's words returned to taunt him. *I've decided that Lady Tansy is the only woman I want.*

But surely he wouldn't.

Surely he couldn't.

Surely seducing his brother's woman was beneath even a true rakehell like Nando.

Wasn't it?

"Maxim," Nando called to him brightly, giving him one of the grins that favored his dimples.

And that was when he noticed Tansy was wearing his brother's coat. Possessive outrage roared to life, leaving Maxim as a strangled growl.

"Why is Lady Tansy wearing your coat?" he demanded without preamble as he reached them.

"She was chilled," Nando explained. "I was merely being a gentleman."

"She should have fetched a wrap," he snapped, wanting to tear the garment from her shoulders and replace it with his own.

He hated the sight of her in something that belonged to anyone other than him.

Tansy dipped into a curtsy, head bowed, refusing to meet his gaze. "Your Majesty."

He wanted to snatch her up and carry her away and cover her with his body and kiss her until she forgot everything and everyone.

But he couldn't do that, because he had just pledged himself to Princess Anastasia St. George. Every stroke of his quill had felt wrong. He'd hated making his mark upon the betrothal contract, the finality of it, knowing Tansy was watching.

"Lady Tansy," he greeted in turn, forcing himself to be polite.

And still, she would not meet his gaze.

He had missed her. The realization was as potent as a blow.

"I would like a word with you, my lady," he added, needing her alone.

Needing Nando to go elsewhere.

Needing, needing, *needing*. Just her. Only her. Had he ever needed anyone more? He frantically attempted to recall what it had been like, those early days with Mina. And try as he might, he realized with a pang, he could not. Too much time had passed. What felt like a lifetime. And he was a different man now than he had been then.

"I cannot fathom what must be discussed," she said, her voice frosty.

She was angry with him; that much was apparent. But he couldn't be sure of the reason. His absence? The signing of the betrothal contract? Perhaps both.

He ignored her protest and looked to his brother, raising an imperious brow. "Nando, if you'll excuse us?"

His brother made a show of looking from Maxim to Tansy and lingering despite Maxim's request.

"Now," he gritted.

Nando glanced back at Tansy. "My lady?"

As if she required protection from him, Maxim thought, stung by his brother's protectiveness where Tansy was concerned. He should be the one protecting her, damn it.

Tansy hesitated before nodding and slipping Nando's coat from her shoulders. "Here you are, Your Royal Highness. Thank you for lending me your coat."

Nando took the raiment from her and settled it back around her with an authoritative air. "Keep it, dear lady. I wouldn't dream of you taking a chill."

Maxim clenched his jaw so tightly that it ached, pinning his brother with a narrow-eyed glare as he sauntered past on the walk. Nando's grin was smug. He knew damned well the effect his antics were having upon Maxim, and he was relishing it.

He waited for the crunch of his brother's footfalls on gravel to retreat, followed by the sound of the door closing, leaving Maxim and Tansy alone. And then he eliminated the remaining distance between them, going to her as he had longed to do from the moment he had crossed the threshold of the drawing room earlier and spied her across the room.

Gloriously beautiful in a demure gown of white embroidered muslin, short, dark curls artfully framing her face. Their gazes had met and held, and for a moment, he'd lost his breath and capacity for thought both.

But then he had recalled the obligation awaiting him, and he had carried out the painstaking process accordingly, hating that she was his audience. Hating that he was binding himself to a woman who wasn't her.

He bowed formally, still nettled by the sight of her in Nando's coat, drowning her as if it were a cloak two sizes too large. "Tansy."

Another curtsy from her, the sleeves of Nando's coat grazing the gravel walk, her countenance wary. "Your Majesty."

"What were you doing out here with my scoundrel of a brother?" he asked, his voice bearing a sharpness he hadn't intended.

"We were walking." At last, her eyes were on his instead of at her feet. "Taking the air."

"It is raining," he pointed out.

A faint smile curved her lips. "So I said to the prince. However, I must agree with His Royal Highness's assessment that it is merely misting."

Absurdly, he didn't like that she was agreeing with Nando. He didn't like that she was wearing his brother's coat.

He wanted to toss it into a puddle and stomp on it like a child who had been denied a favorite toy.

What a colossal arse he was. And yet, he couldn't control the way he felt.

"You should have worn a bonnet," he said stupidly. "You'll take ill."

"Thank you for your concern, Your Majesty. I am quite well without one."

Her crisp tone was distant, as if they were no more than strangers. It sliced through him like a blade.

"What were you and Nando speaking about?" he asked, needing to know.

Had Nando been flirting with her? Attempting to woo her? Nando was loyal to him, but there was no telling what he would do when a woman was involved. Maxim didn't think his brother was capable of resisting anything in petticoats, let alone someone as gorgeous and alluring as Tansy.

"You," she said simply.

Relief rushed over him that Nando hadn't been attempting a seduction, replaced swiftly by dread. "What about me?"

Although, he suspected he knew. Damn Nando and his loose tongue.

Her impassive countenance cracked for a moment, giving way to vulnerability and compassion. "About your wife."

Mina.

His chest tightened. He didn't want to speak about Mina to Tansy, not here in the gardens of a strange town house in London. Not after he had just signed a contract that promised him to another in a marriage that would be a sham compared to the one he'd had with his first wife.

"I see," he forced out, the words almost painful to speak.

"I'm sorry for what happened," she said softly.

He wished Nando hadn't been so free with his knowledge. There were some things he wasn't ready to admit or discuss with others. Mina's death was one of them. But Tansy was standing before him, agonizingly lovely as the mists fell around them, her eyes laden with unabashed care and tenderness.

For him, he realized.

"Thank you," he managed past the lump in his throat.

"It must have been very painful for you."

It was strange to hear Tansy speaking of Mina. It felt… not like a betrayal. But odd just the same.

"Life is filled with pain," he said, trying to keep thoughts of Mina at bay.

Trying desperately to keep from falling into one of his fits before Tansy.

Breathe in.

Breathe out.

Breathe in.

Tansy's concerned face was before him, and the weight on his chest remained, almost crushing. He needed to move. To pace. To do something before he revealed the depths of his madness to her.

"Why did you not tell me?" she asked softly.

And he couldn't bear it. Couldn't stand here in the cold mists with her giving him a look of such raw tenderness when he didn't deserve it, his secret in desperate danger of being revealed.

"Why should I have done?" he bit out, the hair rising on the back of his neck, his skin prickling.

It was coming.

He didn't want to hurt her, but he didn't want her to know. Talking about Mina's death was like pulling a trigger on the pistol of his sanity.

Tansy's countenance changed instantly, the tenderness giving way to hurt.

Her shoulders stiffened. "Indeed, you should not have done. Your past is yours alone, Your Majesty. Forgive me."

She dipped into a half curtsy that was wholly unlike her.

And then she flitted past him, leaving him standing alone as the mist turned into rain and his mind splintered into a thousand tiny shards.

CHAPTER 15

*T*ansy stood before the window in her new chamber at the Palace of Tayrnes in the Varros capital city, staring down at the sprawling gardens below. The voyage to Varros had been arduous and long. She had spent the journey aboard the ship with Princess Anastasia, who had been struck with dreadful seasickness.

They had arrived the day before to much rejoicing and fanfare. Streets crowded with revelers eager to catch a peek of their new queen. A carriage procession from the port to the palace, escorted by armed guards dressed in ceremonial finery. The spectacle had been tremendous.

Had she not been nursing a broken heart, Tansy might have delighted in the enthusiasm of the crowds, their arrival in a strange and new kingdom that felt a great deal like her home in Boritania, only different. Warmer. Wilder.

It was Maxim's home.

And it had certainly felt that way as they had progressed to the bold, beautiful capital with its ancient architecture mixed with stunning new edifices. It was large, it was aloof, it was filled with mysteries she had yet to unlock. The capital took her breath just as the king who ruled over it did.

She was, without question, miserable here.

Miserable as the princess's lady-in-waiting—or Stasia, as her friend had convinced her to call her during the terrible sea passage. Miserable knowing that all too soon, her friend would be marrying the man she loved.

A man who had turned into a cold, harsh stranger that day in London when she had spoken to him of his dead wife. She had gone too far, she knew. But the knowledge had been too new and fresh, and after all she had shared with Maxim, she had naively believed he would open himself to her.

He hadn't.

They had parted that day as the mists gave way to lashing rain, and they had not been alone again since. Soon, they had left England for Varros, Maxim eager for his plan of aiding Prince Theodoric in a Boritanian rebellion against King Gustavson. Their departure had been cloaked in secrecy. The sole relief had been in escaping Gustavson's guards, who had returned to Boritania at Maxim's demand. They had been allowed to proceed to Varros unescorted by anyone other than Maxim's men.

Her chamber had been laden with gifts upon her arrival. Books, a fur, an ivory fan, a pair of gloves, a sapphire parure, even a handsome hat. Gifts of welcome. Or gifts of farewell. Gifts from Maxim? She couldn't be sure. All she knew was that they left her feeling hollow.

A knock sounded at her door, the rapid thumps jarring her from her thoughts.

She turned away from the window and the palace gardens, which were resplendent even in winter. Because naturally everything in Maxim's court, including the man himself, was nothing short of magnificent.

"Come," she called, expecting one of the servants who had been assigned to her.

At home in Boritania, Tansy had not been afforded a servant that was solely hers. But here in Varros, as the lady-in-waiting to the future queen, she had been given three servants. It was an astonishing excess that King Gustavson would never have provided.

She was hardly accustomed to it yet.

The door opened, but it was not one of the servants she had been given standing at the threshold. Rather, it was Prince Ferdinando.

He was dressed formally for the feast that was being held in honor of the betrothal. A vast affair with a rumored half the city in attendance. He grinned when he saw her and offered her an exaggerated bow.

"Lady Tansy, you are a vision."

She curtsied. "Your Royal Highness, thank you." She wondered if she should praise him as well; he was certainly attractive, even if he couldn't possibly compare to his older brother. But then she decided not to do so. Undoubtedly, his legion of admirers could tell him.

"Call me Nando, my dear," he invited, and not for the first time.

She smiled. "You know I can't."

"Can't or won't?" He raised a golden brow.

It was exceedingly difficult not to like the prince. He possessed an easy air and smooth charm that rendered him infinitely affable. Quite unlike Maxim, who was a cold, walled-off enigma.

Of course, he wasn't always cold. But she mustn't think of the passion she had known with him now.

Nor ever again.

"Perhaps a bit of both." She moved toward him, grateful for his presence, for she had managed to spend a small amount of time with the prince on the ship bringing them to Varros. She considered him a friend. "It is lovely to see you on land instead of on water."

"I still feel as if I'm aboard that damned ship," he said ruefully, striking an indolent pose against the doorframe. "I vow, the affliction didn't last nearly as long when I arrived in England. But perhaps that was down to my...activities. I reckon I was distracted."

He was speaking of his conquests, and yet his air was entirely unmoved, as if he didn't care about any of them. Rather as if he found the entire memory empty and unfulfilling. Dull, even.

"Distraction can be potent," she agreed.

Particularly when that distraction was tall, broad-shouldered, and devastatingly handsome.

Prince Nando offered her his arm. "On that, we agree. I've come to offer you escort."

She had been wondering at the reason for his presence at her door. But at his pronouncement, her smile faded, wariness blossoming inside her.

"Escort?"

The prince nodded. "My brother wishes to see you."

Maxim wanted to see her.

She had not expected a summons from him. Not after the distance that had fallen between them over the past fortnight. Nor did she want to see him. It was too painful. Their polite interactions aboard the ship, since that day in the gardens in London when he had been so cold and impervious, had been agony enough. Now he wished to see her?

Tansy stiffened. "Why?"

"He hasn't told me."

"I suppose I haven't a choice in the matter?" she asked needlessly.

Nando gave her a small smile. "You could ignore him, but I don't think it wise."

Of course it wasn't wise. Maxim was king. He possessed all the power, and she must not forget it.

She slid her hand onto the prince's proffered arm. "I'll see him, then."

Questions swirled as she and Nando started down the elaborately decorated hall lined with paintings and gilt. What did Maxim want from her?

"He's been quite miserable these last few weeks," the prince commented lightly as they proceeded, their footsteps echoing on the marble floors. "Perhaps your visit will improve his mood."

"I very much doubt it," she said grimly.

She had no intention of playing the part of mistress, and it nettled that he had snapped his fingers and expected her to come to him and do his bidding.

"Something has changed between the two of you," the prince observed shrewdly. "My brother has been vicious as a thundercloud, and I haven't seen you truly smile since London."

They turned and ascended a grand staircase. "The king reminded me of the disparity in our stations."

And the futility of her love for him.

But her heart still foolishly yearned for him just the same. She couldn't lie; even the prospect of seeing him again had her filled with a complex combination of anguish and eagerness.

"He can be a very difficult man," the prince acknowledged. "The war and Mina's death changed him. He wasn't always so cold."

Because he had loved his wife, and he had lost her. Tansy didn't want to think about that. Didn't want to feel jealousy toward a dead woman, for it was wrong.

"Perhaps he will soften in his marriage to Princess Anastasia," she said, unable to remove the bitterness from her voice.

They reached the door to the king's private apartments, where a guard was stationed.

Nando stopped before the harsh, dangerous-looking man. "Lady Tansy is expected."

She turned to the prince. "You aren't accompanying me?"

He flashed her one of his most charming grins, revealing his dimples. "I'm afraid I have other matters to attend to. I'll see you later at the betrothal feast."

She wanted to protest, for she had no desire to be alone with Maxim. It was far too dangerous. Too tempting, despite her hurt feelings and her every intention of never again succumbing to his sensual lure.

Tansy swallowed hard and curtsied, all too aware of the guard standing as silent audience. "Of course, Your Royal Highness. Thank you for your escort."

Nando bowed solemnly, all traces of levity gone. "The pleasure was mine, my lady."

The guard knocked at the door as the prince took his leave.

"You may enter," Maxim called, his deep voice wrapping around her heart like a fist and giving it a squeeze.

The guard opened the door, and she crossed the threshold, stepping into Maxim's lair. The air within felt as if it bore some manner of charge as the portal closed behind her, leaving her utterly alone with him. He stood by the window, dressed informally in a banyan and trousers, his feet bare. Her breath caught at the sight of his neck, unadorned by a cravat, and the slice of skin revealed by the vee in his banyan.

For a wild moment, she longed to throw herself into his arms, to press her lips against every inch of flesh exposed on him. To fill her lungs with his scent. To wrap herself around him and never let go.

She curtsied instead. "Your Majesty wished to see me?"

How pleased she was with herself for the calm iciness of her voice. Keeping her expression blank required all the restraint she possessed.

He bowed to her and then moved forward, his long-limbed strides closing the distance separating them with ease. "You are well?"

His dark gaze was searching, his lips unsmiling. She wanted to kiss him. Wanted to hate him.

"Yes," she said simply. "Thank you."

"The chamber is to your liking?"

She wondered if he had chosen the bedroom for her but quickly banished the thought, for it hardly mattered if he had.

"It is a lovely room."

His brows snapped together. "You don't like it."

"It's far more than I'm accustomed to," she elaborated.

He clasped his hands behind his back, the action making his banyan gape at the top and reveal more of his chest. "In what way?"

She tried not to stare at the newly revealed skin and failed. "It is opulent and large."

Not as opulent and large as his apartments, which were cavernous. But he was the king, and she was nothing more than a lowly lady-in-waiting.

"You may choose another."

"I've already settled in it."

"Stubborn wench," he said.

There was such tenderness in those words that she tensed beneath the stunning weight of it. His impassive countenance shifted, rather in the fashion of a mask being lifted, and what she saw there made her knees go weak.

"Why did you send for me?" she asked desperately, already perilously close to abandoning her resolve to resist him.

"Need there be a reason?" He unclasped his hands at his back, allowing them to fall to his sides. "I am king."

The mask was back in place.

She should have been relieved, but she was not.

"Whatever His Majesty desires," she mocked.

"You," he said.

Tansy blinked.

"I desire you," he elaborated, stopping before her. "Surely you know that by now."

"You're marrying another, and you've made it abundantly clear that your past is none of my concern. Indeed, you've scarcely spoken more than a handful of words to me since that day in the gardens."

"I'm sorry."

His apology took her aback. Tansy had expected more imperial magnificence, more ice and harsh aloofness.

The fight seeped from her. "You're sorry," she repeated.

"Yes, spitfire. I'm sorry." He extended his hand to her, palm up. "Will you sit with me and allow me to explain?"

She eyed his hand, remembering how wonderful it felt on her bare skin, caressing her. Holding her. Pleasuring her. She should leave. She should tell him to go to the devil and flee his apartments, never to return. Sever all ties.

Yes, she should do all those things.

Tansy settled her hand atop his.

But she couldn't.

⁓

TANSY TENTATIVELY PLACED her hand in Maxim's. So small and delicate. She made him feel like the beast he was. He tightened his fingers on hers, lest she have a change of heart and think to slip away.

He had been waiting weeks to have her alone.

Weeks of torture.

Weeks of endless agony.

Desperate, terrible fucking weeks.

Wordlessly, he guided her to the sitting room, where a servant had laid out a tray of sweets and fresh lemonade was poured and awaiting their delectation.

"Sit," he invited, reluctant to release her now that he was touching her again, and yet knowing he must.

God, her skin was so soft and warm. He wanted to lose himself in her. To forget the world and everyone in it, save the two of them.

But he couldn't. Prince Theodoric would be arriving in Varros soon, and together, they would be formulating the plans for rebellion in Boritania. And after that, his wedding to Princess Anastasia.

Maxim's gut curdled at the reminder.

Tansy seated herself with her customary prim grace. He sat as well, choosing one of the oversized chairs he'd had commissioned especially for his large frame.

"Lemonade?" he asked, wishing it were whisky instead.

"Please."

He offered her a glass, and she accepted, taking a small, nervous sip. "Sweets?"

"The lemonade will suffice for now."

He couldn't prolong his delay a moment more.

Maxim cleared his throat, struggling to form the words. "You wanted to know about Mina."

Her spine went straight at the mentioning of his past. "You needn't tell me."

"I couldn't tell you that day," he forced himself to confess.

"Maxim."

"I couldn't tell you because speaking of it without preparing myself causes me to…" He stopped, not wanting to say the words "go mad." And yet, how else to describe it? "I lose control. I was beginning to lose control that day in the gardens. I didn't want you to see it, to see me as I am."

He was adept at disguising it. When the fits came, he hid himself away. No one other than Nando had ever witnessed them in full.

Her brow furrowed. "What do you mean?"

"Madness," he supplied, hating the word, hating his weakness, the lack of power he truly possessed when it came down to it. "A form of it anyway."

"You're not mad, Maxim."

Her voice was like silk to his senses, a balm to his ragged soul. He didn't deserve it. Didn't deserve *her*. The last fortnight had taught him that.

"I've suffered from this madness since the war," he forced out. "Perhaps it was all the battles, the blows to the head, the deaths I've witnessed and been responsible for. I cannot say. All I know is that it's there, lingering beneath the surface of every moment like a serpent waiting to strike. I never know when it will come."

She placed her scarcely touched lemonade on the table at her side. "Nando knows, doesn't he?"

He nodded. "No one else."

And now, her as well.

But that was how much he longed for her. How greatly he needed her. He was willing to strip himself bare, to reveal the most hideous parts of himself, if it meant she would forgive him. If it meant she would have him.

"Thank you for telling me."

Her voice was quiet, almost hushed, and he was reminded of those endless hours they had spent in London with Gustavson's guards on the other side of the walls. How cautious she had been. For her own sake then, and now, for his.

"No one else can know," he told her. "If word were to spread that I've such a weakness, my enemies would press their advantage."

"Your secret is safe with me," she said.

"I trust you, Tansy," he said, his voice hoarse with pent-up emotion. It was the closest he could bring himself to a declaration. "I would have told you then, but it was coming upon me, and I didn't want you to see me that way. I never want you to see me thus."

"Much time has passed since that day. Why did you not tell me sooner?" she asked.

Because he had wanted to tell her here, in his private apartments, where he felt most at home. Not in a leased town house in London with guards hovering over them. Not on a ship. And not with his future bride nearby.

"I needed to have you alone," he elucidated.

"You'll not tell the woman you intend to marry?"

"No." It was none of the princess's concern.

"And yet you've told me."

There was no other explanation for this, save one.

He held her stare. "You're my woman."

"And she will be your wife," Tansy countered sharply.

It was an endless point of contention between them, the marriage he didn't want to a woman he didn't desire. The endless obligations and duties he faced in his life as king.

"I cannot change our circumstances, spitfire," he said quietly.

How he wished he could.

How he wished he were marrying Tansy instead of Princess Anastasia. But he couldn't be selfish in the future of his kingdom. The attempts on his life in London were brutal reminders of that.

"Nor can I," she said, her voice tinged with sadness.

Sadness he was the cause of, and he despised himself for it.

"I don't want you to be her lady-in-waiting," he said, moving to the other reason he had sent for her.

The reason that had given him purpose through the long days they had been apart.

Tansy's lips tightened. "Yes, you would have me be your mistress, a position I've already declined."

"Then be my lover instead," he told her, determined to have this woman in whatever capacity he could. "Come to me when or if you wish. You'll be free to do whatever you like."

"And where will I sleep?" she asked, ever practical. "I'm a foreigner in a strange land. I know nothing and no one here."

In his bed, damn it.

He couldn't say that, however. He was trying to woo her.

"You have your choice of palace rooms," he said instead. "And if you find palace life too stifling, there are other homes here in the capital that might be more to your liking."

"That would make me a kept woman."

He rose from his chair, going to her and doing the unthinkable, dropping to his knees before her. "It would make you a woman I hold in the highest regard," he corrected solemnly.

A woman he wanted far too much. A woman he wanted so desperately that he had spent their time apart trying and failing to convince himself that they were better off without each other.

"And do you?" she asked, her eyes seeking answers he wasn't entirely certain he could give.

But he didn't look away. "I do."

"Maxim," she said his name softly, half protest, half sigh, as if the mere utterance pained her.

As if being with him pained her. And he knew the feeling all too well, because being alone with her without touching her—having her here in his private chambers—was nothing short of torture.

"Whatever you want, Tansy," he repeated. "I'll give you anything I can."

Except marriage. He couldn't give her that, and they both knew it. The acknowledgment lay between them, unspoken and ugly. But he wasn't free to wed her, not with so much at stake. He had to make every decision on behalf of his kingdom with painstaking care.

He reached for her hands, taking them in his, and she didn't protest. Maxim took that as a sign that her resolve was waning, and he pressed his advantage, lifting first her left, then her right to his lips for a lingering, worshipful kiss.

"Please," he added when she hesitated, not giving him an answer but instead watching him with a gaze that seared him to his marrow.

"What would you have me say?" she murmured, looking as torn as she sounded.

"Say that you'll have me." Another kiss, this time to her inner wrist, where her skin was warm and velvet-soft. "Give yourself to me."

He found the pale blue of her veins and traced them with his lips, his tongue. Desire, so long suppressed, roared to thunderous life. He was aching, his cock hard, his knees beginning to hurt from kneeling for so long, his mind and heart in an agony of waiting.

"Until you're married," she said suddenly.

"Forever," he countered, selfish and greedy when it came to Tansy.

He hadn't known how much he needed her, how much she completed him, until he'd been forced to spend two weeks without her.

"Until you're married," she repeated firmly.

His stubborn spitfire. He shouldn't be surprised. He smiled into her palm as he laid a kiss there, for he considered this a battle won between them, and he had every intention of emerging the victor in the war. He would change her mind. He would keep her in his bed day and night, pleasuring her so well that she never wanted to leave him.

Perhaps he could delay the marriage indefinitely.

Hmm, yes. He did like the sound of that, he thought as he flicked his tongue over her, tasting the salt of her skin. A potent wave of lust overwhelmed him. He wanted to taste her everywhere. To bury his face between her legs and lick her until she screamed.

"Until then," he agreed, running his nose along her inner forearm, inhaling the scent of her skin, floral and delicate and so damned sweet.

"You're..." Her words trailed off, as if her thoughts had escaped her, and her voice was breathless.

Good.

He kissed to her elbow, grateful she was wearing an afternoon gown with little capped sleeves so that he had more of her to kiss and touch. "I'm..." he prompted.

"You're agreeing," she said, her chest rising and falling in shallow breaths that drew attention to the ripe fullness of her breasts straining against her bodice.

He would agree to anything in this moment, as long as he could have her.

"Beginning now," he clarified, releasing her to grasp fistfuls of muslin and begin lifting them to her waist.

"What...Maxim..." He shoved her petticoats and gown into her lap, giving her stocking-clad legs a leisurely caress. "Oh. Now? Truly?"

He skimmed his touch lightly past her knees, intent upon spreading those pale, well-curved thighs. "Now. Truly."

"But…"

Maxim kissed one knee, then the other, fingers trailing higher. Beyond her silken garters so neatly tied with perfect bows. He was touching bare, glorious skin now. She was so warm and soft, so pliant and beautiful. He guided her legs apart with ease. She had loved his tongue on her; he had thought of scarcely anything but the way she had tasted, how wet she had been, the breathy sounds she'd made, how responsive she was.

"I've been dreaming of licking your cunny every night we've been apart," he told her, his fingers daring to venture closer to the heat at her center. "Are you going to deny me, or do you want my tongue on you?"

It wasn't the practiced question of a seducer, but he was no charmer. He never had been. He was rough and ragged and brutal. He was the man his life had fashioned him into. He could only hope that man would prove enough for her.

"Yes," she said.

"Elaborate, sweeting. Tell me."

"You like it when I tell you what I want." Her voice had a husky tenor of pleasure that made his cock even harder.

Maxim smiled, kissing her other knee. "Few things please me more."

"I want you to kiss me."

Her words surprised him. He had been intent upon ravishing her. So close to the exquisite paradise that awaited between her thighs.

He glanced up. "Where, spitfire? I'm afraid you'll need to be specific to get what you want."

"On my lips first." She tapped the lushness of her bottom lip.

And he surged toward her, something about the innocence of that gesture coupled with her command that riled him beyond measure. He cupped her nape and took her mouth with his. She made a sweet sound of helpless desire, threading her fingers through his hair. She kissed him as if she were starved for him, giving him her tongue. He sucked on it and gave her his in return, and she moaned, grasping at his hair with sharp little tugs that made him wild.

He wanted to mark her. To rake his teeth down her throat. To claim her in every way he could, so that she would never forget she was his and, likewise, that he was hers. A stinging rush of need overwhelmed him, the force of it so strong that his hands trembled on her thighs, his fingers likely digging into her skin so tightly, he risked leaving a bruise.

Realizing how firmly he held her, he gentled his hold, tore his mouth from hers to stare at her, his chest rising and falling in ragged breaths, heart hammering so loudly he wouldn't be surprised if she heard its frantic beats.

All for her. Each one.

Somehow, he found the presence of mind to ask another question. "Where else would you have my mouth?"

Wordlessly, she pressed two fingers to her throat.

He followed them with his lips, kissing the skin, opening to suck hungrily at her silken flesh. "Where else?"

His voice was hoarse with wanting. He thought he might explode from the wondrous agony of desiring her.

Her fingers dipped to her bodice, to the faintest hint of the valley between her breasts, almost entirely hidden by the modest cut of her gown. He kissed her there and then moved beyond, his mouth finding the hard peaks of her nipples through the layers of gown and chemise and whatever other feminine frippery that kept her from him. He sucked and licked and bit, gratified by the throaty moan she gave him in response.

He wanted to tear the gown in two. To rip it away from

her and lay her naked in his bed and fuck her for days. To never leave this chamber or her side.

To the devil with obligations. Why could he not have her now? He had intended only to bring her pleasure. To make her come on his lips and tongue and then tend to his own desire discreetly after she had gone.

But now he wanted to be inside her. He wanted her in his bed. He never wanted to pretend they were strangers again. How could they, after this? How could they when the passion between them was so undeniable, so right?

Still, he was proving himself to her. Giving her the control. Allowing her to dictate to him. He tamped down his ravenous needs and raised his head with great reluctance. "Where next?"

"Must I tell you?" she asked, her gaze already heavy-lidded with her own passion.

She wanted him every bit as much as he wanted her. And thank Christ for that. Because he would die if he did not have her.

"Yes, spitfire," he told her thickly. "Tell me."

"Here," she whispered, and then her wicked fingers moved beneath her raised gown and petticoats and chemise. She pressed two fingers to the apex of her thighs. To the gorgeous heart of her.

And ye gods, he nearly came right then, at the sight of her fingers pressing against her intimate flesh. It looked so wicked, so perfect. He wondered if she touched herself there and thought of him.

But then her fingers moved, and her legs widened in further invitation, and he forgot the ability to think entirely. He buried his face between her legs, starving for her, licking her seam and finding her entrance, thrusting his tongue deep. She cried out, her fingers clutching his hair again. He suckled her bud, licked up and down her folds, drunk on the taste of her, musky and delicious.

Still not enough.

He hooked her knees over his shoulders, brought her flush against him, her body angled perfectly for his appreciation. He lapped at her lightly, teasing her until she was writhing against him, and then he gave her what she wanted. More pressure. More suction. His fingers, parting her and sinking deep. She was soaked. Her inner walls clung to him.

Weeks had passed since he'd last been inside her, but it may as well have been a century. She felt like heaven, slick and sleek and hot, gripping him tightly, and his cock was leaking, pressed insistently to the fall of his trousers with the will to replace his fingers.

Soon. First, he wanted her coming undone. Wanted her breathless and flushed and helpless, at the mercy of his relentless need to give her pleasure. He devoted himself to her, using his tongue, his teeth, everything he could. She was close. He could hear it in her voice, in the panting gasps of breath she let out as he nibbled on her tender bud and then sucked hard, fucking in and out of her sultry heat with determined thrusts.

Closer.

He tongued her with wild abandon, feasting on her cunny as he gave her another finger, stretching her tight sheath. And then she was twisting in the chair, her bottom sliding forward, her body stiffening, her fingers tightening in his hair as she cried out his name and she pulsed around his fingers.

"Oh God. Maxim."

Yes. He liked the desperation in her voice. Wanted more of it. He kissed her sex and withdrew his fingers, the need to be inside her driving him to his feet. He hauled her from the chair with as much gentleness as he could manage, and then he scooped her into his arms and carried her triumphantly to his bed where she belonged.

~

TANSY HAD GIVEN IN. Surrendered to her desire, to her need for Maxim. She was weak and wretched.

But none of that mattered as he tenderly stripped her bare of every garment, kissing each new swath of skin he revealed. The brush of his mouth on her flesh was pure sensual torment. She was still throbbing from the release he had given her on the chair, and yet, she already wanted more.

She wanted him inside her, filling her.

Wanted to touch and kiss him everywhere. To explore his powerful body as he did hers.

Wanted, wanted, *wanted*.

He kissed the peak of her breast, his lips closing over the sensitive nipple to suck. He had shrugged out of his banyan and wore nothing but trousers. So much of his body on display to her through the golden afternoon light filtering in the windows. He was all rippling muscle, masculine and brutal, his chest and shoulder marked with scars from his days on the battlefield. She reveled in him, trailing her fingertips over the crisp dark hair dotting his chest, over the smooth, rounded slopes of his shoulders, down his strong back.

When he shifted to peel off her stockings, she made a sound of protest, hating to lose the connection with him.

"You'll have me soon enough, love," he promised soothingly, kissing her knee.

Deft fingers dragged over her calves and ankles in a wicked caress that sent a fresh rush of longing through her. Her stockings were whisked away, tossed over his broad shoulder, and she didn't care where they landed because he was freeing the fall of his trousers now. And his cock sprang forth, thick and long and demanding.

Molten heat pooled between her thighs.

She reached for him, daring to wrap her hand around his hard length, and he growled his approval.

"Yes, touch me. Feel how badly I want you."

How powerful she felt, knowing the effect she had upon him. That his desire for her was so strong. He was soft and yet firm, and hot. So hot. Guided by instinct, Tansy caressed him, her thumb finding the bead of pearlescent moisture at the tip and slicking it over the head of his cock.

He muttered a guttural curse that she didn't understand, which was probably for the best. "Enough, sweeting, or you'll make me spend before I'm inside you."

She released him, then watched as he rose to shuck his trousers, before joining her on the bed again, as naked as she was. He knelt between her legs, gripping his cock and giving it a firm stroke that made her sex throb with achy need. She opened wider, exposing herself to him, feeling the cool kiss of the chamber air on her most intimate flesh mingling with the searing anticipation of his claiming.

"Are you wet for me?" he asked, his gruff voice thick with desire.

Like velvet to her senses.

"Yes." There was no shame in her answer, in her body naked and spread before him.

There was only need.

His head dipped, and he took her nipple into his mouth, suckling as he lowered himself over her, his cock pressing between them in urgent temptation. The weight of him on her was familiar and heady. She wrapped her arms around him again, holding him to her, love for him beating in her heart so ferociously that she thought he surely must know the depth of her feelings for him. That it must be written on her skin, on her face.

He visited the same torture upon her other breast, and then he kissed the place between them where her skin was flat and smooth. "Such beauty." His lips made a sweltering path up her throat to her jaw. He nuzzled her temple, his whiskers rasping deliciously against her cheek. And all the while, he rubbed his cock against her, slicking it up and down, using it to tease her nub until she was restless beneath him, writhing and rolling her hips in a search for more.

His lips slanted over hers at the same moment that he guided his cock to her entrance. One thrust of his hips, and he was inside her, so large and thick and hard. Claiming her, reaching every part of her, or so it seemed. She cried out at the perfection of the fullness of him lodged deep, and he smothered her cry with his demanding lips, kissing her with an intensity that told her he had missed her every bit as much as she had missed him.

Without breaking the kiss, he withdrew slightly, the glide of his cock sending fire straight through her. And then he slowly sank into her again, feeding her his tongue. She tasted herself on his lips and it incited more of the riotous feelings within.

More, more, more.

But Maxim was in no hurry. He made love to her without haste, his hips moving in a rhythm that was designed to drive her over the edge with wanting. Slow, firm thrusts. In and out, his lips hot and demanding on hers, drawing no quarter in his quest to claim her in every way.

Fiery pleasure streaked through her. She kissed him harder, raked her nails down his back, and pumped her hips against his, seeking a release he kept beyond her reach. Every thrust was delicious agony, and she was incredibly aware of everything, as if her senses had been heightened to painful potency. There was his scent enveloping her, his hardness against her softness, his breath on her lips, the harsh bursts of his ragged exhalations through his nose, the slickness of his sweat, the abrasion of his chest hair against her greedy nipples, the creak of the bed in time to his thrusts.

Pleasure was cresting. Rising. Higher, higher. And then he reached between them, finding the place where their bodies met, and rubbed tight, wicked circles over her pearl, knowing just what she needed. It was too much. She couldn't think, couldn't breathe. It was perfect.

Oh dear heavens.

She was coming.

Coming hard, clenching on his cock, moaning into his kiss, scraping her nails over his shoulders. Coming apart. Filled with him. Claimed by him. *Devoured* by him. She was trembling and quaking, the force of her spend rocking her body.

She would never be the same.

This was different from the lovemaking that had come before it.

This was all-consuming.

Only then did he increase his pace, hips flexing as he pounded into her with harder, faster strokes until he tore his mouth from hers.

"Tansy," he breathed against her lips, his body tensing. "My sweet Tansy. You're mine forever now."

A deep thrust, a strangled moan from him, and then there was the hot rush of his seed filling her. And she didn't bother to correct him as he collapsed against her, his pounding heart keeping time to hers. Because she *was* his forever, regardless of what happened in the future.

Because even if he married another, King Maximilian would always own her heart.

CHAPTER 16

"*M*axim."

A gentle, beloved voice was at his ear. Lips grazing.

Tansy's voice. Tansy's lips.

God, he loved her.

The realization settled over him as lucidity returned.

His eyes flew open to find her face hovering above his, her dark hair streaming around her shoulders in disarray, her lips dark and swollen from his kisses. She looked as if she'd been thoroughly fucked. She looked beautiful.

And he was in love with her.

Strangely, the knowledge didn't fill him with dread. Instead, a calm acceptance swelled deep within him. A sense of rightness he hadn't known since...

No, he wouldn't think it. For everything with Tansy was different. *He* was different.

He reached for her, wonder filling him, and sifted his fingers through the tendrils of her silken hair. "You're beautiful."

"You need to dress for the betrothal feast," she said.

Not the words he wanted to hear.

The reminder of the obligations awaiting him this evening was unwanted. Anyone who wasn't Tansy was unwanted. Any task that didn't involve lying here naked with her and fucking her witless was definitely unwanted.

She had the counterpane pulled over her for modesty.

He tugged it so that it slipped free of her hold, revealing her gorgeous breasts. "I don't want to attend it. I want to stay here with you."

Her nipples were hard, jutting toward him in an invitation he couldn't help but accept. He cupped one breast, rubbing his thumb over the rosy peak.

"But *I* must attend it," she protested, even as she arched into his touch.

"Why must you?" Maxim lowered his head and took the tip of her other breast into his mouth, giving her a long, lusty suck.

His cock was rigid. Ready.

To hell with the feast. To hell with dressing or ever wearing garments again. He could rule from this bed with his woman at his side. Beneath him. Atop him. On all fours for him...

"Mmm," she hummed her appreciation, fingers dancing softly through his hair. "Because my absence will be noted."

He slipped his other hand beneath the coverlets shielding her lower body, finding her sex with ease. She was slick and warm, and she shuddered when he found her pearl and teased the plump bud.

"Who gives a damn?" he growled, kissing the curve of her breast and then giving in to some manner of ancient incivility that boiled in his veins and bestowing a gentle nip on her. "Let them note what they wish. I am the king."

"Maxim."

A primness seeped into her voice that he didn't like. He

was going to have to do better to distract her. He flicked her bud back and forth, gratified when she gasped out a breath.

"Spitfire." He dragged his lips over her collarbone, anointing it with adoring kisses, the warmth inside him spreading as if it were rays of the sun itself, shining into the darkest depths of his soul where all the despair had once dwelled.

Happiness.

That was what this mysterious feeling was, this lightness in his heart, in his chest.

Tansy made him happy.

And he was going to reward her by making her come. He worked her nub some more, kissing up her neck before slipping a finger deep inside her wet heat. She tightened on him instantly, making his cock twitch with need.

"Again?" she asked breathlessly, moving restlessly, her legs parting wider.

Despite her protests, she was not as unaffected as she would have him think. Excellent. He had no interest in leaving this bed.

Maxim raised his head and met her gaze. "Darling, my appetite for you is insatiable."

To emphasize his point, he withdrew his finger and rolled her onto her back, settling atop her, his cock rising rigid and demanding between them. He rolled his hips, letting her feel his hardness, his desire for her. Tansy's lashes lowered, her pupils dilating wide.

"We shouldn't."

"To the contrary," he murmured, taking in the picture she made, flushed and lovely in his rumpled bed. "There is nothing we should do more."

"We haven't time."

He moved his hips again, the friction against her slick

flesh nothing short of torture. "Will you deny me, then? Will you deny us both what we want?"

He kissed her before she could answer, claiming her lips with his. Kissed her long and slow and deep, just as he had made love to her. Showing her without words how much he desired her. Her arms twined around his neck, holding him to her, and she arched into him.

When he was satisfied that he had proven his point, he raised his head, strumming over her bud as her breath quickened.

"Your answer, madam. Do you want to dress for the feast, or do you want me inside you again?"

He teased her with greater pressure, then aligned his cock with her entrance, awaiting her answer.

Her lips parted, and he could plainly see her waging an inner struggle between desire and duty. "You know what I want."

He couldn't hide his smile. "Say it."

"You."

He dragged his cock up and down her seam, coating himself in her dew. She was almost obscenely wet. He fucking loved it.

He loved *her*. He should tell her. But in the proper way. Not when he was about to bed her. Later, he decided.

"How?" he demanded instead. "How do you want me?"

Dark lashes lowered over mysterious gray eyes. "Inside me."

Those two words.

He was lost.

Maxim thrust into her to the hilt, gliding in her slick channel with ease, the constriction of her cunny wrapped around him, fitting him like a glove. Here was where he belonged. Not even on a throne. Just here, deep inside Tansy, making her his.

He groaned at the rightness of it, the feel of her, the perfection.

His lips settled on hers, and she kissed him voraciously, as if she could not have enough of him. This time, he had already lost his tight grip on his control. He could not control his motions. He slammed in and out of her, taking her in harsh thrusts as he sought his next release. She sucked on his tongue, wrapped her legs around him, met him thrust for thrust. He fucked her across the bed and into his headboard, using a pillow barrier for protection. Maxim caught her hips in his hands and angled her against him so that he could penetrate her even deeper. As deep as he could go.

He was so close to exploding, pleasure licking up his spine like flames.

Maxim broke the kiss, staring down at Tansy. Her eyes were closed, her lips parted, and she was lost in the throes of her own passion. He'd never seen her look more maddeningly lovely, the rose of a flush blossoming on her cheekbones, her breasts moving with the force of his every thrust. His, all his.

His *love*.

With the feeling came a sudden rush of need, dark and potent. He wrapped her hair around his fist, leveraging himself on the pillow as he pumped into her again and again.

He tugged gently. "Open your eyes, spitfire. Look at me while I'm deep inside your cunny. You're mine."

Her lashes fluttered, then lifted, and he fell into the depths of her eyes. "Yes."

He hadn't expected the acknowledgment to fall so readily from her lips. That it did made the beast within him roar with pride.

"Come on my cock," he ordered, his hips pumping faster as she tightened on him.

"Maxim, please."

Her breathy begging nearly undid him. She was close. He could feel it. He shifted again, his cock slipping from her wetness. And then he slid a pillow under her bottom, inside her in the next second, the angle achieving new penetration.

Ah, fuck. Yes. That was good. So good.

He found her pearl and stroked.

She cried out, her cunny convulsing, milking his cock deliciously, a rush of wetness bathing him, dripping down his shaft to his ballocks. One more slam of his hips, and he lost control entirely. He spilled inside her, body bowing beneath the intensity of his orgasm.

When she had drained him of the last drop, he slipped free of her body, rolling to his back at her side. He should tell her now, he thought stupidly as his heart thundered in his chest. He should tell her that he loved her.

She dropped a kiss on his chest and rose from the bed. "We should dress now for the betrothal feast."

The damned feast. His looming wedding. His duty to his people. She was right. He was obliged to attend. He had been thinking with a lust-addled mind earlier. But now that the poison had been cast out of him, he could think again.

Disappointment came crashing down on him, and he kept the words to himself. Later. He would tell her that he loved her later, he thought as he watched the sway of her hips and felt his cock impossibly stir once more.

He would tell her tonight, after the betrothal feast.

∾

THE HOUR WAS late and the night was cold, but Tansy couldn't bear to remain another minute in the grand hall where the betrothal feast was being held. Pulling her wrap more tightly around her to ward off the chill, she ventured deeper into the walled palace courtyard. A fountain tinkled merrily somewhere in the distance, and torches had been placed strategically along the path, but shadows and darkness blanketed the quiet grounds, rendering it difficult to see. The night was almost starless on account of silvery clouds that had been hanging over the capital since that afternoon when she'd left Maxim's apartments, what now seemed a lifetime ago.

Toasts had been made to the king and his future queen. Maxim and Princess Anastasia had been seated together on a dais at the center of the hall so that it had been impossible not to see them. Neither had appeared particularly happy despite the high spirits of the revelers, who were drinking wine and ale and celebrating with merry delight the impending nuptials.

Tansy had been seated at the far end of the long, intricately carved table where the most prominent lords and ladies of Maxim's court had gathered to dine on a sumptuous meal of so many courses she had quite lost count. And although the food had been elegant and enticing, she had scarcely eaten a bite, sick to her stomach at the vivid picture of her life before her.

A woman on the periphery, watching from afar as the man she loved stood with his wife at his side.

After the frenzied tenderness of their earlier lovemaking and Maxim's revelations to her, watching him with Princess Anastasia, *celebrating* their looming marriage, had been akin to a slap in the face. Tears stung at her eyes even now, far from the glittering assemblage, the ladies with their elegant gowns, encrusted in jewels. The lords with their formal court dress. The laughter, the titters, the lack of familiar faces.

How hopeless her position was here.

Had she imagined that she would be able to remain in Varros after Maxim married the princess, even for a moment? That seeing him with another woman would one day cease to bring her unspeakable agony?

If she had, her mind had been addled. She hadn't been thinking clearly. Or at all.

Loving him and not being able to be with him—truly, in every way—was an anguish she wasn't prepared to bear. She was going to have to leave Varros. To end her service to Princess Anastasia. To carry on was not fair to either of them.

Tansy pressed a gloved hand to her mouth, stifling a hopeless sob.

Crunching soles on gravel somewhere behind her alerted her to the fact that she was suddenly no longer alone in the courtyard. With a deep, shaking breath, she tried to calm herself, blinking furiously to force her tears away. Although it was dark, she would be mortified if anyone were to find her in such a state.

"Lady Tansy?"

The masculine voice, though familiar, was not the one she had been longing to hear.

She turned, hoping there would be no evidence of her upset on her countenance in the lack of light, and forced a feigned smile to her lips. "Prince Ferdinando," she greeted formally, peering into the shadows as his tall form appeared around a neatly trimmed hedge.

But of course it was the prince and not Maxim coming to find her. The king could not leave his betrothal feast without everyone taking note. And despite his earlier insistence that he needn't attend, he had been regal and painfully handsome in his full court dress, seated at the princess's side.

There had been a moment when Princess Anastasia had appeared distressed, and Maxim had covered her hand with his on the table. The smallest of gestures, and yet one that had shattered Tansy's heart and any foolish hope she might have been clinging to that she could watch her best friend marry the man she loved.

The prince stopped before her, the glow of a cheroot hanging from his mouth as he gave her an elegant bow.

He withdrew it to speak and exhaled a puff of smoke. "I thought that was you I spied dashing into the gardens. I know it's terrible form to smoke in the presence of a lady, but I lit it before I saw you, and it's a damned fine cheroot. I'd hate for it to go to waste."

The scent of it curled around her, cloying and unpleasant. She didn't want company, and she didn't want to smell the cheroot. But she was a visitor to the prince's court.

"I hadn't even noticed it, Your Royal Highness," she lied.

"You are to call me Nando," he said smoothly, taking another measured puff of his cheroot, smoking it with the same easy confidence he applied to every action, word, and gesture.

She wondered what it was like to be so assured of oneself. For so much of her life, she had been too terrified to be herself, lest she be cast to the streets. Not by the princess, whose heart was pure and good, but by the princess's uncle, King Gustavson.

"I do not think it wise to adopt familiarity," she told him cautiously.

"Why not? I imagine we will be getting to know each other quite well as the years go on," he said, tilting back his head to puff high into the air.

In an effort, she supposed, to spare her the brunt of his cheroot smoke.

"I don't think so." The words left her before she could think better of them, and not without a hint of bitterness she couldn't hide.

She bit her lip and cursed herself for saying too much.

"And why not? You will be staying in the palace. In

Maxim's apartments, if today is to be any indication." His tone was shrewd. "He has made you an offer, has he not? I assume that was the reason for your visit to his rooms."

"I won't be remaining for long," she admitted, hating that she would leave Maxim, yet knowing that she had no choice.

"In the palace?"

"In Varros," Tansy clarified. "I don't belong here. There's no place for me."

I can't remain and watch the man I love marry another.

But she kept that to herself, tucked safely inside the remnants of her broken heart.

"Does Maxim know of this?" the prince asked, calmly taking another pull of his cheroot.

She shook her head, an ache deep inside her at the thought of leaving him, never seeing him again. "There's no need for him to know. It doesn't concern him. I'll be securing passage to England as soon as I'm able."

She couldn't return to Boritania, not if there was a war about to be waged. England seemed the most reasonable option.

Prince Ferdinando exhaled a cloud of smoke. "If you leave him, he'll be devastated."

She blinked furiously against another stinging rush of tears, fighting to keep them at bay. "If I remain here and watch him marry another, it will destroy me."

Her voice trembled with unspoken emotion.

"You love him."

It wasn't a question, but rather a knowing statement.

She pressed her lips together, staving off a sob, summoning her control to keep from humiliating herself. "Yes."

Desperately.

Hopelessly.

Futilely.

"He should be marrying you instead of the princess," Prince Ferdinando said with great feeling. "To hell with allies and wars. He's sacrificed enough of himself for Varros. He deserves to be happy."

He did deserve happiness. Maxim was a good man. A misunderstood man. A man who had been through hell in the name of his people. But she couldn't bear the agony of watching him with the princess.

"I understand why he must marry Princess Anastasia." The words left her with great difficulty. She had to pause and collect herself before continuing. "But tonight showed me that I can't stay in Varros. It's far too painful. I'm not strong enough to bear it."

"Damn it," the prince cursed, tossing away his cheroot and smothering it beneath the sole of his boot. "You should tell him, Lady Tansy."

"If I tell him, he will only try to keep me here. He can be very persuasive when he chooses to be." Her cheeks heated as memories of just how persuasive he'd been earlier filtered through her, chasing some of the anguish. "He cannot know."

"You do him a disservice in not giving him warning," the prince cautioned.

But she was firm on this. She was weak and vulnerable where Maxim was concerned. She didn't trust herself not to succumb, should he attempt to dissuade her.

"He can't know," she repeated. "Promise me you won't tell him either."

"My lady," Prince Ferdinando protested, clearly not liking the idea of keeping a secret from his brother.

The two of them were close, she knew. And she hated being the reason the prince lied to Maxim. But she was desperate.

"Please," she begged. "Promise me."

He exhaled a weary sigh. "Very well. I promise you.

However, I insist that you allow me to assist you in securing passage from Varros. Maxim would want me to make certain you're safe."

The offer was a relief. She hadn't been sure how to obtain passage in a ship on her own.

"Thank you. I would be most grateful for your assistance."

The prince nodded, looking grim in the flickering light of a nearby torch. "How soon do you intend to leave?"

"As quickly as I'm able."

The sooner she left Varros, the better. Her heart couldn't bear the strain.

Prince Ferdinando inclined his head. "Consider it done."

CHAPTER 17

"*Y*ou look as if you're attending your own funeral, madam," Maxim observed grimly.

The day had dawned dark with storms rolling in from the sea. Rain was lashing against the window-panes where Princess Anastasia stood, wind howling beyond. He had summoned her for the meeting with her brother, who had newly arrived from England in preparation for the invasion of Boritanian shores.

He hadn't failed to note the dark crescents beneath her eyes. Nor her wan complexion and utter lack of joy. Maxim couldn't blame her, of course. He felt the same. He missed Tansy. The damned betrothal feast the night before had kept him from her, and he'd spent the night in his bed alone after finally managing to return to his apartments at half past two in the morning.

By that time, Tansy had long since disappeared from the feast.

His obligations thus far today had similarly kept him from her.

"Forgive me, Your Majesty," Princess Anastasia said, her

tone lacking inflection. "I am merely concerned for my brother."

"And you don't want to marry me," he finished for her, daring to say aloud what he could read in her eyes each time she looked upon him.

"I want to do what is best for the people of Boritania, and that is marrying you," she said, not refuting his claim.

"Do I frighten you, Princess Anastasia?" he asked, frowning at the thought.

He knew that he possessed a certain reputation. That he was bereft of the easy charm his brother possessed. That he was gruff and cold and aloof. But he would never harm a woman.

Her eyebrows rose in surprise. "Of course not, Your Majesty."

"Good." Clasping his hands behind his back, he paced toward the fireplace, feeling distinctly cold. "I wouldn't like to think you fear me."

"There is something I must confess to you."

He turned, casting a curious glance in her direction. "Yes?"

The princess squared her shoulders. "I'm in love with another man."

"Tierney," he guessed instantly.

Her lips compressed into a tight line. "It matters not. He is not here in Varros."

"Then why do you tell me?" he asked, curious.

"Because I wish for our marriage to be an honest one. It seems inauspicious to begin it with lies."

Their very marriage felt increasingly inauspicious to Maxim. He had spent the entirety of the betrothal feast wishing it had been Tansy at his side instead of Princess Anastasia. Wishing it would be Tansy he would make his wife. Tansy who would be his queen.

"Thank you for your honesty," he told the princess. "To be candid, I'm in love with another woman as well."

There. He'd said it. That elusive word he hadn't spoken aloud since Mina.

Love.

He'd admitted he was in love with Tansy.

It felt...liberating.

Right.

Princess Anastasia's chin went up, her countenance turning guarded. "May I ask whom?"

It seemed damned unwise to admit being in love with her lady-in-waiting to the princess. But he wasn't going to lie. His love for Tansy wasn't shameful. He was proud of it, proud of her.

"Lady Tansy is the lady in question," he said simply.

"I'm relieved to hear that, Your Majesty."

He was about to ask why when a knock sounded at the door to the chamber, signaling the arrival of her brother.

Perhaps the interruption was timely. He wasn't certain it was wise to reveal more of the details of his feelings for another woman to his future wife.

"You may enter," he called, turning to the portal.

It swung open, and for the first time, he stood face-to-face with the exiled and rightful king of Boritania.

"Your Majesty," Maxim greeted him warmly.

Theodoric St. George crossed the threshold, bearing a regal air despite the fact that he had never occupied his kingdom's throne.

"Call me Theo," he said.

And Maxim liked the man instantly. He nodded to Felix, who snapped the door closed, giving them privacy.

"Theo," he repeated. "Come and sit. We have much to discuss."

"Brother," Princess Anastasia greeted warmly, her entire

mien changing as she rushed forward, throwing herself into her sibling's arms for an undignified embrace.

Theo clasped his sister tightly. "Sister. Are you well?"

Maxim watched in silence as the two exchanged pleasantries, inquiring after each other's welfare and journeys. It was plain to see that despite her brother's lengthy exile, Princess Anastasia remained close to him. It was also plain to see that her grim demeanor had been entirely caused by being alone in a room with Maxim.

It certainly didn't bode well for their union.

He clenched his jaw, telling himself it was a concern for later.

At last, the conversation between the princess and her brother waned.

"Sit," Maxim invited, gesturing to a grouping of chairs that had been arranged for just such a purpose. "Please."

The three of them settled in their respective chairs.

Theo was first to speak. "Thank you for including Stasia in this discussion."

The gratitude startled Maxim. Did everyone consider him a vicious ogre?

"Why would I not?" He forced a smile he didn't feel. "It is her homeland of which we speak as well, is it not?"

Theo inclined his head. "Other men would not, however, and merely because she is a woman."

Maxim scoffed, thinking of Tansy and her boundless determination. "Other men are stupid."

In Varros, women possessed rights over property. They also had suffrage. Those were some of the many changes Maxim had enacted when he had come to power. He regretted none of them.

Theo chuckled, the sound seemingly rusty, as if he didn't often have cause for levity. "I don't disagree, Your Majesty."

"Call me Maxim," he invited. "Please. We are allies, no?"

And soon to be family, but that reminder came with an unwanted surge of bitterness.

"Allies," Theo repeated, slanting a glance at his sister. "I would like to believe we are."

"Allies," he insisted firmly. "I have an army ready to prove it so, and I've men in Boritania awaiting you. They've been gathering the revolutionaries in preparation for your arrival. My ships are at your disposal. Varros is committed to removing the pretender king from your throne and seeing you placed upon it where you belong."

Theo nodded, his expression tense and stern. "I'm indebted to you for your generosity."

Maxim shook his head. "I'm not a generous man. I'm a wise one. Having you on the throne will benefit my kingdom and my people. Boritania and Varros were close allies once. I hope to restore that bond."

And he was sacrificing himself to do it.

"The time has come for Gustavson to pay the price for his sins," Theo said grimly. "I'll defeat him or die trying."

"We'll defeat him together," Maxim vowed.

~

LYING on her side in his bed, Tansy watched Maxim as he slept. The glow of flickering candlelight lovingly illuminated the sharp angles of his face. Inky hair fell over his brow. He was all stark, brutal masculinity, the emerging whiskers shadowing his jaw, the scars on his body, and the breadth of his shoulders making him appear more warrior than king. How she loved him.

Her heart felt impossibly heavy, weighed down by the certain knowledge that they had made love for the last time. Beyond the heavy curtains, the sun was rising on a new day, painting the sky with rich, gold light. She was going to leave him today.

Prince Ferdinando had made good on his promise. He'd secured her passage on a ship bound for England. In hours, she would be aboard the vessel, sailing back across the sea. She bit her lip to quell the rising tide of grief, so bitter and powerful that it threatened to drown her.

It was better, she told herself sternly.

She couldn't live this way, granted only the smallest scraps of his affections and time. He was a king with many duties to attend to, and yesterday had been a testament to that fact, just as the betrothal feast the evening before had been. She'd scarcely seen him as he had been closeted in meetings with his privy council and the princess and her newly arrived brother. His summons had arrived late in the evening, a liveried servant who had tapped at her door and informed her that His Majesty requested her attendance in his private apartments.

For a wild moment, she had considered denying him. But then she had realized she couldn't bear to squander any of the time she had remaining with Maxim, regardless of its cost to her pride. He had greeted her with a passionate kiss, and they had removed each other's clothing in a frenzied rush. They'd made love twice, the first time hurried and frantic, the second slowly and tenderly.

She'd spent the hours afterward scarcely sleeping, her mind crackling with the knowledge that she would soon have to go. And now, although she had willed the passing hours to progress torpidly, the time had come for her to rise and dress.

With a whisper of a touch, she traced the crisp whiskers covering his jaw.

He was so beloved to her, the powerful warrior king who had fought for years to assume his throne. The man who bore scars on his mind and heart as well as his body. What horrors he must have seen and endured. And yet, for her, he was gentle with his hands, his desire, his kisses. For her, he was vulnerable.

Prince Ferdinando's warning returned to her, taunting her now.

If you leave him, he'll be devastated.

Would he be? Maxim had not spoken of love, and she couldn't be certain there would be room in his heart for anyone else after the death of his first wife. Slowly, taking care not to wake him, she pressed her lips lightly to his, stealing one last kiss.

It would have to be enough to carry her through. Tears burned her eyes as she slipped from the bed, shivering at the chill in the air. The fire had burned low, and the morning air was crisp and unforgiving, an icy rebuke against her bare skin. She found her chemise flung across a chair and pulled it swiftly over her head, trying to think about the future looming before her instead of the pain leaving him would cause.

She had a small amount of funds with which to support herself after her arrival in England. She would need to find a situation. Returning to Boritania in its present state was out of the question, and since she knew no one in England, she would have to find some means. Perhaps she could work as a governess or—

"Where are you going?"

The deep, decadent voice interrupted her thoughts.

Tansy's breath caught as she jumped and whirled to face Maxim on the bed. He had leveraged himself on one forearm, making the bedclothes fall to his waist, and he looked impossibly handsome, his muscled chest on display, his hair mussed, his eyes dark and intense.

"I thought you were asleep," she managed past the emotion clogging her throat.

Heavens, how could she leave him when he was awake? She should have left sooner rather than lingering. She shouldn't have dared that final kiss.

"Someone kissed me awake."

So it *had* been her foolish urge to kiss him, then.

"Forgive me," she said quietly. "I had intended to leave you to your rest."

"I'll only forgive you on one condition." Giving her a sinful smile, he held out his hand in invitation. "Come back to bed, love. I'm not finished with you just yet."

Longing pulsed to life, a restless hunger that would never be soothed. Being with Maxim only made her want him more. And knowing that she could no longer have him, that she would never see him again after today, was breaking her apart inside.

"I should leave your apartments before the servants are about," she protested, wanting to go to him and yet fearing the consequences if she did.

"The only thing you should do is come back to me." He flipped back the bedclothes to reveal his cock, rising thick and hard. "Don't leave me in this state. It's criminal."

As she watched in helpless thrall, he gave his beautiful cock a leisurely stroke. Her sex clenched at the sight. Unabashed desire arced through her. She ached for him to be inside her.

One more time, whispered a wicked voice inside her.

Just one more time.

The ship wasn't leaving until the afternoon. She had already packed her meager belongings.

Her feet were moving of their own accord. She reached the bed, and he caught her waist in his hands, lifting her easily atop him.

"This is how I prefer to spend my mornings," he said appreciatively, his voice gruff, his gaze roving over her with frank admiration. "There's only one thing wrong. You're wearing this blasted chemise."

She grasped handfuls and hefted it back over her head, no longer cold now that the blazing heat of Maxim was beneath her. "Better?"

He took one of her nipples in the velvety warmth of his mouth. "Much."

Tansy ran her fingers through the silken strands of his hair, then kissed his temple at the patch of silver. He suckled her other breast then, and he slid his hand up and down her spine in a gentle caress that incited the flames of wanton desire into a feverish pitch. She was already wet, more than ready for him, their earlier lovemaking leaving her in a heightened sense of awareness.

"Mine," he said against the curve of her breast, as if she were a prize to be coveted.

As if he made the declaration for all the world instead of just the two of them.

She kissed his cheek, the scrape of his stubble against her lips, and inhaled deeply of his scent. "Maxim, I love you."

The confession left her suddenly. Unintentionally. But she had to tell him. She'd meant to all through the night, but fear had made her hold her tongue. Here was her sole opportunity to unburden herself before she lost the chance forever.

He stilled, his head lifting to meet her gaze, an expression of such astonished wonder on his countenance that she felt everything inside her seize. "Say it again."

She swallowed, holding his stare. "I love you."

In one fluid motion, he rolled them as one, so that she was on her back and he was above her, big and strong. He gave her a kiss that was ravishing and ferocious, and with one thrust, he was inside her to the hilt, his cock embedded deep, pinning her to the bed with his hard body.

She moaned into his kiss, feeling her will to leave him flee by the second, her core clenching around him to grip him tightly. Their mouths still fused, he withdrew and then slammed into her again. Tansy wrapped herself around him, arms and legs, clinging like a vine. He withdrew, almost slipping entirely from her body, and then he was inside her again, thrusting with powerful strokes that took her instantly to the edge.

Maxim groaned and gave her his tongue as his hips moved faster. The sounds of their bodies meeting, skin slapping, the bed heaving beneath the force of his thrusts, filled the air. Helplessly, she writhed under him, her engorged pearl brushing against him with each movement. She felt as if she might splinter apart into a thousand tiny shards of herself, exploding from the sheer, raw pleasure it gave her to be so claimed by him.

Her orgasm came upon her quickly, her cunny contracting on his cock with helpless spasms. He tore his mouth from hers and pressed his face to her throat, fucking harder, faster, his hips pumping as he sought his own release. And with each thrust of him inside her, she unraveled more, bliss exploding from deep inside her and radiating outward. His breathing was ragged and warm on her neck, his shoulders stiffening.

With a growl, he came, filling her with the hot spurt of his seed.

Tansy held him to her as he collapsed atop her, their bodies both slick with a sheen of perspiration from their unrestrained efforts, and closed her eyes tightly against the renewed threat of tears.

She couldn't bear to leave him.

And yet, she couldn't bear to stay and watch him become another woman's husband.

She only hoped he could forgive her.

~

AFTER SPENDING the morning closeted in meetings with Prince Theodoric, his general, and his privy council, Maxim was exhausted and ravenous. He was also longing for Tansy. Mere hours had passed since she'd left his bed, but already, he missed her.

Pacing the length of his sitting room as he awaited her arrival in his private apartments, he exhaled a heavy sigh. Everything was in place, the plot to invade Boritania coming together flawlessly. He would soon have what he wanted, and his army and naval fleet were both far superior to Boritania's depleted ranks. With the revolutionaries stirred and ready to join forces with Theodoric, victory was almost certain. The elite soldiers who had been tasked with infiltrating the August Palace and secreting the remaining St. George princesses to safety had completed their mission. Princess Anastasia's sisters would soon arrive safely on Varrosian shores. No detail had been overlooked.

And yet, Maxim couldn't shake the unsettled feeling lodged in his chest, an instinctive premonition that something was wrong.

A knock sounded at his door, and he instantly halted his pacing, the lure of seeing Tansy again chasing the tension from him. She loved him. It seemed a dream, a miracle. He'd been basking in the wondrousness of those words ever since she'd uttered them this morning. When she'd said the words, a burst of possession had struck him with so much force that he'd been able to do nothing but show her he felt the same. He had made love to her with almost brutal abandon.

So much so that he had feared afterward that he might have hurt her in the fever of his passion. When he had worried over it, she had soothed him with a kiss that had stolen his breath, and then she'd taken his cock into her mouth, and he'd forgotten his own name.

"Come," he called now, expecting to find his gray-eyed enchantress crossing the threshold with one of her soft, sultry smiles.

God, he'd missed her.

Instead, it was the frowning servant he'd sent to fetch her. Maxim was instantly on edge.

"Where is Lady Tansy?" he asked, a sharp note entering his voice.

The footman bowed in a show of respect before reporting, "She's gone, Your Majesty."

Gone?

"You mean to say she isn't in her room at present," he corrected.

The footman's expression turned pinched. "Forgive me, Your Majesty, but Lady Tansy has left the palace. I made some inquiries, and I was told a carriage was called for her by His Royal Highness, Prince Ferdinando. Her cases were loaded into it, and she left."

Maxim went numb.

Gone, indeed. But no, it couldn't be. Just this morning, she had been in his arms, in his bed. She'd told him she loved him. Why would she leave him without word, slipping away no better than a thief? He couldn't believe it of her.

"All her cases?" he asked hoarsely.

"I'm afraid so, Your Majesty," the footman answered, his tone laced with regret.

She was leaving him. Tansy was leaving him.

It was true. There was no other explanation. His mind

whirled, his gut clenching, his heart seizing as if gripped by a merciless fist. And Nando had called for the carriage.

Damn him. Nando was behind this. He was going to throttle his brother. No, that was far too merciful. He was going to send him to the fucking dungeons.

"Do you know where Prince Ferdinando is?" he asked tightly.

"I believe His Royal Highness is in his rooms, Your Majesty," the footman said timidly.

Maxim bit out his thanks before rushing past the footman, intent upon finding his brother and finding out what the hell was happening and where Tansy had gone. His long-legged strides ate up the distance easily. Through the marble hall, down a flight of stairs, until he reached Nando's door.

Stifling the urge to roar, he pummeled the door with his fist. *Bang, bang, bang.* "Nando, open the damned door."

"I'm indisposed at the moment," his brother called from within. "Come back later, if you please."

Maxim tried the latch. The door swung open, and he stalked inside, slamming it at his back. Nando was in a state of half dress, his valet stilling in the act of applying some manner of pomade to his annoyingly perfect blond curls.

"Your Majesty," the valet greeted, sweeping into a courtly bow.

But Maxim scarcely noticed him. He was intent upon his brother's guilty face.

"Where is she?" he growled.

"Brother, as you can see, I'm in the midst of dressing," Nando said calmly. "Can you not return later?"

"No, I can't," he snarled, not even bothering with the pretense of manners.

He didn't care if they had a wide-eyed audience. All he cared about was finding Tansy and bringing her back to him, where she belonged.

Nando sighed deeply, as if he'd just been interrupted whilst performing a task of the utmost importance instead of having his valet dress his hair. "Thank you, Leonardo. That will be all for now. His Majesty wishes to speak with me alone."

"Of course, Your Royal Highness." With another deferential bow, the valet took his hasty leave of the chamber.

Maxim stalked the rest of the way across the room when he had gone, grasping a fistful of his brother's waistcoat. "Where. Is. She?" he demanded through gritted teeth.

"If you're speaking of the widowed Countess of Leavarra, I haven't seen her since this morning when we parted at dawn," Nando drawled.

"You know who I'm speaking of." He gave his brother a shake. "Tansy, you bastard. What have you done?"

Nando took a step back, disengaging with him and smoothing a hand down his shirtfront. "I've done what she asked of me."

"She came to you for help?" This in itself felt like a betrayal of the worst sort. "I don't believe you. Why would she come to you instead of me?"

"Because she didn't want you to stop her."

Denial soared through him. "Where has she gone? If she didn't wish to live here in the palace, she only needed to say the words. I would give her anything. I'll give her ten houses if it pleases her."

"She doesn't want ten houses, Maxim," Nando said quietly. "She wants you, but she can't have you."

The urge to plant his fist in his brother's irritatingly perfect nose was strong, but Maxim resisted.

"Of course she can have me," he countered. "She already has me. She has my heart in her hands."

"She can't bear to stay in Varros and watch you marry

another," Nando explained. "Lady Tansy asked me to secure her return passage to England."

She was not just leaving him. She was leaving his kingdom.

He nearly doubled over at the blow. "Why did you not tell me this?"

"Because she made me promise not to."

"And when have you ever kept a fucking promise in your ne'er-do-well life?" he roared. "You've done nothing but bed everything in skirts, and now you've chosen to be honorable for the first time with the woman I love? Damn you, Nando. If you weren't my brother, I'd thrash you to within an inch of your life right now."

Nando flinched, and Maxim knew a pang of guilt for the harshness of his words, spoken in anger and the furious need to find Tansy before it was too late.

"Thrash me, then, Maxim. I don't regret helping her to flee your selfish plan of keeping her as your mistress when it's as plain as the nose on my face that you love each other and should marry."

"You know why I can't marry her."

Nando made a show of flicking a speck from his immaculate sleeve, effecting a mien of boredom. "I know why you *say* you can't marry her."

Maxim raked a hand through his hair and hissed out a frustrated sigh. "I need Theodoric as my ally, and I can't have him as my ally if I jilt his sister in favor of her lady-in-waiting. This is bigger than my own needs and wants, Nando. Perhaps if you bore the responsibilities I do, you'd understand."

"And perhaps if you'd stop being so damned selfish, you'd look at the matter from Lady Tansy's perspective," Nando snapped. "Do you want her to spend the rest of her life as your wicked little secret? To bear your bastards and never know respectability? To always know that you've chosen the throne over her?"

His brother's words shook him. Maxim couldn't deny it.

"I would give her everything I'm able," he said, some of the fight leaving him.

Was he being selfish in wanting Tansy at his side despite being obliged to marry Princess Anastasia? Such an arrangement was not uncommon. Royal marriages were made for dynasties and not for love. When he'd married Mina for love, he hadn't been king. He hadn't had the weight of the kingdom's future bearing down upon him. He'd been young and reckless, a soldier on the battlefield who didn't know if he'd live to see another day.

"But it wouldn't be enough," Nando said quietly. "You see that, don't you, brother? That's why she's left you. She wants more than you're willing to give."

It wasn't that he wasn't willing. It was that he was mercilessly trapped by obligation and duty. But what if there were another way? What if Nando was right? What if he could marry the woman he wanted to marry instead of the woman he felt compelled to marry for the sake of future alliances and the kingdom?

"When is her ship leaving?" he asked, needing to see her.

To speak with her.

To beg her to stay.

Just...*needing* her.

"At two o'clock this afternoon," Nando answered.

Maxim extracted his pocket watch and consulted the time. "I've an hour." His mind spun. His carriage was slow, and assembling the outriders he required for leaving the palace gates would take far too long. He'd miss her. He had to reach her before her ship left. "What is the name of the ship?"

"You're not going to force her to stay, are you?" Nando asked instead of answering his question.

Not precisely a testament to what his brother thought of his character.

"I'm going to speak with her," he ground out. "Now tell me the name of the blasted ship before I blacken your eye."

"Always threatening me with harm." Nando shook his head and gave a tsk. "What would our mother say?"

"She would say that you should give me the name of the fucking ship," he growled.

His brother arched a brow. "Mother never swore."

"Nando, I'm begging you."

"*La Reina*," Nando said finally.

Maxim didn't hesitate another moment. He turned and quit the room, his booted feet carrying him as fast as they could travel. He was going to fetch his woman and bring her back to him where she belonged.

And damn it, one way or another, he was going to make her his wife.

∽

In less than an hour, *La Reina* would set sail for England.

Tansy should have been filled with a sense of peace, if not relief.

Instead, as she waited to board the ship looming before her at the docks, all she felt was the unbearable weights of dread and regret. She felt like a delicate piece of porcelain which had been left teetering on the edge of a high shelf, only to fall and smash to bits, and regardless of the attempts anyone would make to reassemble the pieces, she would never again be whole.

She'd told Maxim that she loved him. And despite the ferocity of his response and the sensual abandon with which he'd claimed her, he hadn't spoken of loving her in return. It was just as well. If he had told her he loved her, leaving him would have proved impossible. As it was, she'd needed all the strength she possessed to see her cases loaded into the carriage Nando had arranged before climbing in herself. As the carriage had driven away, she'd looked back, the fanciful notion that she might see Maxim running after her lingering in her foolish mind.

Instead, the palace had disappeared from view, and the carriage had been swallowed by the capital city street traffic. And there she'd sat, alone on the oiled Moroccan leather squabs, leaving the man she loved behind forever.

A cold wind whipped off the water, nearly claiming her bonnet.

Tansy wrapped her pelisse more firmly about herself, shivering. It was difficult to believe that mere hours ago, she'd been in Maxim's bed. In his arms.

No, she mustn't think of him now. Already, tears burned her eyes, threatening to spill. She needed to keep all thoughts of Maxim from her mind. To turn her thoughts solely to the arduous journey awaiting her.

A sob rose in her throat, and she pressed the back of her hand over her mouth to suppress it. She didn't want to leave Maxim. Didn't want to leave his kingdom. To never again see him, touch him, kiss him, make love with him…

Do not weep now, she ordered herself firmly. *Don't humiliate yourself by turning into a watering pot before all your fellow travelers.*

She inhaled sharply. She could leave him. She *had* to leave him, for the sake of her own self-preservation. She had no other choice. Just a few more minutes, and then she would be aboard the ship, and even if she changed her mind, it would be too late. She couldn't weaken in her resolve now.

For if she returned to the palace, she would fall back into his arms, into his bed. She would never leave, and she would spend the rest of her life in the anguish of knowing he belonged to another, that she could never truly claim him as her own. That her children would be born out of wedlock and that she would be relegated to the periphery of society.

Leaving him was for the best.

It was her only choice.

Yes, she could do it. She would be strong enough. She would—

"Tansy."

His voice broke through her madly churning thoughts, and she whirled about to find somehow, impossibly, Maxim striding toward her, his cheekbones flushed as if he had ridden to the docks from the palace as quickly as he could. He had come to her, and for a moment, her heart rejoiced at the sight of him, so beloved. So handsome.

He stopped before her, his greatcoat swirling about him, his hat pulled low on his brow. It required every bit of restraint she had to keep from launching herself at him.

"What are you doing here?" she asked.

He grunted. "I might ask the same of you, madam."

His tone was displeased. His expression impossible to read.

"I am waiting to board the ship," she forced herself to say.

"You're leaving me," he said bluntly.

And how she hated the hurt in his voice, the pain in his dark eyes. She felt it as surely as a blade slicing into her skin.

"I'm leaving Varros," she protested. "This isn't my home."

"Neither is England your home," he countered, his voice sharp as a lash.

His fury didn't surprise her. He was a man long accustomed to getting what he wanted. No one denied him.

"Maxim," she began, struggling to find the words to explain herself.

He held up a silencing hand. "I would speak to you in privacy."

Her fellow passengers were gathered everywhere around them. She doubted anyone knew it was the King of Varros among them, and yet she well understood the need for discretion.

She nodded. "Very well, but I can only spare a few minutes. We are preparing to board the ship."

His nostrils flared in displeasure, but he offered her his arm. "Come with me."

Reluctantly, she accepted his escort, wrapping her hand around his elbow. "I don't have much time," she cautioned again.

"Are you so eager to leave me, then? Did this morning mean nothing to you?"

A flush crept over her cheeks as they walked a few paces, drawing nearer to the water, separating themselves from the gathering of travelers. "Of course it did."

"And yet, you left me without a single word." His voice was harsh, his face impassive. "You told my brother of your plans, enlisted his aid, but you said nothing of your decision to me."

How to explain?

Tansy took a fortifying breath. "I didn't want you to—"

The rest of her words were swallowed up by the unmistakable report of a gunshot echoing through the air. A searing pain stung Tansy's arm, making her lose her balance. She stumbled and fell from the docks, splashing into the cold, murky depths of the sea.

～

"Tansy!" Maxim reached for her as she stumbled, but he was too slow, his motions impeded by shock. She slipped through his fingers, falling into the churning waves below.

Good, sweet God. He didn't know if she could swim. Without thought, he dove into the water after her.

Fuck, the water was frigid. Where was Tansy? Frantically, he reached for her, trying to find her, his arms empty. He swam to the surface, desperation making his heart pound and his mouth go dry. When he emerged, she wasn't anywhere in sight. He had a vague impression of horrified bystanders on the dock above, women swooning and men calling out. Keeping himself afloat, he searched the waves for a sign of her and thought he saw a shadow.

Maxim dipped below the surface, swimming in the direction he thought he'd spied her. Mercifully, he found fabric. Clutching it tight, he hauled her to him, pulling her to the surface with the force of his kicks and one arm alone.

When they reached the top, she sputtered, coughing out water, eyes wide with fear, choking out his name. "Maxim."

"I've got you, love," he said in as soothing a tone as he could manage, keeping her anchored to him even as the weight of her sodden skirts threatened to pull them asunder.

"My arm...hurts," she managed, her lips trembling, pale from the cold.

And that was when he noticed blood.

Blood on her. Blood in the water, swirling around them.

"My God, you've been shot," he murmured, heart hammering as he made the discovery.

She'd been wounded. Hit in the arm.

Fucking hell, he had to get her out of this blasted water.

"Someone help us!" he shouted to the men and women watching in horror above. "The lady has been wounded."

He was keeping them afloat, but weighed down by his boots and her garments, he didn't know how much longer he'd be able to keep their heads above water. And he needed to stop the loss of her blood, to determine the extent of her injuries.

A flurry of movement caught Maxim's eye—a skiff rowing toward them. He called out, desperate to get Tansy into the boat and safely onto shore. The man at the oars nodded, rowing swiftly to them.

"She's been wounded," he told the two men in the skiff. "Be gentle with her arm."

"Lift her up to me if you're able," said the fellow at the front of the boat. "I'll take care."

"Maxim," Tansy said weakly, her face pale, lips devoid of color, teeth chattering. "Please. I'm afraid."

The words were like a knife to his heart. Fear for her powered him. With inhuman strength, he clung to one side of the boat, hefting her up with the other. The effort took every bit of strength he possessed. Arms wrapped around Tansy, taking her into the boat. And then the man returned, his hand extended for Maxim to take.

Driven by the need to see Tansy safe, he hauled himself into the boat, rolling to his back, cold and sodden, struggling to catch his breath.

"Get us to the docks," he managed.

Tansy was shivering, blood seeping from her torn pelisse. He hauled her to him, knowing he was soaked to the bone as well and yet somehow thinking he could warm her. Comfort her. Heal her.

Damn it, he couldn't lose her.

Not now.

Not ever.

He murmured words to her, switching between her language and his own, uncertain of what he was even saying beyond the need to comfort her. To soothe her. To somehow give her the motivation to cling to this world rather than surrendering to the next.

Hot tears scalded his cheeks. He wept openly, without care, without thought. And in his mind, he saw Mina, pale and streaked with soot, her face bruised and swollen almost beyond recognition. He had found his way to her too late to save her. But he wouldn't allow the same to happen to Tansy.

"Live for me, spitfire," he begged, holding her close to him, the wind whipping cold and brutal around them as the skiff frantically journeyed toward the docks. "Live for *us*."

~

MAXIM PACED the hall outside the room where Tansy had been taken in the palace, looming madness warring with fear. His personal physician had been summoned to attend her, but she'd been weak and cold. The ride back to the palace from the docks had seemed an eternity, and at some point as his carriage had swayed over familiar roads in torpid agony, she'd swooned in his arms.

"Maxim, you should at least bathe."

Nando's voice was at his ear, his brother's booted footfalls matching his, his presence a comfort that nonetheless lacked the impact it ordinarily had upon him.

He couldn't bear to lose her.

All he could see was her face, so wan and fragile.

She'd been limp as a doll in his arms. Pale and lifeless.

He wouldn't lose her.

"Maxim," Nando pressed when he ignored him.

Pace, pace, pace. Neat steps, even time, rhythmic and unending. But not even the old routine could heal him now. Marching with Nando didn't erase the memory of Tansy crumpling into the waters, Tansy bleeding, the terror of realizing she'd been hit by a damned bullet. His chest seized.

Who had shot her?

And why?

He had a suspicion the bullet had been intended for him. He hadn't taken his customary outriders with him in his haste to find her. His carriage had been marked with his coat of arms. Anyone could have spied him. They could have followed him into the crowds on the docks, taken the opportunity...

He'd been responsible for Mina's death, and now, he was likely responsible for what had happened to Tansy too.

"Maxim."

Nando's voice, insistent, pierced the haze of thoughts whirling in his mind.

He stopped at last, turning to his brother. "What do you want?"

"You're soaked," Nando said. "You'll catch your death. A hot bath has been drawn for you in your apartments. Go and warm yourself, change into dry clothes."

"Do you think I give a damn about what happens to me?" he roared, fists clenched at his sides in impotent fury. "I'd lay down my life for hers." He jabbed a finger toward the closed door, on the other side of which Tansy was closeted away with his physician. "I'd give anything to be in her place."

"I know you would, brother." Nando's effortless charm was nowhere to be found. Instead, he was somber and grim. "As would I. It's my fault she was at the docks to begin with."

But Nando wasn't to blame, and Maxim knew it. *He* was. Just as he'd been to blame for Mina's ruthless murder.

He shook his head. "If I hadn't chased after her, she'd be safely aboard that ship right now, sailing away from me."

And God help him, as much as he couldn't bear for her to leave him, he would happily send her away any day if given the choice between her living and leaving and her dying because she'd remained.

"You cannot know that," Nando countered, reaching out to him.

"I do know it," he snarled, shaking free of his brother's touch. "The bullet that hit her was meant for me. If I hadn't

269

gone to the docks, if I hadn't taken her aside, if I had asked her to marry me instead of holding that fucking betrothal feast…"

"How do you know the bullet was meant for you?" Nando asked. "There could have been a footpad in the crowd, and mayhap his shot went astray."

"No." Maxim shook his head again, for he'd been turning those few moments over in his mind again and again in endless search of the answers. "I had pulled her aside, away from the crowd, begging her to speak to me in private. And that was when it happened."

"But why would someone shoot at you?"

"Given what happened in London, need you ask?" He scrubbed a hand over his jaw, feeling helpless and furious and terrified all at once. "The rebels have grown bold. They could not kill me when I went abroad, so they're determined to slay me here on my own soil."

Yes, that was what had happened to Tansy. He had no doubt. Another one of Charles's loyalists, striking with the intent to undermine the kingdom and the line to the throne. Their uncle was dead, but not all his supporters had been stamped out. They had been silently waiting, biding their time. Perhaps the knowledge that he would soon possess a wife and heirs had been the spur for their murderous plans.

And Tansy was paying the price.

"You think loyalists to Charles are trying to kill you?" Nando asked.

"I know it." He thumped his chest with a fist, directly over his heart. "Here. My instincts have never been wrong. That bullet was meant for me, and instead, Tansy was shot, and she might well die. Because of me."

His voice trembled and broke on those last three words. It was as if, eighteen years later and in an entirely different world, he'd suddenly found himself thrust into the same hell he'd inhabited on the day he'd held Mina in his arms outside the burning ruins of her family's home.

His chest tightened; his head pounded.

He had to move. Couldn't remain in the same spot another second.

His waterlogged boots resumed movement, measured paces. *March, march, march.*

March to keep the madness at bay. March to keep the demons that inhabited his skull quiet. March to forget.

"I blame myself," Nando was saying, keeping time at his side. "You cannot blame yourself. This is not like what happened with Mina."

The urge to strike something had never been stronger, but Maxim tamped it down with brutal determination.

"This is everything like what happened with Mina," he countered harshly. "You don't know because you were scarcely more than a whelp. A lad still on his mother's teat."

He regretted the lash of his outburst the moment it left him, but damn it, all he wanted was to know how Tansy was faring. To know if she would live.

To see her. To touch her. To beg her forgiveness.

"I'm reasonably certain I wasn't on our mother's teat at twelve years old," Nando said smoothly.

"You were a boy," he said hoarsely, raking his fingers through his still-damp hair. "You know what I'm saying, Nando. You weren't there that day. You didn't pull her body from the burning remnants of her home. Didn't see what they'd done to her…"

A shudder racked him.

No, he wouldn't lose himself in the past now. Mina was long gone. He had to keep his lucidity about him. To be here for Tansy. She needed him.

"I understand, brother." Nando wrapped an arm around his shoulders, and this time, Maxim didn't retreat. "I'm so sorry for what happened to her. But you need to retain your strength and your health, for Tansy's sake and for the sake of Varros. Your people need their king. And Tansy will need you as she recovers."

He stopped pacing, the aching sting of tears he couldn't quell burning his eyes and pouring down his cheeks. "What if she doesn't recover?"

"She will," Nando insisted with far more certainty than Maxim could muster. "Now go and at least change your clothes, brother. You stink of fish."

Before Maxim could answer, the door opened and the doctor emerged, looking wearied, blood on the cuffs of his shirt sleeves.

Tansy's blood.

"How is she?" he rasped.

"She is alive, Your Majesty," the doctor said grimly. "The next few hours and days will determine her fate."

CHAPTER 18

*T*ansy woke to a strange, burning pain in her left arm.

As lucidity returned to her, she became aware of her surroundings.

She was in Maxim's apartments. In his bed. Confusion swirled through her, along with recollections. She'd been at the docks, preparing to leave, and Maxim had come to her. Then there had been the gunshot. She'd been hit and had lost her balance, falling into the frigid water. And Maxim had been there, jumping into the water. Saving her.

He was here now as well, she realized, slumped in a chair beside the bed, his long legs stretched before him. Dark hair fell over his brow, his lashes fanned on his cheeks. He was asleep, and for a moment, she studied him, drinking in the sight of his masculine beauty in repose, love for him beating fiercely within her heart.

But then she shifted, and a twinge of pain had her gasping.

He jolted awake with a start, the intensity of his stare colliding with hers. "Tansy? You're awake?"

She licked her dry lips, feeling terribly parched. "I seem to be."

Her attempt at a joke failed.

Maxim leaned forward in his chair, reaching for her hand and taking it in a warm grasp. "Thank God. How do you feel? Are you thirsty?"

Before she could answer, he was on his feet, fetching her water from a gilded pitcher and returning to her side, his face etched in worry. "Here, my love. Take a drink."

She reached for the cup, their fingers brushing, but she was terribly weak, her hand trembling, her arm not cooperating with her body's needs and her mind's intentions. Water splashed on the coverlets over the rim.

His fingers chased hers. "Let me."

She did, taking a tentative sip from the cup, allowing him to tend to her as her uninjured arm fell back against the downy softness of the bed. Then another.

"Slowly," he cautioned sternly, pulling the cup away. "You've been ill for days."

"How many?" she managed.

"Three," he said, watching her closely, his expression guarded.

Three days. Sweet Deus.

She moved again, trying to find a more comfortable position, and winced at the pain in her arm. "What happened?"

"Are you in very much pain, darling?" he asked instead of answering her question.

He was frowning, hovering over her.

"It's bearable," she reassured him. "More water, please?"

Her throat seemed endlessly parched. She felt as if she could drink an entire ocean of water and still not be satisfied.

"Another sip," he allowed, holding the cup to her lips for her. "You were shot. Fortunately, the bullet passed through flesh and not bone. However, an infection set in. I've been praying it would pass."

Dark circles marred the skin beneath his eyes.

"Have you been tending to me all this time?"

"Of course," he said simply, as if it were a foregone conclusion. "Where else would I be?"

"With your betrothed," she said, and not without accompanying bitterness. "Where you belong."

"I belong with you," he countered.

How she wished it were true. But her wounding had changed nothing. She couldn't stay here in Varros. As soon as she was well enough, she would go. She had to, for the sake of her own self-preservation.

"Surely there are more important duties awaiting the king," she said quietly.

"We'll discuss that later. For now, the doctor should see you." He was frowning ferociously down at her, worry evident in his gaze and his tone.

"I don't want to see the doctor," she protested weakly, disliking the notion of being prodded and examined.

She felt as if she'd been at war, every part of her body aching in some strange new way. Surely an examination by the physician would only enhance her pain.

But Maxim remained impervious, his face a stern, impassive mask. "I'm not taking any risks with you, spitfire. You're too precious to me."

Before she could offer further objections, he stalked to a bell pull, calling for a servant.

≈

IT HAD TAKEN one week of sheer, absolute hell for Tansy to fully fight off the infection that had claimed her in the wake of her wounding and regain her strength. And it had taken one week for Maxim's men to find the bastard responsible for it.

He approached the prisoner who had been chained to the walls of the palace's dungeon. The man was familiar, save the scar marring half his face and the patch he wore over one eye. He'd last seen that face covered in blood on the battle-field years ago.

Maxim had left him for dead.

"Rodrigo," he spat in greeting, the name like a curse.

The other man sneered. "The bastard who pretends to be king."

"I'm the rightful King of Varros," he countered with a calm he didn't feel. "It was your leader who was the pretender."

Maxim would show Rodrigo no weakness.

Rodrigo released a bitter, mocking laugh. "You'll never be the true king. You were born of a false union."

Inside, his heart was galloping. The madness that was never far lurked at the edges of every moment. He kept his cool façade in place by sheer force of will.

"My father's half brother was born of an annulled union, and he was disavowed," he countered. "He seized control through bribery and other nefarious means, and he led a pack of brutal, ravening murderers in doing their damnedest to destroy this land."

Mina's soot-streaked, badly beaten face rose in his memory. And then he thought of Tansy falling into the water, blood everywhere. Rodrigo would pay for the pain he had inflicted upon those weaker than himself. He would pay dearly. Maxim would make certain this time that the villain could never harm anyone again.

"King Charles was the rightful heir to the throne."

He smiled grimly. "And yet, I am the one who now occu-pies the throne whilst he rots in the dirt."

"If my hand had been steadier, you'd be rotting with him," Rodrigo growled, tugging at his restraints, to no avail.

He was secured to the ancient stone walls. Maxim had made damned certain that the hold the devil had been placed in was their most secure. There would be no escape.

"And if the assassins you sent after me in London had been trained half as well as my men, I wouldn't be here now," he acknowledged. "But none of them could do the job properly. Not any more than you and your men could win the war."

Rodrigo's glare was venomous. "We may not have won the war, but we did enjoy passing around your whore. Pity I couldn't manage to kill the new one the same as I did the old."

His blood went cold, rage making his shoulders tense and his fingers ball into fists at his sides. "You ordered the attack on the village that day."

It wasn't a question; Maxim already knew the answer. It was why he had faced Rodrigo in battle. Why he had done his best to slay him. His best hadn't been sufficient. But this time would be different.

Rodrigo grinned. "It was a great pleasure to watch the torches set flame to the houses and burn the traitors to the ground."

"You murdered my wife, you wounded my future wife, and you tried to kill me," he accused, lethal menace rising within him, threatening to overtake him.

"I would do it all again in the name of the one true king," Rodrigo said defiantly.

The urge to do him violence, to thrash him to within an inch of his life, was strong. Perhaps the greatest temptation Maxim had ever known. But he knew that the worst punishment he could inflict upon Rodrigo was to suffer. To live the rest of his days caged like an animal, never again seeing daylight. Going mad in the bowels of the palace, existing on gruel and water and nothing else.

"The only thing you will do in the name of the pretender king is stay chained up in this dungeon for the rest of your miserable days," he told the other man dispassionately. "You will be tried for your crimes, and I'll turn over every rock in this kingdom to find the rest of your traitors and to send them here to hell along with you. That's not a threat, Rodrigo. That's a promise."

With that, Maxim left the cell, closing his ears to the obscenities and hatred Rodrigo called after him. He'd just made one promise, and now he had another to break.

~

"MY SISTERS HAVE ARRIVED SAFELY," Theodoric St. George told Maxim after performing a perfunctory greeting. "I'm indebted to you. If anything had happened to Annalise or Emmaline, I wouldn't have forgiven myself, and yet I was in no position to retrieve them."

They were seated in Maxim's formal study, a decanter of Scotch whisky laid out on a table before them, fortification he feared might prove necessary, given the information he intended to impart.

He nodded anyway, pleased to hear the news. "Excellent. I know you wished for their removal from Boritania before we press our advantage, and now we have one less obstacle in our path."

St. George raised a brow, his look turning questioning. "You speak heavily, as if there is something weighing on your heart."

"Because there is." Maxim reached for the whisky, pouring a measure into his glass before taking a healthy sip.

"There is the matter of my marriage to your sister, Princess Anastasia."

The other man's countenance turned guarded. "Oh?"

"My intention in forming such a union was to solidify an alliance between Varros and Boritania," he elaborated carefully. "With you on the throne, our particular corner of the world will be much more stable. Meanwhile, I've still been fighting an ever-smaller group of traitors who remain loyal to my father's half brother. I need all the stability I can achieve for the sake of my people."

St. George passed a hand over his jaw. "I understand the need. Stasia has already explained as much to me."

He took another swift sip of his whisky. "Did she also tell you that she is in love with another man?"

St. George appeared stunned. "Stasia? Of course not."

"As it happens, I'm also in love with another woman," he continued. "Lady Tansy Francis, the princess's lady-in-waiting."

"Lady Tansy," St. George repeated.

"Yes." He held the other man's stare, refusing to change his mind or relent. "It's my most sincere wish to make her my wife."

"I cannot imagine Stasia has any objections to the match."

How odd it was to hear Princess Anastasia referred to so informally. Maxim had never been on such intimate terms with her, and now he hoped he never would.

"What do you mean by that?" he asked sharply.

"Forgive me for being blunt, Your Majesty," St. George said, "but my sister has made it more than plain to me that she considers a marriage between the two of you an obligation. She is sacrificing herself so that you will aid us in securing Boritania and the removal of Gustavson from the throne."

"And what of you?" he asked, for although the answer

would not alter his decision, it was best to know where he stood. "Would you have objections to a match between myself and Lady Tansy instead?"

"If it is what Lady Tansy wishes, I would be well pleased." St. George smiled. "She has been like a sister to Stasia these years, strong and true. Varros will always have the support of Boritania when I am king. This, I vow."

Relief washed over him, along with a new, freeing rush. A lightness in his chest. A rightness in his heart.

Happiness.

He raised his glass in salute. "To Boritania."

The other man followed suit. "To Varros and the forging of a true friendship."

They clinked glasses. "Now, all we have to do is win the war."

And all he had to do was convince Tansy to become his wife.

CHAPTER 19

"The both of us shall bear scars," Princess Anastasia said, smiling sadly. "All because of love."

Today was the first day Tansy had finally managed to gather the strength to not just leave the bed for ablutions and bodily necessity, but to sit and take tea. To feel almost like herself again, despite the continued pain in her healing arm.

"On our hearts as well as our limbs," Tansy agreed, smiling back at her friend with an equal amount of sorrow. "Do you forgive me for leaving without telling you?"

"Need you ask?" The princess gave her hand a reassuring pat. "I understand your reason for wanting to go, even if I hate the thought of no longer having you at my side as you've been all these years."

"You will have Princesses Annalise and Emmaline to keep you company now," Tansy pointed out, for her friend had just delivered the news that her sisters had arrived safely in Varros, freed of their uncle's tyrannical rule.

"It won't be the same," Stasia said quietly, sipping at her tea. "I'll miss you dreadfully. When do you think you will be leaving?"

Tansy sighed, hating the thought of leaving now just as much as she had before, if not more. "Very soon. My strength is returning to me."

Maxim had been solicitous, tending over her with dedicated persistence. He had also refused her request to be moved from his apartments, and until this morning, she'd been too weak to leave. Finally, she'd been able to return to her own room, where Princess Anastasia had joined her.

"I wish you would stay, but that is a selfish desire, I know," Princess Anastasia said. "I wish for so many things. At least there is comfort in knowing my brother will soon be on the throne, my sisters are free, and the people of Boritania will no longer be trapped beneath the hateful rule of an evil tyrant."

"Do you think you'll be happy in Varros?" Tansy dared to ask, hoping that neither Princess Anastasia nor Maxim would be miserable in their future together.

Although she was keenly envious of her friend becoming Maxim's wife, she still understood the necessity for both of them. Even if she couldn't bear to watch it happen.

Stasia sipped quietly at her tea, her countenance turning pensive. "Perhaps in time. Right now, my heart aches far too much for me to hope I'll find contentedness here."

Tansy took a sip of her own tea, understanding the sentiment all too well. She didn't know if she would ever find happiness in England. Indeed, she very much doubted it.

A knock sounded at the door then, taking her by surprise, for she was expecting no one. Indeed, she had only just returned to her rooms earlier.

"Who is there?" she called.

"Me," came a deep, growly voice that was as beloved as it was familiar.

Maxim.

She shot from her chair with such sudden motion that

her dish of tea tipped, splashing hot liquid over her hand as she tried to right it, and then she switched to the hand of her injured arm unthinkingly. A gasp of pain tore from her, and before she could bid him entrance, Maxim was bursting over the threshold, a warrior king prepared to go to battle.

"What's happened?" he demanded, stalking toward her. "Are you hurt?"

"Perhaps my pride and just a sting to my hand," she reassured him shakily. "I spilled my tea, burned myself, and then attempted to right it with my injured arm."

"Thank God." He was there in an instant, blotting up the tea, gently cleaning her hand. "What are you doing here? You should be in my apartments, where you belong."

A warm flush crept over her cheekbones at his blatant, masculine display of possessiveness, with Princess Anastasia as their audience. "I'm well enough to return to my rooms, Your Majesty."

"Princess," he greeted, as if belatedly realizing Tansy wasn't alone in the room.

Her friend dipped into a curtsy. "Your Majesty."

He looked from Tansy to the princess. "Am I interrupting something?"

How like him to belatedly have such a thought occur to him, after he'd already barged through the door and stalked into their tête-à-tête. Tansy would have smiled had her heart not been aching with the bittersweet knowledge she would soon leave him again.

"Princess Anastasia and I were taking tea," she said pointedly.

"Tea?" His expression turned disgusted. "Coffee is superior."

"To you, perhaps," she countered gently.

"To anyone with a tongue capable of tasting," he quipped.

"I find tea to be delicious," she argued with him, allowing herself to be nettled over his customary arrogance.

Perhaps if she clung to that, she wouldn't be thinking about how she would soon be an ocean away from him.

"We shall have to agree to disagree on the matter," Princess Anastasia intervened brightly.

"It's fortuitous that you're here, Princess," Maxim said. "There's a delicate matter I need to discuss with you."

Tansy's heart plummeted. Did he truly intend to speak privately with his betrothed before her?

"Can it not wait?" she asked desperately. "I cannot think such a discussion appropriate for me to intrude upon."

Maxim gave her a look that smoldered with intensity, a look of such blatant tenderness and—dare she think it—adoration that she swayed, feeling as if she were back on the ship that had brought them to Varros.

"There's no intrusion," he said quietly. "Indeed, it's a conversation best held with the two of you at once."

She couldn't fathom what manner of conversation that was.

"Please, Your Majesty," she said weakly, "do not force me to participate."

"I'll not force you, but as the discussion very much concerns you and your future, you may wish to join us," he drawled.

They hadn't spoken of the future since she'd been wounded. Instead, their every interaction had been almost insufferably polite. Maxim inquired after her health, her strength, the pain in her arm. He hadn't talked about the inevitability that she would leave Varros, leave him. And this time, she wouldn't be returning.

"I've already told you I won't remain here in the capacity you request of me," she reminded him tightly, unwilling to say the word *mistress* before Princess Anastasia, for it was too uncomfortable.

"That's just as well," he said, a faint smile curving his lips. "Because there is only one capacity in which I want you to stay here in Varros."

Confusion washed over her.

Surely he didn't mean what her fragile, foolish heart dared to hope he meant. Did he?

"Princess Anastasia," he said, turning to her friend, who was watching the two of them bemusedly, as if seeing them both for the first time. "You are in love with another. Are you not?"

The princess nodded. "You know it's so."

"We find ourselves in a similar predicament," he continued. "I propose a solution."

Every part of her caught on those three words. A similar predicament. Was Maxim saying...

Surely not.

It couldn't be that he was saying...that he loved her.

Could it?

Tansy couldn't seem to speak, but fortunately, the princess found her tongue first.

"And what is your solution?" she asked Maxim warily.

"I propose that we both marry the people we love," he said simply.

"But the betrothal bargain," Princess Anastasia said. "You promised me you would aid in Theodoric claiming the throne in return for marrying me."

Maxim nodded, his countenance going stern. "I've spoken with your brother. He knows that Varros will proudly support him with men and resources and help him to dethrone the usurper king. I've also told him that we haven't any desire to marry each other, and that there's only one woman I want to make my queen."

Tansy's heart pounded hard.

Surely he wasn't serious.

Was he jesting?

She couldn't bear it if he was.

"Maxim," she whispered, feeling as if she were in a dream. "What are you saying?"

As if, at any moment, she would wake to discover none of this had truly happened, and she would be shattered anew.

"I'm saying that I am humbly requesting Princess Anastasia's agreement in the annulment of our betrothal contract," he said, giving her another look of such raw, unfettered tenderness that she had to press her lips together to stifle a sob. "Doing so will leave both myself and the princess free to pursue those we love instead of forcing ourselves into a marriage of obligation." He paused, turning back to the princess. "What say you, Your Royal Highness? Will you take the opportunity to be free to pursue your English puppy?"

The princess's eyes narrowed. "He's no puppy."

Maxim shrugged. "As you wish."

"Yes," Princess Anastasia said without hesitation. "I agree to the annulment of the betrothal. How soon can I go back to England?"

"It's too early to be certain. I expect a swift defeat, given the size of the Varrosian army and those of the rebel forces in Boritania compared to the size of what—according to our spies—remains of the Boritanian army. But if there's anything I've learned from my years at war, it's that a man should never underestimate his opponent. It won't be safe for you to return to England until the war is won. If you return prematurely, not only will you be at peril, but so will your Englishman. I'll not mislead you in that."

War.

A shiver went down Tansy's spine, for she knew all too well the cost that Maxim had paid in war before. The thought of him having to go to battle again filled her with fear.

Princess Anastasia nodded. "I'll wait forever for him if I must."

"I understand the sentiment," Maxim said, gazing at Tansy.

She longed to run to him. To throw herself into his arms. To hold him close and never let go. And yet, there was much that needed to be said, and Princess Anastasia was still present in the room.

With great effort, Tansy remained where she was, gripping the back of her chair to keep from tumbling over beneath the weight of this sudden turn of events.

"I should leave the two of you alone," Princess Anastasia said, sending a sly smile in Tansy's direction. "I'm sure there is much you need to speak about together."

Dazed, Tansy watched her friend take her leave from the chamber, as effortlessly elegant as always.

The door had scarcely closed behind her when she turned to Maxim. "What is the meaning of this?"

He went to her, setting two fingers gently beneath her chin and tilting her face toward his. "I want you to be my queen."

Once again, it was so very Maxim, to make a decree rather than to ask permission.

"But what of your duties, your obligations to your people to form a great alliance between Varros and Boritania?" she demanded, knowing how it had weighed upon him.

Knowing why he had made the decision to marry Princess Anastasia.

It was a decision she had respected, even though it had crushed her.

"My brother is an idiot," Maxim said wryly, "but sometimes he is wise beyond his years. When we were in London, he said to me, *You're the King of Varros. Can you not choose the woman who will be your queen?* At first, I dismissed his words as recklessness. Nando being his wild, ne'er-do-well self with nary a care in the world and no sense of duty. But those words haunted me." He caressed her cheek lightly with the callused pad of his thumb. "And the more I thought about them, the more tempted I was to heed them. I thought my first duty was to my kingdom and my people, to the throne. I was wrong. My first duty is to the woman I love. To you."

Tears blurred her vision, made her blink to clear them so that she could see his harshly handsome face, and then she reached for him, wrapping her uninjured arm around his neck and anchoring herself there, bringing their bodies flush. "You love me?"

"I love you, spitfire," he rasped. "I should have told you sooner. I intended to, but everything has been such a damned whirlwind, returning to Varros and planning the invasion. It wasn't until the moment I realized you were leaving me that I knew I had to find you and tell you. I had to beg you to be my wife, and I had to do anything and everything I could to make that happen."

The day she'd been wounded, he'd intended to ask her to marry him. And meanwhile, she'd been plotting to leave him again.

"Why didn't you tell me this sooner?" she demanded.

"You were badly injured and ill. I didn't want to pressure you into making a decision when you weren't well enough to think clearly."

"I could have been on my deathbed, and I would have told you yes," she murmured, twining her fingers through the soft strands of hair at his nape. "The answer for you is always yes, my love."

His expression became serious, his eyes burning into hers. "You'll marry me?"

"I'll marry you."

"Thank God," he breathed, as if he had doubted her answer.

And perhaps he had.

He kissed her swiftly, softly. A quick meeting of mouths before he was frowning down at her again. "What happened to you at the docks… Tansy, I'm to blame. An enemy of mine was attempting to kill me, and you were wounded in the process. You could have died because of me, because of my recklessness."

"You couldn't have known what would happen," she protested, hating that he believed himself to blame, when he already shouldered so much responsibility in what had happened to his previous wife.

"There had been assassins in London," he revealed grimly. "We traced them back to some remaining loyalists. I'd believed them dead, but they were in hiding, lying in wait until the most opportune moment to strike against me. I need you to know that I'll never again be so careless with you. The man responsible for what happened to you has been captured and imprisoned, and my men will have the name of any and every conspirator still on Varrosian shores. But I will see that you are protected in every way. I can't bear to lose you. I'll do anything you ask of me, but please, Tansy. Just don't leave me. Never leave me."

"Never," she echoed, rising on her toes to press her mouth to his, sealing the promise.

He made a low sound of helpless need, kissing her hard before lifting his head. "There is more we need to discuss. With the war looming, it isn't prudent for us to make Gustavson aware of the broken betrothal until the invasion begins. Otherwise, he may suspect us."

"I understand." She searched his gaze. "You're not intending to go to battle yourself this time, are you?"

"My battlefield days are done. I have faith in my generals and my soldiers." He leaned his forehead against hers. "The only place I'll go to battle is in the bedroom with my stubborn queen."

She smiled through her tears. "I like the sound of that, my king."

He kissed the corner of her lips. "We'll win the war, I vow it, and we'll catch any remaining loyalists intending to do harm. I'll not have you living in fear. You're mine to protect."

"I have faith in you, Maxim. I trust you above all others. That's why I fell in love with you."

"Thank you." Another kiss fluttered over her mouth. "Say it again."

"Always so demanding," she teased. "Might you not ask nicely?"

"Say it again, please," he growled.

"I love you, Maxim," she said, falling into the glittering depths of his dark gaze. "I love you, and I'll never leave you. I'm yours, always."

His mouth was on hers again, possessive and voracious, stealing her breath. "And I'm yours, spitfire."

EPILOGUE

ONE YEAR LATER

*M*axim was marching.

One, two, three, four.

One, two, three, four.

One, two—

"Damn it, brother, I think I'm getting a cramp in my leg," Nando complained at his side.

"It's been hours," he seethed without pausing his strides. "Fucking hours."

"What manner of hours?" Nando teased with a light air that was wholly inappropriate for the moment and made Maxim want to punch him in the mouth.

"*Fucking* hours," he repeated grimly. "Don't test me, brother. I doubt your legions of women would be tripping over their petticoats to get into your bed if you were missing some teeth."

Nando grinned. "But I've all my teeth. And they're remarkably straight and neat, too. All my women compliment them."

"I imagine they do," he allowed icily. "However, I'm referencing what will happen when I slam my fist into your mouth for making a jest when my lady wife is down that hall and behind those doors birthing my child."

"You love me too much to punch me in the mouth," Nando countered, unperturbed.

And damn him, he was right.

"I'm not in the mood for levity," he snapped at his brother.

"When *are* you in the mood for levity?" Nando grumbled with good-natured humor.

He didn't hesitate with his response. "Whenever my wife is near."

Tansy made him smile. She filled him with happiness, the sort he'd never known possible. They'd been married in secret one year ago as the rebellion had unfolded in Boritania. The victory, as Maxim had predicted, had been swift. Within months, Theodoric St. George had assumed the throne that was rightfully his, and Gustavson had been not just removed from power, but from the earth. St. George had taken an English wife as his queen, and Princess Anastasia was happily wedded to her English puppy, Archer Tierney. Love stories all around. But none so great, in Maxim's less-than-modest opinion, as his and Tansy's.

He was admittedly biased.

"Is now the wrong time to remind you that you have me to thank for my matchmaking efforts?" Nando asked as they continued pacing.

"Your matchmaking efforts," he repeated incredulously. "Need I remind you that your so-called matchmaking efforts resulted in my wife almost leaving me?"

"You needed a kick in the arse. Only think of how miserable you'd have been had you wed the princess instead, all because you had some cork-brained notion about duty."

He glowered at his vexing brother. "Duty is not cork-brained. I was doing what I believed was in the best interest of the kingdom at the time. We desperately needed stability in Boritania and an ally on the throne."

And Theodoric St. George had proven a most reliable and worthy ally. Already, he had created vast improvements in the kingdom. Boritania and her people were beginning to flourish again, and Varros rejoiced in it. The last of the loyalist rebels had been arrested for treason, and a much-needed sense of peace had blanketed the land.

"But now, you can see that marrying Tansy was in the best interest of Varros," Nando said knowingly.

"And I suppose you would claim responsibility for my marrying her as well," he drawled, secretly grateful for the distraction his brother provided.

He was maddening.

And reckless.

And irresponsible.

Not to mention depraved.

But Nando was his brother, and he'd been a steadfast presence in Maxim's life.

Nando beamed at him. "Of course I would. I am, after all, responsible. Someone had to break through that thick head of yours with some common sense. As a reward for my service to the kingdom, I humbly request you name your firstborn in my honor."

"Ha!" Maxim bit out a reluctant laugh at the suggestion.

"Only think… If the babe is a girl, she can be called Ferdinanda, and if the babe is a boy, he can be called Ferdo."

He shook his head. "You've been giving this thought."

"Why wouldn't I? You aren't the only one eagerly awaiting the birth of my niece or nephew."

"Those are terrible names," he said without heat.

Nando grinned at him. "Give it some time. Ferdinanda is a particular favorite, although Ferdo certainly possesses an elegance all its own."

"I suggest you name *your* firstborn after yourself," he countered with a snort.

"I've no intention of marrying," Nando said easily. "One woman could never tame me."

Maxim raised a brow at him. "You only think so because you've yet to find the right woman. The one who makes your heart whole. The one you cannot possibly live without. The one who brings you to your knees."

Nando clapped him on the back. "I do believe impending fatherhood is making you maudlin, brother."

Perhaps it was.

Maxim didn't give a damn.

Before he could form a blistering retort, however, a servant approached them in the hall.

"Your Majesty, Your Royal Highness." The woman dipped into a formal curtsy. "Her Majesty has asked for Your Majesty's presence."

His heart lurched, his gut tightening with sickening fear. "Is something amiss?"

"All is well," the servant said, smiling. "The royal baby has arrived. Her Majesty and the child are healthy."

Relief washed over him, so powerful and potent that his knees trembled and his legs almost gave way beneath the brunt of it. "Thank God."

"My felicitations, brother," Nando said quietly, giving him a hearty pat on the back. "You should go to the queen."

"Yes. Thank you." He nodded, feet moving, eating up the distance between himself and his wife and child.

His child.

Ye gods, he was a father.

He hastened his stride, and by the time he reached the chamber door, he burst over the threshold without a hint of grace. But he didn't give a damn about that either, because the most beautiful sight he'd beheld yet greeted him. His beloved, beautiful wife sat propped by a mound of pillows, her dark hair neatly swept away from her face, a swaddled babe in her arms.

"My love," he said, fairly flying across the chamber to her. "How are you?"

Gray eyes met his, not filled with secrets and mysteries now—for he had learned hers just as she had learned his. But sparkling with love and happiness instead.

"I am well," she said, her voice sounding a bit hoarse and weary, yet laden with warmth. "Come and meet your son."

His son.

He had a son.

Maxim seated himself with ginger care on the bed at her side, and with a trembling hand, he drew the swaddling back so that he could see the pink, wrinkled face of his new baby. Love, abundant and rich, hit him.

"He's a handsome little lad," he said shakily, awestruck by the tiny, wriggling bundle, who rooted toward his finger as he stroked his son's soft cheek.

"He takes after his father," Tansy said tenderly.

He looked up, smiling, tears suddenly blurring his vision. "Thank you for giving me a son."

She reached for him, cupping his cheek in one hand, smiling. "As I recall, I'm not the only one responsible."

He chuckled at her daring, and the tears spilled free, falling down his cheeks in hot trails, and he didn't give a damn about that either. Maxim turned his head and pressed a reverent kiss to her palm. "Excellent point, spitfire. But I meant thank you for carrying him all these months, and for giving him life."

"Nothing has made me happier," she said, looking down at the baby in her arms. "For so long, I was without a family, and now, at last, I have a family of my own. My heart is filled with joy."

"As is mine," he said, joining her in gazing at their son in wonder.

The baby made a small sound, and then his eyes opened, meeting Maxim's.

"You should hold your son, Papa," Tansy told him.

He opened his arms, and she placed the baby into them carefully, the small weight so precious, the tiny life just beginning a source of endless wonder to him.

"Son," he said, trying out the word, so strange and yet so glorious. "Papa loves you."

These were words that had grown easier to say with time. And he had Tansy to thank for that.

His son's face screwed, going red, and he opened his mouth to emit a small, princely roar of protest, likely at having been removed from his mother's arms.

"I don't think he's pleased with me," he observed wryly.

"Rock him gently and pat his bottom," Tansy instructed. "That seems to calm him."

He did as she said, and the baby quieted.

"We must name him." He glanced up at Tansy. "Nando recommends Ferdo."

Tansy laughed. "That's a terrible name."

Ah, vindication.

"That's precisely what I told him." He traced the bridge of his son's nose in awe. "If you're in agreement, I would like to name him Caspian the Second, after my father."

And the king who had been denied his throne, who had never lived to see the House of Tayrnes vanquish their enemies and rule victorious.

"Caspian," Tansy repeated. "Caspian Ferdinando."

"Nando would be most pleased."

"Since we're indebted to his matchmaking, the least we can do is honor him with our son's name."

Maxim gave her a searching look. "Has Nando been crowing to you as well?"

She smiled, a beautiful smile, one that was weary and yet filled with so much love and hope, so much promise for the future. "Of course he has."

"He's fortunate I love him," he muttered, gently stroking the silken tuft of dark hair atop Caspian's head.

"We're all fortunate you love us," Tansy said softly.

He leaned forward, slanting his lips over hers for a swift kiss. "No one is more fortunate than I am, my love."

~

As THEY HAD every night for the last three months since they had welcomed Caspian into the world, Tansy and Maxim watched their baby son sleeping soundly in his crib, swaddled in his blankets.

"He's an angel," Maxim said reverently.

"Only when he's sleeping," she returned wryly.

Their son, in the fashion of his father, could be quite demanding. But she adored all the joys of being a mother, even when her refusal to use a wet nurse meant that she'd had precious little slumber each night in between feedings. She was exhausted and more content than she'd ever been.

"Papa says he's an angel," Maxim said. "That's a royal decree, and it cannot be argued, not even by the queen."

She chuckled softly. Watching Maxim dote over their son only made her love for him grow. He was a wonderful father, just as she had known he would be.

"Something tells me that Papa will have no end of royal decrees where his beloved son is concerned," she said.

"And where his beloved wife is concerned as well." Maxim drew an arm around her waist, pulling her into his tall, lean form. "Shall we retire to the library?"

After she settled Caspian down for a few hours of sleep in the evening beneath the watchful eye of his nurse, she and Maxim went to the palace library, a cavernous room laden with every manner of book imaginable, and spent a few precious hours alone.

But this evening, she had something else in mind.

"I think that perhaps I'll retire to my apartments for some rest instead," she told him as they left the nursery, careful to close the door softly at their backs, lest they wake their sleeping son.

"I'll leave you to your rest, then," he said solicitously.

She laced her arm through his, leaning into his delicious masculine heat and strength. "Perhaps you might join me for a nap."

He glanced down at her, his dark eyes curious. "If you wish for the company."

Tansy smiled back at him. "I very much wish it."

Understanding flared in his expression. "Are you well enough, my love?"

"More than well enough," she promised, restless yearning unfurling in her body.

They hadn't made love since she'd been heavily with child, and she missed his touch. Missed his body moving in hers. Missed the searing intimacy they'd known. She had needed time to heal after Caspian's birth, but she was ready.

More than ready, in fact.

"You haven't been reading that filthy book of yours again, have you?" he teased.

Her cheeks warmed. "Perhaps."

He chuckled. "My wicked queen, whatever shall I do with you?"

"I have a few ideas."

"Mmm." His strides quickened. "Show me."

He was moving so rapidly that she could scarcely keep pace with him. "Is that also a royal decree?"

"Oh yes," he said darkly.

They reached her door, and he threw it open, pulling her inside and kicking it closed with a booted foot. She was breathless and giggling as he hauled her into his chest for a ravenous kiss. They worked together in a flurry of motion, lips clinging as their fingers flew over buttons and hooks. Her gown, his coat. Her stays and petticoat, his shirt. Chemise, stockings, and trousers fell away.

She knew a moment of self-consciousness as her naked body—changed from her pregnancy—was revealed entirely to him for the first time since she'd given birth to their son. Tiny violet marks marred the skin of her belly and breasts, and she was more rounded now than she had been before. But any fear she had that he wouldn't find her attractive faded when he joined her on the bed, raining reverent kisses over her bare skin, his mouth lingering over the places of change.

"You're so fucking beautiful," he murmured, making a low rumble of appreciation deep in his throat as he kissed over her stomach, his big hands spreading her thighs. "I've been desperate to lick your cunny again."

She was already on edge after being denied his love-making for so long. His wanton words brought the ache in her sex to an acute crescendo. She opened wider for him in welcome and moaned, arching shamelessly into him when he lowered his head and gave her one tantalizing lick.

"Maxim," she gasped out, grasping a handful of his hair as her body bowed from the bed. "Please."

"As perfect as I remember," he said worshipfully, drawing her bud into his mouth with a hard, delicious suck that made her toes curl.

He sank a finger inside her and spoiled her with his

tongue. Her inner walls clenched on him, the intrusion almost unbearably good. And yet, still, she wanted more. Her hips moved, chasing him, seeking, demanding.

He gave her another finger, moving tentatively in slow, deliberate strokes.

"I'll not break," she ground out. "You needn't be so gentle."

With a groan, he gave her what she asked for, pressure and friction, his fingers fucking her with deep strokes and his mouth lavishing her with licks and sucks and the maddening nip of his teeth. When he found that place inside her that made her wild, she couldn't maintain her control. Her orgasm slammed into her with frenzied fury, making her cry out his name and grasp him to her as wave after wave of bliss rolled over her.

She scarcely had a chance to catch her breath before he was looming over her, the slick head of his cock pressing against her aching softness. He bent, catching the peak of her breast in his mouth before releasing it. "Are you ready for me, my love?"

"Yes," she moaned. "Feel how wet I am for you."

He groaned and pushed into her, one smooth stroke. And she was stretched so full of him, deliciously, gloriously full. He felt wonderful inside her, thick and rigid.

"Ah God," he murmured. "So wet for me, my love. Tell me what you want."

Tansy didn't hesitate. "I want you to make love to me."

"As my queen commands." He withdrew from her almost entirely and then pressed forward, gliding easily through her slick passage, sinking deep before retreating and then stroking forward again.

She planted her feet on the mattress, meeting him thrust for thrust. She clung to him, hands finding purchase on his broad shoulders, her nipples scraping against his chest with every movement. Their rhythm became feverish as they raced together to reach fulfillment. He took her mouth in a ravishing kiss, gorging on her lips and tongue. She moaned, body writhing, twisting, seeking.

Already, she was so close. She'd been denied him for too long, and now that she had him inside her where she longed for him most, her restraint had been entirely banished. She was aflame. Tansy collided with him again and again, their bodies slamming together, feeding him her tongue, wrapping a leg around his hip to increase the angle. Needing more. Needing him so deep inside her he would never leave.

And then, she was splintering into a thousand shards of light, the rush of bliss so heady that she could do nothing but close her eyes and cling to him as the wild force of her orgasm hit her. Pleasure licked up her spine, fanning over her body in furious ripples. Her head fell back against the pillow, her breaths leaving her in harsh pants.

Maxim kissed her jaw, her shoulder, his magnificent body on proud display as he made love to her. She watched the glow of candlelight on his muscled torso, loving his strength, his battle scars, the unguarded heart he'd given to her.

Loving *him*. Her king, her husband, her lover.

"Ah, my love," he whispered into her ear. "How you undo me."

He moved with greater urgency, and she felt his big body stiffening beneath her touch. Knew he was on the edge of finding his own release.

"Yes," she urged him on, nails digging into his shoulders now, raking up and down the broad planes of his back. "Come inside me, my love. Fill me."

"Fuck," he growled harshly. "Tansy."

"Come," she said again, begging him, longing for him to reach completion. "I want to feel you. Please."

And, spurred by her words, he did. With a lusty groan, he slammed deep one last time, emptying himself into her. She felt the pulse of his cock, the hot rush of his seed bathing her with his spend, her cunny quivering around him. Another small tremor rippled through her, her body insatiably greedy for his.

He collapsed atop her, a welcomed, beloved weight, his chest rising and falling as he struggled to calm his ragged breaths in the wake of his release. "My God, spitfire."

She smiled, happiness joining the bliss that never failed to blanket her whenever they made love. "I missed you."

"I'm likely crushing you," he muttered. "I'm an oaf."

She wrapped her arms around his neck, holding him where he was. "Don't you dare move. I've waited far too long to have you where I want you to be denied now."

He raised his head, giving her one of his private smiles, all tenderness and love. "If my queen demands it, who am I to deny her?"

Tansy smiled back at him, smoothing a lock of hair from his brow. "A wise king would not defy his queen."

He was still inside her, and she felt his spent cock stiffening with renewed interest.

"Let it never be said that the King of Varros is not a wise man." Smiling, he lowered his head and claimed her lips with his.

∼

THANK you for reading *How to Love a Dangerous Rogue*. I hope you loved Maxim and Tansy's forbidden royal romance every bit as much as I loved writing it. You can find Princess Anastasia's happily ever after in *Her Wicked Rogue* and you can find Theo's happily ever after in *Her Dangerous Beast*. You may also remember *The Tale of Love* from my Wicked Winters series. It, like the kingdoms of Varros and Boritania, is a product of my imagination, though it's based loosely on similar texts of the era.

Please stay in touch, particularly if you want to be notified about the next book in this series! The only way to be sure you'll know what's next from me is to sign up for my newsletter here: http://eepurl.com/dyJSar. Please join my reader group for early excerpts, cover reveals, and more here. And if you're in the mood to chat all things steamy historical romance and read a different book each month together, join my book club, Dukes Do It Hotter right here: https://www.facebook.com/groups/hotdukes because we're having a whole lot of fun!

DON'T MISS SCARLETT'S OTHER ROMANCES!

Complete Book List
HISTORICAL ROMANCE

Heart's Temptation
A Mad Passion (Book One)
Rebel Love (Book Two)
Reckless Need (Book Three)
Sweet Scandal (Book Four)
Restless Rake (Book Five)
Darling Duke (Book Six)
The Night Before Scandal (Book Seven)

Wicked Husbands
Her Errant Earl (Book One)
Her Lovestruck Lord (Book Two)
Her Reformed Rake (Book Three)
Her Deceptive Duke (Book Four)
Her Missing Marquess (Book Five)
Her Virtuous Viscount (Book Six)

DON'T MISS SCARLETT'S OTHER ROMANCES!

League of Dukes
Nobody's Duke (Book One)
Heartless Duke (Book Two)
Dangerous Duke (Book Three)
Shameless Duke (Book Four)
Scandalous Duke (Book Five)
Fearless Duke (Book Six)

Notorious Ladies of London
Lady Ruthless (Book One)
Lady Wallflower (Book Two)
Lady Reckless (Book Three)
Lady Wicked (Book Four)
Lady Lawless (Book Five)
Lady Brazen (Book 6)

Unexpected Lords
The Detective Duke (Book One)
The Playboy Peer (Book Two)
The Millionaire Marquess (Book Three)
The Goodbye Governess (Book Four)

Dukes Most Wanted
Forever Her Duke (Book One)
Forever Her Marquess (Book Two)

The Wicked Winters
Wicked in Winter (Book One)
Wedded in Winter (Book Two)
Wanton in Winter (Book Three)
Wishes in Winter (Book 3.5)
Willful in Winter (Book Four)
Wagered in Winter (Book Five)
Wild in Winter (Book Six)

Wooed in Winter (Book Seven)
Winter's Wallflower (Book Eight)
Winter's Woman (Book Nine)
Winter's Whispers (Book Ten)
Winter's Waltz (Book Eleven)
Winter's Widow (Book Twelve)
Winter's Warrior (Book Thirteen)
A Merry Wicked Winter (Book Fourteen)

The Sinful Suttons
Sutton's Spinster (Book One)
Sutton's Sins (Book Two)
Sutton's Surrender (Book Three)
Sutton's Seduction (Book Four)
Sutton's Scoundrel (Book Five)
Sutton's Scandal (Book Six)
Sutton's Secrets (Book Seven)

Rogue's Guild
Her Ruthless Duke (Book One)
Her Dangerous Beast (Book Two)
Her Wicked Rogue (Book 3)

Royals and Renegades
How to Love a Dangerous Rogue (Book One)

Sins and Scoundrels
Duke of Depravity
Prince of Persuasion
Marquess of Mayhem
Sarah
Earl of Every Sin
Duke of Debauchery
Viscount of Villainy

Sins and Scoundrels Box Set Collections
Volume 1
Volume 2

The Wicked Winters Box Set Collections
Collection 1
Collection 2
Collection 3
Collection 4

Wicked Husbands Box Set Collections
Volume 1
Volume 2

Stand-alone Novella
Lord of Pirates

CONTEMPORARY ROMANCE
Love's Second Chance
Reprieve (Book One)
Perfect Persuasion (Book Two)
Win My Love (Book Three)

Coastal Heat
Loved Up (Book One)

ABOUT THE AUTHOR

USA Today and Amazon bestselling author Scarlett Scott writes steamy Victorian and Regency romance with strong, intelligent heroines and sexy alpha heroes. She lives in Pennsylvania and Maryland with her Canadian husband, adorable identical twins, and two dogs.

A self-professed literary junkie and nerd, she loves reading anything, but especially romance novels, poetry, and Middle English verse. Catch up with her on her website https://scar lettscottauthor.com. Hearing from readers never fails to make her day.

Scarlett's complete book list and information about upcoming releases can be found at https://scarlettscottau thor.com.

Connect with Scarlett! You can find her here:
    Join Scarlett Scott's reader group on Facebook for early excerpts, giveaways, and a whole lot of fun!
    Sign up for her newsletter here
    https://www.tiktok.com/@authorscarlettscott

facebook.com/AuthorScarlettScott

x.com/scarscoromance

instagram.com/scarlettscottauthor

bookbub.com/authors/scarlett-scott

amazon.com/Scarlett-Scott/e/B004NW8N2I

pinterest.com/scarlettscott

Made in the USA
Las Vegas, NV
30 April 2025

21509336R00184